Praise for *Bound*

"A small gem . . . sharp and deeply moving."

—*Kirkus Reviews* **(starred review)**

"In her new novel *Bound*, set mostly in Wichita, Kansas, Antonya Nelson compels you to linger, makes you take in the shimmer of the long gray highway beside the strip malls, the promise and punishment of the steely blue sky. This America is her stage, and its characters are her people . . . It's a liberation to read Nelson here in the long form. There's no question of her superlative gifts for the short story . . . In *Bound*, Nelson makes her story as big as it should be, and gives her characters room to run."

—*New York Times Book Review*

"An exploration of the delicate, painful connections among us . . . Gripping . . . Nelson explores these connections and disconnects in understated, exact, and frequently witty prose."

—*Boston Globe*

"Nelson illuminates the ugly questions that shadow our intimate relationships."

—*New Yorker*

"Antonya Nelson is a brilliant storyteller. With whip-smart prose, she describes the just-another-day-ness of our lives . . . with precise candor and pathos . . . *Bound* is one of those rare books that can be hilarious and snarky and heart-bruisingly moving all at once. Nelson's work feels brazenly honest because her characters' relationships are as richly textured and complex as our own. This familiarity makes Nelson one of the best writers of contemporary desire we have."

—*Dallas Morning News*

"Nelson's prose [is] as sleekly tough-minded as ever . . . Essential for those serious about contemporary literature."

—*Library Journal*

"*Bound* is almost effortless to read—which is remarkable when one considers the number of complex relationships at work and the cutting truth with which each character is depicted . . . That a novel can accomplish so much in such tight space is otherworldly, and it speaks to Antonya Nelson's gift for writing great fiction."

—*TheRumpus.net*

"Nelson is a remarkable writer . . . This is a wonderful collection of characters, deftly drawn and expertly unveiled."

—*Slate*

BOUND

BY THE SAME AUTHOR

Novels

Living to Tell
Nobody's Girl
Talking in Bed

Short Fiction

Nothing Right
Some Fun
Female Trouble
Family Terrorists
In the Land of Men
The Expendables

BOUND

a novel

ANTONYA NELSON

BLOOMSBURY

New York • Berlin • London • Sydney

Published by Bloomsbury USA, New York

All papers used by Bloomsbury USA are natural, recyclable products made
from wood grown in well-managed forests. The manufacturing processes
conform to the environmental regulations of the country of origin.

LIBRARY OF CONGRESS CATALOGING-IN-PUBLICATION DATA

Nelson, Antonya.
Bound : a novel / Antonya Nelson.—1st U.S. ed.
p. cm.
ISBN: 978-1-59691-575-6
I. Title.
PS3564.E428B68 2010
813'.54—dc22
2010009791

First published by Bloomsbury USA in 2010
This paperback edition published in 2011

Paperback ISBN: 978-1-60819-299-1

1 3 5 7 9 10 8 6 4 2

Typeset by Westchester Book Group
Printed in the United States of America by Quad/Graphics, Fairfield,
Pennsylvania

To Laura Kasischke, in friendship

FALL

CHAPTER 1

T HE DOG HAD two impulses. One was to stay with the car, container of civilization, and the other was to climb through the ruined window into the wild. Wait with the woman, or dash toward the distant rushing water?

The woman hung suspended, patiently bleeding, barefoot, allover powdered by deployed airbag dust, one palm open like a forget-me-not in her lap, the other hand raised unnaturally high, as if thrown up to respond to a question, fingertips caught in the teeth of the ripped-open moon roof. A signal chimed, tiredly announcing that a door was not latched, or a passenger was not buckled, or a light had been left on, or that some other minor human infraction had been committed. The machine was made to attend to these. Additionally, the tape player played on, a man reading aloud. In other instances, recorded sound sometimes roused the dog's interest—animals on television or computer, the doorbell at home in Houston—but not this man's voice.

This was the car's third accident today. For nearly thirty years, its driver had not had an accident, not since high school. Then in one day: three. First a bashed bumper at the liquor store parking lot in El Paso, she and another woman backing out directly into one another. From above, it might have looked choreographed, perfect comic symmetry, a gentle jolt, the sudden appearance of a car bumper right where there hadn't been one in the rearview mirror. Or like film footage, run in reverse, people parking, un-parking. This first accident, which had produced no problems, bumpers doing their jobs, had been in Texas, the next one in New Mexico, and the third in Colorado. The second accident, in New Mexico, was clearly the fault of the dog's owner. Headed north through a tiny town made of trailers, she'd run its only shot-blasted stop sign and been clipped by a westbound pickup. Its driver jumped furious from his cab, shouting and pugnacious before she'd even shifted into park. Her right taillight had been sheared off by his too-big tow bar. The dog would not stop bark-ing at the angry man. For ten minutes the two drivers had had to circle and study their vehicles, the man venting his significant frustration, which took the form of rhetorical questions con-cerning the whereabouts of her mind, not to mention her driv-ing barefooted.

"What are you, *drunk*?"

Hungover, the woman thought, but not drunk. She shook. Her response, often, was to retreat to silence. This had made her a formidable adult, although she'd been mistaken as sullen or dull-witted when she was young. The man finally convinced himself that he wasn't at fault, nor was his truck damaged. And he couldn't much care about an unpretty woman. The drivers left the scene of the accident without reporting it. The other cars that passed—both local and tourist gawkers—slowed but did not bother to stop, interested to know if the verbal antics would esca-late into something truly entertaining, since clearly there'd been no carnage.

They wanted mayhem.

The dog had not ceased barking until her owner settled behind the wheel, slammed the door, blinked into the setting sun from behind sunglasses she had not removed, and turned over the engine. Then they were restored to their humming, air-conditioned peace. For miles, the woman talked to the dog as if to prove that she could, her hands trembling when she finally put in the first cassette of her borrowed book on tape. "Heart of Darkness," its narrator intoned, and thus began the story.

Now the dog was busy navigating a nervous figure eight between back seat and front, stepping gently past the gearshift, tightly circling the passenger seat, her tail inadvertently sweeping beneath the driver's upraised arm, near her hinged, leaking mouth, then squeezing once more over the gearshift, onto the back seat and into her metal kennel, which was intact, although upside down. There she made the motion of settling, albeit on the ceiling rather than the floor of her cage, hopeful that obedience would reinstate known order.

Obeying was her first instinct; she'd been performing these moves, tracing this circumscribed looping path, every minute or so, since the car had gone off the highway and down the cliff. She stepped from the kennel and shook in her abbreviated space, sat suddenly and awkwardly on her tail, like a bear or raccoon, and curled forward to lick at her belly, tempted once more by the sense of the flowing stream beyond the car, yet dutiful to the woman inside. Far above, on the highway from which the car had fallen, a truck downshifted, straining against its own massive weight and force, roaring gradually by. The dog had been whinnying every now and then, an uneasy chatter in her throat, but now squared her front feet on the car console and barked close to the woman's head, teeth snapping unnaturally near the pink cheek flesh, tail waving with hope, anxiety. She had eyebrows, this dog, which gave her the appearance of intelligence, as if she could read minds or understand complicated speech. The woman was in the habit of talking to her. Certain words—Walk! Treat! Home!—as well as certain tones of voice inspired a reply. The dog barked again, as if to begin their usual exchange, taking the lead, and then again, insistently, demanding a response, even one of anger, then put her nose to the woman's temple, tasted the blood there, whimpered, her tail now swinging low, pendulum of shame. The man's voice, steadily reading. The other sound, the one she could more truly heed, that of the stream.

She stepped gingerly over the woman, dropped to the damp cool ground outside, stood for a moment with her nose to the air. Without its familiarities, the car evaporated from her attention, sucked into the overwhelming enormity of the rest of the world. She dashed headlong toward the water. Plunging in, she was startled by the current; she flailed and her eyes rolled, panicked and wild. She raised her neck, scrambled, and only occasionally, and only momentarily, found purchase on the rocks beneath. Down the stream she flew, borne on an icy journey, through a slight and shadowy canyon, her body thrown sideways around one bend, backward around another, her chest scraped lengthily over a jutting cluster of boulders in the last rapids, again and again her muzzle submerged and blasted, and then, finally, she was deposited into a still pool, a wide clearing where the water abruptly sprawled, stalled, where its temperature gradually rose, milder. On the banks, grazing deer.

The dog climbed out through tall saturated yellow grass, through dying pussy willows and stagnant silt, and onto a large flat red stone that still held the late-afternoon warmth from the sun. Here she lay panting, quivering. Her feet were tender and there was a new rip on her belly from the rocks. Wet, she showed her wolflike physique, the slender sneaky profile of her face, the alert damp fan of her tail. Her coloring was dark, her thick fur stippled, and her tongue mottled, like a chow's, but her slender skeletal underpinnings were those of a wild creature, fox or coyote, something nocturnal and sly. Her owner had liked that about her, the grateful and frightened girl whose appearance daunted, her loyalty and love that of something rescued from cruelty. She'd lived on garbage; she'd slept with her eyes open. She was strange looking, skittish, intimidated and intimidating. She answered to Max. On her neck she had worn a collar, but now it was gone, torn from her when the car flew off the mountain and rolled over the talus and into the trees below, or snatched away in the turbulent trip down the stream. In the flesh of her neck she had had a surgical procedure to install a microchip that identified her. Some shelters, some veterinarians, knew to scan lost animals for those. Some didn't.

She lay on the rock, cleaning her wound, her eyebrowed forehead nudging stubbornly, her teeth briefly bared so as to gently pull, precise as tweezers, at something in her fur. Glass, perhaps; it had left tiny cuts on her tongue before she'd begun nipping it out with her teeth. She paused to glance around, holding absolutely still—water, trees, wind, diving swifts and wary deer, gathering night. She had undomesticated origins; the dark did not worry her.

Upstream at least two miles, a man's voice continued reading sonorously, as it had for an hour now, a curiously old-fashioned voice, overly dramatic, an actor from the continental school, reciting for the third time the opening chapters of Joseph Conrad's *Heart of Darkness*. The tape reversed; the story continued, repeated. The car's driver had been trying to improve her mind. Through New Mexico she had been listening to National Public Radio, and had been fascinated to hear yet another installment of a story from her old hometown, from her own long-ago adolescence, where a serial killer, dormant for decades, had once again been taunting the media, a killer who'd hovered on the periphery of her formative years, his first victims having been neighbors of hers. Strangers, newcomers, but neighbors, nonetheless. Their house, a few doors down from hers, with the precise same floor plan; her uncle, who lived with her then, had been among the many men in the neighborhood initially considered a suspect. Fingerprinted, interrogated, eyed uneasily. Until the killer struck again, elsewhere, they'd all been wary of one another in the vicinity of Edgemoor and Murdock streets. Now the radio said he had made another public overture; he'd been doing it on and off for the last few months. The woman felt a prickling pride in being from the city where he'd killed people, the curious emotion of by-proxy notoriety.

Only after the radio signal fizzled completely, somewhere within the Navajo Nation, just after her second accident, had she been reduced to the book on tape. It was an effort to attend to the story, its teller so sinister with foreshadowing gloom, its language archaic, the syntax unnecessarily convoluted. Plus, she kept suffering the surprising sensation of the truck, from nowhere, jarring her when he clipped her car, a recurrent jolt thereafter, a flash of heat in her sternum, her bare foot leaping briefly from the pedal.

Her daughter was reading this book. She attended boarding school in the East, and the driver, the mother, wished to impress the girl, come Christmas. She wanted badly to make up for what she'd not taken seriously, earlier in her life, which was also what she was now, against intense teenage resistance, insisting that her daughter take seriously.

Affording tuition, fifteen-year-old Cattie had let her know after orientation, did not put them in the same class as her classmates. "Give it a shot," the mother had said. "That's all I'm asking."

"Okay," said Cattie. "But I don't want to."

The car in which the woman had been traveling, the car she'd handled so heedlessly today, was an expensive one, its interior designed to protect its passengers no matter the external damage, the vehicle boasting its own protective cage. Two months ago it had delivered her and Cattie to Vermont, to the quaint village that held the esteemed school. The mother had driven back across the country alone, then, alone and lonely; she'd taken this trip out of loneliness, too, but in the opposite direction, and without particular destination. She and the dog had traveled across Texas yesterday, stopping in El Paso for the night. Tempted after a few drinks, she'd refrained from dialing her daughter's cell phone; she'd made that mistake the last time she called Vermont. Then today, sober, she couldn't think what she'd say to the girl.

She'd crossed the state of Texas yesterday as if to be done with it; today she appeared to have the same agenda with New Mexico, traveling through and out of the rocky desert, *So long!*, and into Colorado, climbing above 7,000 feet, passing signs announcing the Continental Divide, ascending. The temperature had ranged from 95 to 26 degrees in the course of the journey, its decline in direct proportion to the car's progress north, and up.

Maybe she would make it her mission to drive through every state, say good-bye to each as she exited.

The animal had yipped when she caught the new air circulating in the cabin, wind that had passed over and brought with it glacier and pine, the scent of falling yellow leaves. She'd shoved her snout at the kennel's clasp, clicking her clever teeth at the latch, and her owner had reached back to free her, simultaneously cracking a back window so that the animal could further enjoy the mountain air, the car steered momentarily by knees. The dog wouldn't have perceived the Alpine vistas, the purple mountain tops iced with snow, blue spruce and blonde aspen. She might not have even registered the sharper curves, the way she slid on her padded bed inside the cage. Or she wouldn't have complained. But something in the air had alerted her, alarmed her, and she'd thrust her nose through the bars, madly licking the driver's hand. Frustrated, the woman had released her seat belt, and the car, always on call for such foolish maneuvers, sounded its nagging chime. The curve was no more dangerous than others, but there was neither shoulder nor railing, and the drop beside it precipitous. The mystery and whim of the highway engineers, who ran miles of sturdy guardrails in just such precarious places, and then without obvious reason, left a section open—opportunity, break, entry, and access to the yawning firmament.

The car had gone over without skid marks, directly into the lapse of barrier, then rolled longways, head to toe, rather than side to side. Its roof had peeled back on one revolution, and on the next, the windshield had landed in the driver's lap, a sheet of sparkling pebbles like chain mail. Her neck had been broken during the first tumble, her arm flung over her head by centrifugal force, the fingers snared by the sheered metal moon-roof rim. The dog had been saved by the doubleness of her enclosure: inside the kennel, inside the car's venerated metal egg. At the bottom of the hill, the vehicle landed on its wheels, finally at rest, not hidden from the highway but not in a location where anyone would be looking. After all, it was the peaks in the distance, the wide-shouldered majesty of Mounts Sunshine and Wilson, brilliantly snow-capped against the purple sky, somehow more vibrant than ordinary three-dimensionality, as if accompanied by the tonal shimmer of a clanged bell, there with a vague shrugging of bluing clouds, golden beams radiating as if from a godly crown, simmering red sun sinking behind. To encounter it was to shiver with pleasure and awe, overcome by beauty. Why would anyone glance down?

"That's not firewood, that's a tree," said the young woman to the young man who'd dragged his prize to their campsite.

"It'll last all night," he said. "It's huge." He grinned, baring his teeth. He'd dragged the tree by one of its tender speared ends, the heavy broken trunk creating a furrow behind. When he dropped it, he sniffed, frowning at his fingers.

"It's green. See, it just fell, it's got buds, it still bends." She illustrated by flexing a branch of the poor juniper back and forth like rubber. She did not say that this was more shrub than tree, that what he smelled on his fingers was the unique odor of its berries, which were edible, and which also, by the way, provided the source of his favorite liquor, gin. "Fires are made of dead wood. *Dry* dead wood." Her boyfriend hadn't wanted to go camping. He preferred bars and live music for weekend entertainment, sex on a queen-size mattress, in air-conditioning. Everything he'd done on their camping trip so far seemed like sabotage. Maybe he meant these efforts to be funny? He had a strange sense of humor, which had originally attracted Elise to him. He carried his lunch in an iron pail better suited to a factory worker from the forties, Mr. Wannabe Tool and Die. His only shoes were thrift-store Florsheims, his hat a fedora. Now he lit a joint and sat uneasily on his springy tree.

"How's there ever a forest fire if only old dead trees burn? How's the whole fucking state of California in flames if only the properly seasoned antique shit will go up? You already told me I couldn't dismantle the fence." The historic horse paddock and corral, long abandoned, rails merely suggesting the creatures they'd once contained.

This former Colorado summer camp had belonged to Elise's family and ancestors, sold off over the years one waterfront segment at a time. Officially, she was trespassing here. Yet she felt the heavier privilege of ownership, kinship, and did not worry about arrest. Arrest was the only enticement the boyfriend understood. She wished that Lance would make a real try at seeing the place as she wished him to: uniquely beautiful, an old horse pen beside a stream, the pen built on an even more ancient deer park, the perfectly circular deer park centered in the cluster of deciduous trees, cottonwoods and aspen and willows, small forest with spongy ground space for tents and hammocks and fire pits, the nearby stream from which her family had pulled fish and water, in which they had bathed and laundered and swam and built dams and floated rafts. Near which they'd gathered and laughed for decades. On its other side, the mountain stretched fantastically upward, its green-treed base evolving into a craggy cliff face on which you might reasonably expect to see Dracula's castle. Its brooding height provided miraculous mid-afternoon shade; elk stepped from the cool shadows to approach the water. The corral had been the final family parcel to sell; eventually a trophy log mansion would be built here, a fence and locking gate, a far more elaborate system of No Trespassing signs, a hired man in a combat-worthy vehicle patrolling day and night. Perhaps this was the bittersweet farewell visit, and how unfortunate to have to share it with Lance. Moreover, once they left here, she might be done with Lance for good. She had not conceived of camping as a litmus test. And yet.

This was the second day of their trip. Rain had forced them into Lance's car, the night before, where they'd eaten corn chips and drunk all of the liquor. The Sentra seats folded back far enough to have been sufficient for passing out. Their entire supply of drinking water had disappeared today to combat hangover. Now they were really camping, preparing to boil stream water over a fire. "I'll find wood," said Elise. She had already erected the tent and unpacked the makings of a camp stew, each act building on an argument in her favor, as if they were engaged in a competition or lawsuit, he more and more clearly the unquestionable loser. He once more fished around in the icy slosh of the cooler box, wishing for another bottle of beer, settling for a tainted chunk of ice.

Elise carried a canvas tote, collecting twigs and branches first, then sticks and bark, finally logs. The ground was soft with fallen leaves, a muffling cushion of yellow and orange and red. She built the pyramid in stages, Lance now sitting on the thick end of his too-fresh juniper, cup of foul cooler box water in one hand, glowing joint in the other. Elise lit a paper grocery sack at the bottom of her tidy pile, then headed out one final time for a last load of dense logs, the ones that would be a pulsing silver ruin by morning, when it was time to start all over again.

Behind her the fire had taken hold, a crackling, pleasing beacon in the moonless night. She was not afraid of the woods; she was proud to think she could survive in the wild. Last night Lance had locked the car doors, securing them inside while the rain and then hail pelted the hood and windshield; it had been amusing, when they were drunk: What did he expect would try to get them? "Opposable thumb," Elise had tried to teach him. "We're the only thing out here with opposable thumbs." Now Elise felt a tiny flare of embarrassment spark in her. It was embarrassment for him, Lance, who was so far out of his element, so inept at mere basics such as these: wood-gathering, tent-pitching, any outdoor skills, any entertainment that didn't involve electronics or drugs or sex, and embarrassment for herself, who had only just learned this about him. He had spent the day smoking weed, twitching and slapping his head to discourage the season's last blackflies, alarmed by the lazy clicking crickets whose mating season it seemed to be, snacking on recognizable snacks, wandering like a dowser with his open cell phone, seeking reception. Later, napping back in the car, radio set at a murmuring volume to override the noise of flowing water and jeering magpies.

"I grew up in L.A.," he explained, shrugging: What could he say? If only he'd been awed by the splendor. If only he'd perceived his lapse as a personal flaw, one he wished fervently to correct. Penitential, he would have been bearable. And, last resort, if only he cared enough about Elise's opinion of him to at least pretend these things, lacking them in fact.

She'd not found quite enough logs, sap-sticky canvas bag over her shoulder, flashlight in hand. It had grown finally truly dark; she refused to consult her watch, poke its lighted stem. Time, while camping, depended on rhythms other than those dictated by civilized devices. Was there a way to send Lance back to Phoenix, where she'd found him, without having to leave herself? The car was his; he'd grimaced and clenched over every rock and rut on the dirt road in. His oil pan, his precious oil pan.

At the corral, Elise detoured into the woods, there where the ancient fallen trees lay. Set next to the blaze, they would fizz and sputter, moss and dampness evaporating, and later would put out a rosy radiant heat, mesmerizing. Ants might emerge, rushing from the center. How would Lance react to that? She might move her sleeping bag outside, beside the fire and under the riotous profusion of stars, leave Lance in an anesthetized slumber inside the tent. She wondered, Would he worry that he could not lock that flapping door?

And then she heard a low animal hum. Her light fell from her hand, and she caught in its weak beam movement in the brush. Wildlife encounter information abandoned her. Play dead? Run? Make eye contact? Scream? Stand (this unlikeliest of all) with arms upraised and roar? Like any stunned being, Elise froze. The animal stepped from the brush, its eyes the first thing visible, glowing gold with reflected light, demonic. Coyote, she guessed, by its size and the cunning low-to-the-ground slide. But why would a coyote approach a person? Protecting its den, she reasoned. Rabid, she panicked.

She knelt for the flashlight, prepared to use it as a truncheon on the creature's crazed/maternal/rabid skull. But now the coyote crept closer, not predatory but groveling; not a coyote but a dog, its ears lowered not in menace but in supplication, fear, appeal. Another hapless domesticated beast, like Lance, loose in the woods, lost in the wild.

This one, however, she felt she could pity rather than scorn. Save rather than abandon.

"What the fuck?" Lance said mildly, when she brought the dog back to the fire. The woods, he was discovering, were full of surprises. For its part, the dog slid behind Elise, as skeptical of the man as the man was of it.

"I found her. She found me. I think we should let her sleep in the car. I'm afraid she'll run off." The dog was somebody's pet. Her coat was glossy and she followed commands, sitting when told, chewing delicately at the beef jerky Elise handed her, one piece at a time, her teeth sharp and white, her tongue two splotchy colors. Behind her ears, the thick tufted fur was slightly damp. Only the gash on her underside spoke of mishap, a newly scabbed twelve-inch cut, as if somebody had attempted to fillet her. As if she'd escaped that.

Lance said, "And we want her to not run off why?"

"Otherwise she'll die." Like you, Elise was tempted to say. She's as unprepared as you are, for this.

"Not in my car," he said.

Elise was thirty-one years old; for the last several months, she'd stopped taking birth control pills, ready to push her entanglement with Lance further. It had always been she who moved them to the next step, from work acquaintances to lovers, from occasional dates to daily monogamy, from separate dwellings to the shared town house (hers). Otherwise, it seemed he would be content to remain in stasis, adhere to a routine, plan no further than a day in advance, perhaps a week if there were a band in town he wanted to hear. He still worked for the temp agency; he had favorite weekly TV shows; his long-term dealer was his cousin, safe as houses, close as kin. He was, in general, sedentary, unadventurous, incurious, steady—maybe that was how Elise had sold him to herself, once upon a time.

How was it, she wondered as they bickered that night, as the thick-pelted dog laid her chin on Elise's thigh and blinked beneath Elise's distracted scratching of her head, that she so clearly foresaw that this animal's unlikely manifestation—tamed wild thing emerging from the black forest, stepping then into the middle of Elise's limping relationship—would be that relationship's coup de grâce?

And still the voice spoke the words. Still the chime chimed. The headlights would have been lit, safety day-runners, had they not both shattered on impact, so that only the inside dome shone. Far above, on the highway that had once-upon-a-time been a rail bed, carved at great mortal risk into the mountainside by men greedy and heedless for gold, a winding two-lane ledge that hugged the geologic formation, a station wagon crept past. At the wheel a man clutched fiercely, his gaze fixated on the centerline. His wife slept oblivious beside him. In the back, his little girl glanced through the window, up at the stars, then down over the fathomless drop. For a second she caught a glimpse of a faintly lighted box, a woman inside. "Snow White," she said aloud.

"Shhh," her father warned. "Your mother is asleep."

WINTER

CHAPTER 2

THEY HAD AN ONGOING HABIT of standoffs concerning phone calls. One would outwait the other, time and again, proving that *she*, mother or daughter, needed the other, daughter or mother, less. Cell phone technicalities meant that they couldn't call without consequence, without the effort being recorded, the need noted later by the smug recipient, winner, whether a message was left or not. The loser caught caring. Proud, stubborn, superficially tough, secretly tender: these were the traits shared by mother and daughter. They'd rather throw a punch than shed a tear, burn bridges than mend fences, always an eye for an eye; after only a month at boarding school, Cattie had been put on three kinds of probation (knee sock violation; absence of footnotes; and going off grounds after curfew).

They were in one of those phone standoffs when Misty Mueller's car flew off the road. For days afterward—for days *beforehand*, truth be known—Cattie Mueller assumed they'd been playing their cellular version of Chicken, two people declining to dial the other.

If she'd called her mother, the phone would have chirped like a muted bird on the forest floor, insulated there between the fallen and the falling leaves.

It was late autumn in the Rockies, and not long after the accident, snow reached the road and river. Hunters—poachers, trespassers—had made an anonymous tip at the Rico Conoco; the alerted stoned teenage counter help had waited until she was no longer high before notifying the sheriff, who had brought along his rock-climbing neighbor in order to verify the car and body, a wrecker with the county had then cleared the scene, and only then, finally, had a long chain of phone calls begun. Sheriff to the state of Texas and to the State Farm Insurance office, State Farm Insurance agent Dick Little who actually knew Misty Mueller, and had had occasion to catch sight of her daughter. Dick Little prided himself on a personal approach to insurance, as if Houston were still (was it ever?) a small town. Misty lived in the neighborhood; she'd come to his Montrose office a few times on the January Sunday morning when the annual city marathon took place, when Dick threw his party, watching from the office deck, serving mimosas, and cheering the runners. He and Misty had been drinking orange juice minus the champagne; sometimes she attended the same AA meetings he did, one or the other of them providing rides. Dick had mistaken her for a lesbian.

It was Dick Little who first began to search for Misty's daughter, Cattie, and he was successful only because he'd been wily enough to guess that her cell number would be only a digit different from her mother's, which had been logged on a form she'd updated just six months ago. *Cattie here*, said a flat gruff voice just like Misty's. *Gimme what you got, mothafucka.*

"Whoa," said Dick Little; he didn't know any teenagers.

The lawyers were slower to react. The will had been filed a decade earlier; her address had changed since then, as had her job, her phone numbers, the vehicle she drove. Her daughter had

grown out of adorable toddlerhood into troublesome adolescence and been sent to Vermont, to a boarding school, and that
information had been garnered only because the woman who
picked up the phone at Houston's Lamar High remembered
having faxed multiple transcripts and immunization records east
on behalf of Catherine (Cattie) Mueller. It was as if that private
school thought the child might be feral and her home state negligent.

Still, by the time Cattie learned of her mother's death, it had
been weeks since they'd spoken. It seemed unthinkable that a
standoff could end this way, one of them having finally gotten
the indubitable last word, and now being told, in the head of
school's office by no fewer than three adults, that Cattie had, in
effect, won. Cattie sat without speaking, staring at her uniformed
thighs, a plaid that vibrated if she let her eyes go loose in focus.
All disciplinary action taken against her at this school had involved her refusal to speak—to provide justification or explanation for persistent rule breaking (uniform knee socks: lost; laptop
computer: neglected; nighttime curfew: ignored). Each adult had
a style of handling youth; none of them was effective with this
girl, not the head of school's tart British professionalism, not
the school therapist's hip liberal understanding, not the band
director's goofy know-nothing nerdiness. They'd been aware of
her isolation, not the ordinary shy newness of a recent enrollee
eager for friends but the more entrenched solitude of the loner
who didn't care if people liked her. In her unwavering stare one
saw the adult looking out. By and large, people declined to challenge her.

She nodded in answer to all of their questions and assertions.
She understood they were there for her. She agreed that it was
tragic. She heard them say that she was stunned, that they were
stunned—who *wouldn't* be stunned? Other students had lost
parents. The school was not unfamiliar with this dilemma. There

was precedence, contingency plans, a series of next steps. She understood everything they had so far said. She did indeed wish to be left, for a moment, alone.

As a group, this trio of adults decided the girl must be in shock. This was what they told themselves when they finally left her by herself (simply vacated the head of school's office, prepared to wait out her shock in the waiting room with the receptionist and college counselor, the plate of organic, gluten-free, non-transfat cookies someone had brought). Alone, Cattie had reached for her cell phone and gone to her saved voice messages. With shaking hands she extended the stay of one of them, her mother's fatigued call from some night last summer, when they'd been back in Houston. Cattie hadn't come home on time—not because she was doing any of the things her mother assumed, but because she was carrying out an experiment. One needed friends to do what her mother feared she'd be doing, and Cattie didn't have friends, really. It seemed like so much work, having friends. From the moment she'd weighed the costs and benefits, Cattie had not consciously sought out the companionship of others. Young, she'd had a neighbor friend, a boy whose sidekick qualities had been second nature to her. There he'd been, for as long as she could recall, and friends they'd inevitably become. Since then, it seemed that friendship required foresight and effort and connivance. To Cattie, it seemed not only like work but vaguely false. People accused her of being selfish; maybe not needing others was what they meant.

Her mother both wanted her to make friends and feared what would happen if she did, where she would go with those friends when night fell. But Cattie's worst behavior—shoplifting, smoking cigarettes, skipping class—occurred during the daylight hours, and always alone. She felt, sometimes, too old to be the age of her peers. Why did they take pleasure in the ridiculous acts they performed together? She studied them at school, at the mall, on the streets near her house, which was located in the neighborhood where teenagers ran wild, there among the tattoo parlors and gay bars, the condom emporium and the comic-book shop, the neighborhood of the creative anachronisms, the addicts, the artists, the homeless, and the giddy tourist wannabes who were Cattie's age. She agreed with her mother: teenagers were irritating. And maybe Cattie was too lazy to be a proper one. Why attract attention, suspicion, penalty?

At night, when her mother worried, she was out committing the most harmless of activities: walking. Dangerous, it might have seemed, except that nobody bothered Cattie on her walks. At her side, her dog, that unpredictable deterrent. She navigated away from her own neighborhood to the mild one to its south, the one that held Rice University in its damp heart of trees and pulsing frogs, its ochre-colored streetlights, under which she wandered with fascination over the buckling sidewalks, glancing in windows, letting sweat drip down her back, murmuring occasionally to her pet. She would never walk to school or to the grocery store, never with a specific destination or errand, but she had an endless energy for walking after dark. She thought. She liked the quality of thinking that aimless walking brought on, of being invisible, the sensation of her inside and outside merged and therefore untroubled. She was often out testing her theory of invisibility, the dog panting reliably alongside.

The cell had vibrated in her pocket on one of those late-night walks. She had been at the Mecom Fountain, into which somebody had poured laundry soap. This happened with regularity, a grand bubbling disaster, slick suds spilling into the traffic roundabout, causing cars to slide. "No," she told the dog as it stepped forward to take a drink. "Dummy," she admonished. As soon as the message had been left, she listened. She might not pick up when her mother phoned, but she paid attention. She retrieved the message, and covered her exposed ear against the noise of cars, of people leaning out their windows to point and laugh at the festive bubbles. She listened then. She listened now.

"I hate that greeting," her mother said. She always started her messages that way, she couldn't help it. *Gimme what you got, muthafucka*. Her mother had been annoyed that evening, and worried, furiously fearful, that Friday-night feeling, but in the middle of this message there'd been a strange pause, a hiccup, an intake of breath, as if, while talking, her mother had seen something that startled her out of her single-minded task of reprimanding her daughter. Misty was suddenly hearing her own words. Cattie knew enough about Misty's own adolescence to recognize the shift, the way the woman took ironic note of the fact that she was talking to herself as she addressed her daughter, the bemused consciousness that entered her voice, its doubleness, and its uselessness. She badly did not want Cattie to lead the life she'd led. Even as Cattie once argued against this logic—"I have to learn by making my own mistakes!" she'd heard herself self-righteously wail—she'd known only an idiot would believe that. Along with taking long walks, Cattie read a lot of books. They'd taught her a fair amount about mistakes. She thought of herself, often, as a character in a book, in the third person, wandering a world that could be described as if from above, or beyond. Narrated. Seeing herself in a scene, rather than feeling caught up in that same scene, was a sensation she had lived with for a long time. It was one of the ways invisibility worked, after all. Did others feel that way, she wondered, or was it the explanation of her freakishness?

Her mother shared that freakishness, Cattie thought. They knew each other well. They could have traded places. Their voices and their penmanship and their dress size were the same. When Cattie had gone for braces, Misty did so, too.

Cattie had saved a more recent message from her mother, but she erased it now without replaying it. An act of loyalty, there in the head of school's office in Vermont. "Why did you call me in the middle of the night?" she'd asked her mother, the morning after missing the call. Her phone had been right beside her head, right beside her bed, but she'd slept through.

"I didn't call you," her mother said.

"Yes, you did. You left a message."

On the other end, silence. To spare her, Cattie had invented the reason: a pocket or purse call, made inadvertently, the phone dropped or bumped and then, all on its own, dialing out to the world. Not tears and laughter and slurred affection, but simple noise—the television, no doubt!

But her mother of course would know otherwise. And so had begun their standoff. Her mother had been drunk. The message was proof. They both knew, they were both not saying. Not saying was maybe more communication than saying, Cattie considered. And erasing it now was an act of love larger than saving it. Cattie then listened once again to that more coherent mother, the one who, last June on a Friday night, had been waiting at home for Cattie to come safely back.

Cattie sighed, wishing she could exit the head of school's office without encountering the adults, but they'd effectively made themselves a gauntlet on the other side of the closed door. Eventually somebody knocked on it—Ms. Windhall *had* to, because, well, it was her office. With her she brought Ito Black, the only student at school any of them could recall seeing Cattie speaking to in her first weeks here. He was the gay boy on a hardship scholarship from only forty miles away in New Hampshire who wished to become a fashion designer. He was seventeen, had already swept the school fashion show two years running, and had latched on to Cattie because he had heard her one day in band, honking away on a borrowed, crappy saxophone. He wanted her to work up some sort of musical accompaniment to a winter collection for small children. Her playing reminded him of the way a three-legged elephant walked, he said. His freewheeling creativity, his out-and-out silliness, interested Cattie; he followed her around without her permission, liking her against her wishes, just like her old next-door neighbor friend Ralphie, the tagalong. She who never smiled, seen now everywhere pursued by the boy who couldn't stop grinning. He was the only one she personally told that her mother had died, there in the office, the two of them now outnumbering the adults in the room, effectively sending the head of school away once more, Cattie a frightening figure, it seemed, her orphaning a form of empowerment.

Even when he wept, clutching her head awkwardly from a standing position, Ito smiled. It was as if some significant nerves and muscles had been severed around the bottom half of his face, leaving him afflicted with inappropriate, even frightening, glee.

"Boo!" he said through this toothy rictus. "It's so bad!"

"I don't want everyone to know."

They found out anyway. They loved to hug you, those private-school people. They loved a reason to actually discern her, finally, invisible, stone-faced Cattie. But before their sympathy could grow epidemic, she left, driven by Ito to his stepsister's home in Montpelier. Ito said that Cattie reminded him of Joanne; for a few days Cattie tried to see what it was about the petulant stepsister that she resembled. Joanne rolled out of bed pissed off every morning, as if the night had served her up one bad dream after another, as if people had been insulting and blaming and humiliating her for hours, as if she'd been waiting on them and was exhausted, along with being unappreciated. Gradually, however, over the course of the day, her mood improved, until, by evening, she was somewhat conversant, pleased to be watching television, smoking cigarettes, eating the only kind of food she kept in her kitchen, either snack- or industrial-size everything, and drinking diet beer.

"How come you aren't going home?" Joanne asked, on the third evening of their odd cohabitation.

"I don't have any relatives. I'm afraid somebody will put me in a foster home."

"I was fostered," Joanne said, suddenly pissed off again.

"No offense," Cattie said. On the rare occasions she opened her mouth, in went her foot. "But I'm from Texas, you know."

"Ah," said Joanne, suddenly understanding everything, insult forgotten. The East Coast thought very little of Texas, Cattie had discovered. When she hadn't displayed much of a drawl, her new classmates seemed disappointed. What good was she, if not to provide novelty, to spice up and enrich their experience?

Like most children (surely like most children, she reasoned; perhaps like no other children, she feared), Cattie had often fantasized that her mother died. Maybe it was this elaborate and frequent imaginary scenario that now accounted for her relatively affectless reaction to the reality. She'd played out too many times her own lostness—walking bereft in the night of the big city, positing an existence of need and wits—for the fact to totally distress her; she and her mother were the only two members of their family; some part of Cattie's fictional narrated life had maybe already taken in and adjusted to orphanhood. She had, perhaps, foreseen it too clearly, and could not now claim surprise. And her new roommate Joanne seemed okay with that. She was passing time, not paying attention particularly to what or who walked through her door. Along with Cattie, there was a man in the attic who'd been in the army, off to war. Cattie heard him at night when he came down the foldout stairs in the hallway ceiling, crawling quietly from his hideout to eat some snack food, shower, clack away on the Internet for a while, then creep back up.

"PTSD," Joanne hissed knowingly. Cattie had no idea what she meant.

The room Joanne had assigned to Cattie was a child's bedroom. She slept on a single bed under a pile of dusty quilts. The bedroom had belonged to a boy, who was maybe eight or ten, and whose boyhood had been captured and preserved at least twenty years in the past. A stereo turntable and a collection of story records, Disney sound-track albums from movies Cattie had grown up watching on video. *The Jungle Book, Dumbo, The Aristocats*. Tunes she turned on when she went to bed, strangely soothing as they scratched and popped along at low volume. Also empty boxes of Legos, the pieces themselves fashioned into a chaotically colored simple house. A set of Hardy Boy books. Stuffed animals that smelled of mold and whose plushness had been worn flat by time, perhaps by affection. Whose room had this been? Not Ito's.

Joanne daily donned her waitress uniform and grumbled out the door, slamming it behind her. Cattie would then always look up, toward the ceiling, tuned abruptly to the other human presence in the house, the man in the attic. She was not sure what she'd do when her cash ran out, the five hundred she'd wisely withdrawn and hoarded since arriving at St. Christopher's, now to be parceled out sparingly until she decided what next. When asked, Ito had told the head of school he'd accompanied Cattie on foot to the double-wide bar at the edge of the village, top of the list of places in the village students had been warned to avoid, where she'd probably hitched a ride with a logger in one of their ubiquitous thundering trucks. That would send her south, back to Houston. Who would think to look north and west, over in blameless Montpelier, upstairs at a shabby house near the bottom of a hill right alongside the train tracks? Why would anyone run away there?

Cattie wondered herself, after a couple of weeks. Could foster care be much different? Dwelling with strangers, one a grumpy woman, the other a vaguely scary, shadowy man? Wasn't that sort of the hallmark of foster care?

Ito's visits were what kept her at Joanne's, provided a routine and purpose to her days. The house itself was not very welcom-

ing. Its rooms were dim, its windows filthy in the way of the neglected aquarium, and the assortment of furniture not just ugly
but uncomfortable or broken or bad smelling, stuff that had been
discarded, second-, third-, fourthhand stuff, warehoused here
rather than being hauled to the dump. Joanne had inherited the
home and its contents from one of the parents that the two step-
siblings did not share, a father gone in the usual gone-father way,
off with a new wife, having left his first set of children the way he
had his belongings, trading up. Joanne was trapped here by fi-
nances, not ambitious enough to pull herself out of a hand-to-
mouth existence, her gesture toward a savings account the recent
development of tenants, her nod to possible change the ancient
For Sale by Owner sign teetering in her yard. "It's totally don't
ask, don't tell," Ito gleefully explained to Cattie. "She can't be
harboring a fugitive if she doesn't know you're a fugitive."

"I always heard that ignorance of the law was no excuse."

"*Bliss*, dude," Ito corrected. "Ignorance is bliss."

"Your stepsister is not blissful," Cattie told him. He came as
often as he could, parked in the alley alongside the house, and
then wandered with Cattie around Montpelier's downtown for a
few hours. Ito's car was a forbidden thing, unknown to the school
administrators or his parents, left when he drove back to St. Christopher's behind the village bakery whose owner didn't mind.

Ito loved the subterfuge he'd engineered for Cattie, his small
part when he joined her. She wasn't sure what she'd do without
his energy for the project. Go back to Houston? Finish the year at
boarding school? Her mother had made no excuses about their
lack of family; Cattie's father was literally unknown to her, one of
three—bad, worse, worst—possibilities, men from her promiscuous and renounced past. "Wasted," Misty said of her own youth,
dispensing with it. She had been raised by her grandmother in
Kansas, and the old woman had died many years before Misty
had left her old hometown of Wichita, never to return. Theirs was

a corrupt bloodline, Cattie was given to know; the closest kin Misty had was a cousin who, during the final encounter, had attempted to kill her, leaving her with a broken nose and a concussion. "The only reason he didn't succeed is because the phone rang, broke his concentration. I'm a person who actually was saved by the bell. You call that family? You want anything at all to do with that bullshit? 'Cause I sure don't."

When she found out she was pregnant, Misty had quit drinking. Until Cattie left town, she had been sober. Maybe that one night, that one phone call, was her only lapse. Cattie was not unhappy to have erased the drunk message, yet the fact remained: her mother had been alive, and sober, when they lived in the same place.

"Don't you love it here?" Ito shrieked.

"I don't love it here," she replied, and he laughed as if she were joking, bluntness her brand of deadpan wit.

Montpelier absorbed them, clerks greeted them when they came through doors, Ito always eliciting a smile, a free cookie, a bit of banter in the music shop, the outdoor store, the antique emporium—snotty barista, self-righteous hippie, dumb kayaker, deaf old lady. He found all novel human traits hysterically amusing, as if he were living in a cartoon, where unexplained action and nonsequitous dialogue were the norm, where violence and tragedy need not lead to tears. He trod lightly, he skimmed like a water walker, he smiled and chattered like a monkey and then moved on. He had a very short attention span, so although he asked a lot of questions, they never tired Cattie. From him she had not had to hide her nonplussed response to her mother's death. She supposed this could actually be what those school officials had assured one another was shock. Eventually shock would wear off. But her mother had never trusted melodrama, and Cattie had grown up keeping her cool. Not so Ito. You might think somebody as flagrant and noisy as he would irritate people, but the opposite seemed true. He radiated too much cheer, too wide a smile, too contagious a curiosity. People reflexively smiled back.

And after his visits, off he went back to what they called St. Sincere. Everyone was so serious there, so *concerned*, from the head of school to the groundskeeper. Cattie had never been to school as a customer before. Before, it was always as an annoyance, an obstacle to a clean floor, impediment to a quiet hallway, interruption to a perfectly lucid lesson plan.

On Friday, during her last shift at the restaurant, Joanne asked Cattie to come help her vacuum and scrub and refill. The manager took Fridays off; Joanne accepted Cattie's help as partial rent payment. They also stole food, which was easier to do with an accomplice. The last bag of trash they left in the Dumpster was perfectly edible goods; later, they returned to retrieve it, spirit it home in Joanne's back seat. Frozen burgers, chocolate wedge the size of a brick, a thousand catsup packages.

Aside from Ito and Joanne, Cattie had no other encounters. When Dick Little the Houston insurance agent phoned, she didn't answer. "Whoa," he said, the first time he heard her message. It always drew a grown-up's comment. His lispy southern voice was soothing to Cattie, no disputing that; she had to admit that she missed the languid drawl of her hometown. The school also called, the brisk head of school and the soppy band teacher, both itching to scold her phone etiquette. By now her disappearance was registering with all the strangers who thought they knew her, that force field of adults, no doubt phoning one another, too, a crisscross of calls, a peculiar net overhead, yet still unable to locate or trap her. She listened to their voices on her machine, erasing before they finished speaking. Only her mother's message did she save, over and over, every day. She waited always for that pause, in between the righteous rage at Cattie's lateness, at Cattie's endangering herself out there in the perilous night world, in the streets among cars and men, bad drivers and bad desires, with the endless possibility of collision and injury and death, and then the switch, the hesitation, and next the awareness that Misty was an aged miscreant herself, nearly a chuckle, the little comic self-check. Who was she to judge? the hitch said to Cattie, who was this pot to name the kettle black? And this was the small vacillating space that roused a flutter in Cattie's esophagus, just behind her ribs and in her throat, trapped moth, powdery wings.

CHAPTER 3

THE WICHITA SERIAL KILLER was back. Every morning, every night, the self-named BTK appeared once more in the news; for twenty-five years he'd lain dormant. Incarcerated, the city speculated: insane asylum or correctional facility; how else to explain the hiatus? Once, it could have been plausible that he'd moved on, to another town, to another smorgasbord of potential victims. In leaving, he might have changed his methods, no longer binding, torturing, killing, but some other set of signature initials. Strangling, dangling, mangling, the SDM of, say, Sioux Falls or Grand Rapids.

Nobody believed he'd have reformed. Neither did anyone really want to think he'd one day conveniently, coincidentally, have died. And of course bad guys did not simply disappear.

There would always be bad guys; evil was one of the rules.

At the nursing home the occupants—those who were free to come and go, those who were not—gathered around the television news at dusk the way their ancestors had around campfires, convening to bask in the glow, compare notes, agree and disagree, recall and invent, horrified and thrilled to have their despicable killer indisputably returned. For a little while it overrode the

other monotonous sounds of the place: the moaning and complaint that came drifting out of one room or another, all the
time, day and night; the Haitians' lilting voices in the break
room; the security person's ludicrous buzzing walkie-talkie; the
burbling oxygen tanks, beeping monitors, clattering carts; the
creaking old building itself, former private psych hospital from
the 1970s, as it stood up to the relentless prairie wind—all faded
under the shrill sense of a more pressing alarm.

In the circle of the lighted screen tonight were: the former university professor and her visitor; the former city magistrate who
now cradled a scruffy stuffed animal on whom she bestowed constant maternal affection; the former housewife and mother who
was now known only as The Woman Who Wept; the former
school-bus driver and Girl Scout leader who read the same line of
her children's book over and over again, "Jesus *loves* the little
children"; the former college student, a too-young brain-injured
girl, no more than thirty years old, who was an advertisement for
motorcycle helmets; the three look-alike old men, former minister, postman, Cessna engineer, lined up now in Barcaloungers
like benched players on the team of the curmudgeonly, murmuring their bitterness and complaint; and the keepers, in their colorful pajama-like scrubs—the obese white lady who was in charge,
the tattooed Chicano intern, and the kind Haitian woman who
was fixing the hair of the unkind Haitian woman. All over town,
people sat, together or alone, to study their local celebrity, that
naughty prodigal son.

This was the hour Catherine Desplaines chose to visit her
mother. From watching crime drama, she had learned to spread
mentholated ointment beneath her nose when entering a fetid
space. She had a gag reflex like a cat's.

"Grace Harding," she said to the lumpy security person at the
front desk. Probably a woman, given the Christmas ornament
earrings, two plastic Rudolphs with blinking noses. They flashed

intermittently, the only less-than-dull aspect of the woman, who wasn't even reading a magazine. Just looking blankly at the parking lot she faced, the tin-pan-colored December Kansas sky. Was she medicated? Contemplative? Merely depressed, as any person might be, by her job? No. She was watching the news, which was reflected in the glass of the door, the talking head on the giant screen behind her, the excited newscaster who'd not yet been born when the BTK was first around.

Guests were supposed to check in; residents were not supposed to leave without paperwork. Yet there were no other signatures besides Catherine's on today's roster. The woman had not met her eyes when she punched in the code on the door's outside keypad. The numbers, inside and out, made a song, a simple tune that could have been easily decoded, had anyone been paying attention, had anyone wanted to break in or out. It was always on Catherine's mind to mention this flimsy arrangement to somebody, merely suggest they change the code now and then. But to whom would she take her thought? Certainly not the security guard.

She heard that tune at night sometimes, just running through her head, reminder of the grim place her mother had ended up.

"I like your earrings."

"Hmm," the guard replied, still studying the reflection just over Catherine's shoulder.

Catherine moved timidly around the woman. She tried never to make trouble here. She wanted no bad feeling to surround her mother, nothing for this security person, nor the caretakers or volunteers or administrators, to hold against her. The home wasn't classy enough to require kindness from its employees or residents. Only the most modest of efforts had been made to hide its institutional aspects—standing lamps in some rooms to take the place of the overhead fluorescents; a volunteer harpist who arrived on Tuesdays to roll her battered instrument out of its closet, ready to play for whomever requested it; and the three fat cats who lived in the television lounge, leaping lazily from lap to lap, heavy staticky creatures who'd been rescued from their Alzheimer's-afflicted owners. Did they mind that they had several different names? That they, like the others who lived here, could not step outdoors at will? That every now and then they would be injured by an errant cane or wheelchair or walker?

"How was Green Acres?" her husband would ask, when Catherine came home. He never joined her. He preferred to treat the place like a joke. He was only a few years younger than his mother-in-law.

"She could live with us," Catherine had said to him once, hesitantly, a test.

"No," said he, "she absolutely could not." And Catherine was terribly relieved.

Professor Emeritus Grace Harding sat in the lounge among the others, although in general she preferred the newspaper to the television as a place to receive information. Beside her, unfortunately, sat her only other regular visitor, Yasmin Keene.

"Hi Mama," Catherine said, resting her hands on her mother's shoulders. "Hi, Dr. Keene."

"Catherine," said Yasmin primly, unhappy as always; her tone of voice always suggested that Catherine had earned yet another demerit. She sat wedged in a wing chair, her brow creased, her heavy lips down-turned, looking for all the world like the chastising high priestess of a disappointing African tribe. This impression was aided by the ebony walking stick she habitually grasped in her right hand, with its fierce carved knob and spiraling length, like a giant corkscrew she might decide to plunge through the heart of somebody, and gladly. She used the stick to walk, to point, to tap against the floor like a scepter as if to call order to a meeting. If one of the cats threatened to approach her chair, Yasmin used her stick to wave it away. Her short Afro was white now, like a cap of popcorn on her black, black head, and her customary outfit was faded, a once-vibrant kente weave, a loose covering that, on anyone else, would be named a muumuu, the tentlike thing with random pleats. Under her incensed gaze, and in spite of the debilitating heat of the room, Catherine decided not to remove her coat and hat; Drs. Yasmin Keene and Grace Harding had always taken a dim view of the attention Catherine paid to dressing herself.

Dress up was for little girls, not grown-ups. Would Catherine never grow up?

"It's looking like snow," she said brightly to the group at large. The curmudgeons had initially turned her way, anticipating the moment when Catherine would strip off her coat and display herself, then looked back at the television when she didn't. Her mother was the only resident without a designated easy chair and blanket out here in the lounge. Struck by stroke, she could no longer speak, but she made her statement regardless: she had a purely temporary relationship to this room and its occupants, to television and the low culture it encouraged. Her damage was a specific cruelty, Catherine thought, her lack of speech. Or it was poetic justice, some scolding moral lesson from myth or fable, her mother the pontificating professor, never without an opinion she could articulate in lengthy, grammatically correct extemporaneous paragraphs, persuasively, downright aggressively, the person who treasured speech above all else, now utterly mute.

Yasmin said, "She didn't get her *Times* today." Her tone of voice said that this was Catherine's fault. She treated the home like a prison sentence her old colleague had been mistakenly made to serve. Her visits, as a result, were like those of a lawyer to her wrongly accused client. Moreover, Yasmin's own children, unlike Catherine the frivolous clotheshorse, had all become exemplary citizens in the world of ideas and culture. Surely they would never have moved their mother into a place like Green Acres.

If Catherine were braver, she might say aloud what she often thought: Why didn't Yasmin offer to share *her* house with her mother?

But Catherine wasn't very brave. "I'll go look," she told Yasmin, concerning the *New York Times*.

She located it in the break room, its parts separated, her mother's room number buried now beneath classifieds and inserts from the local paper. In the past, at the breakfast table, her mother had narrated ceaselessly over the morning's news. Catherine could still see her father's colluding smile to her, his nearly imperceptible shrug that forgave and indulged and defused his wife's tiresome habit, and, as usual, this brought on Catherine's most frequent recurrent fantasy: her mother and father dying together, both swiftly taken on the same day, neither left to suffer the loss. In her fantasy, her father was not alone when he died but sitting beside her mother. Then he could reach out his hand for her mother's hand, and the merciful aneurysm that had hit him like a sudden bolt of lightning would carry sufficient buzzing currency to extinguish them both. Tears, as usual, came to Catherine's eyes.

This was the kind of soft-boiled thinking her mother abhorred. In another wishful fantasy, Catherine granted herself a few helpful siblings with whom she could share this guilty exasperation and wretchedness, an older sister to give her advice, and a couple of older brothers for protection and adoration. Catherine was not made to be an only child. Not made to be half orphaned, either. And who, in the real world, was ever going to witness or reward or punish her for her daily service?

"Earning some stars in your heavenly crown," her husband would say drolly. Despite the mentholated ointment, Catherine could smell the remains of dinner—breaded meat, boiled root vegetables, some sickening pureed sweet. The residents ate all of their meals depressingly early, and on plastic divided trays nicked and faded from multiple trips through the scalding dish-washing machine. Her mother wasn't finicky about food, thank God; imagine if Catherine's husband Oliver lived here.

Not so difficult to imagine; one day he might be in a home. Not this one, of course; he'd design and build his own, a model facility, classy as all of Oliver's businesses were. He was an en-trepreneur, a so-called idea man who had helped start dozens of businesses in Wichita—restaurants, spas, movie theaters, bars, coffee shops; he found locations, financed the start-ups, trained the personnel. He had an uncanny ability to predict what the next logical need could be in this affluent yet conservative market—and the place to locate it. He'd been succeeding at this calling for decades, by now; Catherine had met him when she needed a job nearly twenty years ago, when his first restaurant/bar had already spawned its offshoots. He was much older than she, a fact her mother had gone out of her way to decry, long ago when Catherine had married, mourning her daughter's refusal to see Oliver as an antifeminist decision, a throwback desire for male dominance. "He'll be like another parent!" she'd said, as if any fool could see the doomed predicament of that.

Moreover, he'd had a vasectomy. Her mother's objections had been thoroughly laid out, an argument built on sound logic, one that would have held up in court, had such decisions been reached that way, were there justice.

Catherine had appreciated her father's submissive silence on the matter; he understood the vagaries of love, its curious tendency to illogic. And like his daughter, he was accustomed to being the listener, the respondent, to Grace's opinions.

"Your mother needed a son," Oliver diagnosed. "Not a pretty daughter."

Trophy wife, her mother might have said, concerning Oliver's motives. Her colleague Yasmin Keene would have nodded in agreement.

It was as if her husband had battled her mother for possession of Catherine, and won.

As a result, he refused to visit Green Acres. Catherine held it against him, although he might not realize that. To punish him, she imagined him here, debilitated in a wheelchair, locked inside this building with a bored security guard between himself and freedom, paralyzed, say, so that he couldn't do anything about the annoying cats who would keep leaping into his lap, shedding on his black clothing. The harpist and her cloying music . . .

Only accidentally, only because there was so little here to stimulate the imagination, to fill the torpid passage of nursing-home time, did Catherine notice the bundle of mail on the counter, there behind the basket of Splenda, the plastic cup of stirrers, the sticky spill of Cremora, mail for the residents, some of them deceased. She picked through it idly, seeking the odd bill or card that might have her mother's name on it, the usual gruesome coupons from funeral homes and insurance companies. Instead, she found her own name, her maiden name (her mother had sorely wished she'd kept it). The envelope had been forwarded from the old house, where she hadn't lived since she left for the college dorm in the fall of 1979. It was from a lawyer's office in Houston, Texas. The postmark on it was weeks in the past.

She took both it and the newspaper back to the lounge.

Her mother received the *Times* with her working hand, and Yasmin said, "Hmmph." Catherine decided to take off her coat and hat; as long as Yasmin was going to disapprove anyway, she might as well treat the curmudgeons to a little flash of cleavage and knee, her tame, game striptease. Then she lowered herself to the floor by her mother's chair, wrapping an arm around her mother's calf, leaning her cheek to her thigh. It was easier to be affectionate, now, when her mother couldn't scold her for being sentimental and silly, for a fondness of hugs and kisses and endearments.

Catherine sort of relished the change, to have lost that former mother, the teacher, the talker, the person in charge; that giver of grades, bestower of allowance, withholder of gifts. Noisy and imperious, possessing moral certainty and a confident no-nonsense heart, her mother would bully you into agreement, either bully you or assume that she had when you didn't disagree. Catherine now savored not having always to listen, to agree, to pretend to agree, to pay attention to what she was pretending or not pretending to agree with. Passivity could be exhausting.

But also, curiously enough, now that she couldn't know precisely what was going on in her mother's head, Catherine found herself occasionally interested in knowing.

The television blared as if to make up for the living human diminishment in the room; how would this place seem, minus laugh tracks and commercial jingles, one large grinning orange face after another, and the patriotic orchestral flourishes that announced the news? The serial killer's comeback and his recent letters to the station were a fascinating unfolding story, a new clue every time the city seemed poised to forget him once more. The broadcaster's attempt at showing concern would have been comical, had Catherine been watching at home, safe in her husband's ironic attitude. But here, at Green Acres, surrounded by the dying and their keepers, she could not feel confident disdain.

"Local authorities have no doubt of the authenticity of these souvenirs," the blond woman was saying in that iconic newscaster voice, so sincerely fascinated, every fourth or fifth syllable dipping down. The serial killer's most recent overture had been a package left in a park, in it a PJ doll with a bag tied round her head, hands and feet bound with panty hose. Also a driver's license belonging to one of his victims. "Police were a*lert*ed to the package *weeks* ago," she declared, this token woman on the team. But it was an ordinary pedestrian, much later, who finally found it. Catherine's husband was always pointing out that both the killer and the cops were total bumblers.

"This monster has apparently returned to his favorite hunting grounds," said the woman. She straightened her blank papers on her phony desk, swiveling her earnest glance toward her co-anchor, the token black man on the team.

"Scary stuff, Kelsey," said he.

Favorite hunting grounds? Last spring, when the killer began his teasing communications after such a long absence, the press had seized upon his so-called "reign of terror." They meant the years 1974 until 1979. "My adolescence," Catherine had said to Oliver then. "Age thirteen to eighteen. I'm sure my mother thinks of it as a reign of terror."

"Adolescent girls are nightmares," he had agreed, shuddering at the thought. The younger of his two daughters had briefly lived with him and Catherine, during her own reign of terror.

Without warning, Dr. Yasmin Keene abruptly laughed—a startling bark, something you might mistake for a cry for help, or someone suddenly choking. A few of the caregivers glanced over, but Yasmin's fearsome expression precluded commentary, her walking stick in her gnarly grip like a weapon. Catherine remembered her from many afternoons at the old house, Yasmin and her mother sitting at the kitchen table drinking wine, ranting about their colleagues in, first, the English department, and then, later, in the women's studies department, which they'd founded. Founded out of passionate rage, their righteous indignation fueling a cause, a partnership, *sisterhood*, and, as a probable side effect, a friendship.

The wineglasses were always in danger of tipping over.

It had been Yasmin who wanted to watch the evening's news, not her mother. Dr. Harding wouldn't want to visit the lurid territory of local gossip. Catherine's high-minded mother preferred ideas. Now she gripped her beloved *Times* tighter, in its pages no mention whatsoever of this sick Kansas clown.

Yasmin would have to do the talking for both of them, as her interest in the killer was personal.

"He took one of my classes," she said to the group. The caregivers turned once more in her direction.

"What did she say?" demanded the feeblest of the curmudgeons. "What did you say?"

"It's true," Catherine added, seeing in the staff's collective bemused expression the usual tolerance of delusional thinking, those wacky stories that the tellers could not be convinced weren't true—enemies in the basement, taunts coming from the air ducts, furniture mistaken for kin, food for poison, fiction for fact, and vice versa. The kind Haitian, Catherine's favorite, aimed the remote at the screen to silence a screaming car salesman.

"Her with the stick, what'd she say?" asked the curmudgeon of his comrades.

Yasmin spoke more loudly. "One of his missives, after the seventh incident, was a parody of a folk song from a textbook I assigned for a few semesters." She leaned back and lowered her chin into her neck as if expecting gasps and questions. None came. *Missives, incident, parody, textbook, semesters*: this was not the vocabulary of serial killing. Beside her, Catherine's mother stiffened in her seat, her desire to aid the tale a vibration in Catherine's ribs.

"It was this crazy old folk song," Catherine announced reluctantly, "and he imitated it when he told the newspaper about how he stalked this poor woman, and he left a copy at the library, the building right beside Dr. Keene's office, in the Xerox machine. So he had to be one of her students, you see? The police went through her class lists. She had to have taught the BTK." Catherine ransacked her mind for any other titillating morsel; the thing was, this particular "victim" had gotten away. The letter was a lament about having missed her. It wasn't much, really, in the grand scale of things. Yasmin was scowling at her.

"Excuse me?" said the Haitian politely to Dr. Keene, "but what is your teaching specialty?" She gave the word five syllables.

Women's studies, Catherine almost said. This would be the moment to fashion as an anecdote for her husband's amusement. Ha! Women's studies, indeed.

"Folk culture," Yasmin reported.

"Ah," said the Haitian, smiling brightly.

"Unmute," ordered one of the curmudgeons in the Barcaloungers, the one on Yasmin's other side.

It was the sports announcer's turn to ply his trade.

Catherine's letter from Houston was puckered, with a coffee ring on it. She worked open the seal and began reading. The language made no immediate sense to her. *Decedent*, it said. *Pursuant to wishes.* If anyone were watching, she would have been horrified to reveal her struggle in comprehending, her panic at her obvious lack of intelligence, her poor heart racing as she labored to wrest logic out of yet another page of information that would not avail itself to her. She could bring home what confounded her to have her older husband rescue her. As her mother had predicted, he would be her parent, protector, translator. He wouldn't be scornful of her uncertain, flustered response. But by instinct, she had leaned away from her mother's knee, not wanting her interference. She needed only be patient, read the language over and over again. Her mother valued quickness, and Catherine wasn't quick.

In the amplified and overheated atmosphere of Green Acres, she applied a methodical attention, slowly taking in what would otherwise simply overwhelm her, send her to the grown-ups to relieve the burden. Here, Catherine could take her time. She had another half hour to kill, after all; there were still the meteorologist's bantering antics to anticipate.

After several readings, there in her pretty dress at her mother's feet on the lounge linoleum floor, Catherine eventually discerned that she was the named legal guardian of a minor child.

CHAPTER 4

T HE FIRST THING Oliver Desplaines did was turn the letter over to his lawyer. "You have a lawyer?" his wife said.

"Of course I have a lawyer."

"You don't have to get testy. Why would I know that?"

"You might ask why you *wouldn't* know it."

"No need?" she posited, turning her perplexity into a grinning bit of fun. What Catherine knew and did not know continued to surprise Oliver; women, with the possible exception of his mother-in-law, appeared to undergo some other educational preparation than men—a charming, idiosyncratic, mushy curriculum that privileged people-pleasing over practicality. In the extreme case of his wife, he suspected she'd rejected an interest in the workings of the world in order to thwart her mother, an act of vixenish rebellion, one he'd mostly found quite charming. Mostly, but not wholly.

The document in question had languished at the nursing home after languishing at the post office; his wife might never have received it. Much of her life seemed haphazard that way, unplanned, her calendar of days only sporadically penciled in. She couldn't have located countries or continents on a globe, yet it was she who remembered the birthdays of managers and the names of their offspring; it was she who came smiling and waving through the doors of their businesses every now and again to remind them that they were a sort of family, Oliver the distant dad with the wallet and spreadsheets and the authority to punish, Catherine the cheerful slightly zaftig mom to whom you could go in tears.

"Roe and Roe and Roe," he told her, naming the law firm.

"As in 'merrily, merrily, merrily'?"

"Verily. Will you do this?" he asked, holding up the razor. They were dressing for an evening of holiday partying, wandering in and out of the bathroom and bedroom, their reflections in half a dozen different mirrors. They looked, he thought, as if they'd fallen off a wedding cake, the too-skinny, too-tall man in the tux, the lovely voluptuous lady in the ivory dress.

"I adore it when you ask me to take a weapon to your neck," said Catherine. Because long ago he'd been called vain for requesting this same service of a previous wife, he was always visited by her irritating words when he requested the favor of this wife. *You're so vain*, she sang in his head. He wasn't *vain*, he argued back to YaYa, wife number one; he was *handsome*, and he attended to his grooming, that was all. Catherine, like his other two wives, was less fastidious—wine stain on her sleeve, lipstick on her teeth—but she was also much younger. She could get away with laxness. Not forever, not for much longer, but for now.

He watched her in the three-way bathroom mirrors as she scraped away his errant hairs, her tongue between her lips and her eyes intent, so serious in making sure he was smooth. He smiled at her, felt a frisson of fondness when she finished by giving him a little nip on the ear with her teeth. "Good to go," she said.

When his Sweetheart asked Oliver if he felt guilty about lying to his wife, Oliver provided a simple answer that was also a lie: "Yes," he said, and tried to seem contrite, torn. But he didn't feel guilt concerning love. In his life it was the sacred experience; he refused to turn away when it arrived. He had not invited it, after all; like any truly holy happenstance, it could not be found by conscious seeking. He might have felt guilty, doing that. But love had come regardless, in the form of the Sweetheart. She was one of his employees, a young woman who reminded him of Catherine twenty years earlier, a little awkward with herself, as if she'd woken one morning in a beautiful body that was not her own. She inhabited it in a slightly astonished mood, startling easily, sometimes glancing down at her own wrists or ankles and turning them, as if mesmerized by their perfection.

They *were* perfect, after all. And so was every other part of her, yet all this time it seemed she'd never quite noticed that fact, or never been told by someone to whom she was beloved. She had not been properly loved, Oliver decided. There was nothing more powerful than to be in the position of offering proper adoration to someone. He was still, after a month, meandering around in his own mind and heart about how they'd arrived at the amazing situation of having one another. It had happened before, and yet he never could be prepared for being struck by love. It fell upon him like an accident, like a car crash or knife cut, out of nowhere, without permission or intention. It was like luck, and he would not turn away from such a thing. He was stubborn, that way.

Loyal, he told himself. Loyal to love.

"Ready?" he asked the reflections in the mirror, dabbing at his wife's upper lip, where she routinely rolled an extra bit of color.

"Ready," she replied.

Coincidentally, the lawyer's party, Roe and Roe and Roe's holiday bash, happened to be taking place this evening just across the street from the charity auction the Desplaines were attending. Oliver appreciated the convenience of mixing business with pleasure. A young man stepped out of a ballroom at the downtown Hyatt, his necktie loosened and askew, as if he'd had second thoughts about suicide. He was redolent of gin and now standing too close. He had been stuck with a crooked name badge, *Hello My Name Is* JOSHUA, the words ornamented with hand-drawn mistletoe. Some chubby secretary had spent the morning making those, Oliver guessed.

Catherine offered her hand. She refused to heed Oliver's warnings about germs and random intimacies. She would embrace and kiss anybody who felt the urge. She liked to monitor him at public functions as he maneuvered around greetings, avoiding being touched. Later she would congratulate him on his evasions, letting him know that he wasn't fooling her. In this instance with JOSHUA, he suddenly patted his pants pockets, as if checking for the car keys or valet parking receipt. Catherine ducked her head, smiling.

Oliver thought of his hands in the Sweetheart's hair, his heedless unwashed enthusiasm for touching her, that virtual stranger, that potential harborer of contaminants.

"You're the godparents!" the drunk Roe and Roe and Roe minion told them, as if in congratulations. It was a week before Christmas, after all—season of office parties, candy platters, forgotten grudges, goodwill toward men, plus eggnog. This charge he made had the quality of gift, generosity, salutation. *From me to you, with all good wishes, a girl! God Bless!* In some other season it might have been presented differently, the general mood easily otherwise; in spring it might seem a sorrow or a tax, in July patriotic fanfare in the street or sky, near Halloween a disguised arrival, witch or ghost, costume concealing a secret body, inside of which ticked a tricky heart. A frightening youngster who thrust out a demanding empty bag: Gimme.

"Feliz Navidad!" the hotel's sound system insisted, over and over. The tune was so catchy that it no longer required the words, they were there regardless. Oliver had been unwillingly whistling this and songs like it for weeks, snippets snared together in his head like fizzling flies in a web. A person could feel possessed. And as for the whistling, he knew it was a habit he had to suppress—it announced two things that he did not wish known about him. One was his happiness at being newly in love, and the other was his pitch-perfect ability as a whistler, a trait that dated him.

"You ran all this by one of the Roes?" he asked.

"*I'm* a Roe," Joshua said. "Not one of the Roe and Roe and Roe, but grandson and son and nephew." He spun suddenly to show them another markered name tag, slapped on his back: *Hello My Name Is* JUNIOR. "Anyhoo," he said, "You're the godparents, basically." He looked back longingly at a crescendo in the raucous jollity of the ballroom behind him. "Although 'godparent' is hardly legally binding. I spoke with Houston. It's pretty cut-and-dry, really. You can refuse, of course. And by the way, any decent attorney would have made sure there was a mutual agreement in advance, but whatever. And of course there's always foster care, duh, if you decline. She'll be an adult, sooner or later, and get a nifty little chunk of change, not to mention the trust, from which you all will be generously remunerated. It's kind of a sweet deal, if you think about it. Depending—is she a good kid, or a bad one?" He raised his eyebrows inquiringly, a little blearily: Had he spelled it out?

"What about the father?"

"No father."

"No father?"

"No father."

The subject of the legal document was a fifteen-year-old girl; her mother, who had died six weeks ago, had been his wife's friend from high school. There was no father listed anywhere,

Junior now explained with wearied irony, not on a birth certificate, not on the documents at the school, not in the mother's insurance or work or homeowner's paperwork. No. Father. "Immaculate conception," guessed Joshua Roe.

"Highly doubtful," said Catherine. "I mean, I knew her mom. Immaculate would hardly be the way."

Snowflakes had begun falling outside in festive complicity, covering the ugly, muting the unpleasant. Downtown Wichita had the aspect of snow globe, insular object of rapt sentimentality, a hush of love and hope, forgiveness and averted judgment. Sentences were being commuted, sins absolved, lips loosening, optimistic music as sound track. Oliver glanced out dreamily toward the convention center across the street, where the Sweetheart was setting up hors d'oeuvres.

Catherine began explaining why the circumstance seemed so peculiar. "We don't really know this woman . . . I mean, it's been years. And we didn't agree. It's like wow, out of the blue she's given us her daughter!"

Joshua nodded, taking her in now under his bloodshot, tired eyes, holding out the well-traveled and -researched package. "Well, actually? It's not actually *godparents*, plural, but god-*parent*, singular, you, Mrs. Desplaines. The deceased listed you. Catherine Anne Harding," he added, as if she needed reminding. From being inside his jacket pocket, the packet now appeared to be damp. Oliver had asked him to verify its contents. It had traveled from Texas to Kansas, been forwarded, then forgotten, finally found, then driven to Oliver's office, next couriered across town tucked away in a larger, less soiled envelope, now returned, like an elaborate relic, certified real.

"Happy holidays," said Joshua Roe Jr., giving Catherine a hug, extending his hand once again to be shaken but then lifting it to his temple instead, offering Oliver a kind of awkward salute.

"You like to menace people," his wife told him as they headed to the elevator, laughing.

"I don't." But maybe he did. He was old enough to be Joshua's father, he was old enough to be Catherine's father. He scrolled briefly through a mental file of the people he'd spent the day with—was he old enough to be everyone's father? In general he enjoyed having them look to him as they would any elder, teacher or preacher or boss, waiting for orders and/or approval. He was very tall, his head heavy, his hair still thick. His gaze was necessarily down.

The Sweetheart. He could be her father, too. Earlier they had met at her grandparents' house. The grandparents were in Florida; the Sweetheart house-sat, an annual arrangement from December through March. Strictly speaking, Oliver was of her grandparents' generation, give or take. And had his Sweetheart grown up in Wichita, she would have graduated a few years behind the younger of his daughters. They might have been featured in the same yearbook. But her alma mater was in Portland; her grandparents' aesthetic was suburban, traditional, dismissible; they could have been Oliver's grandparents, the identical conventional furnishings and odors. He and the Sweetheart made love in the guest room, unaccustomed headboard knocking against the wallpapered wall. They drank Folgers afterward, sitting at the kitchen nook gazing over the salt and pepper shaker collection on the windowsill—ceramic pigs, anthropomorphized appliances, curtsying bumblebees—to the array of empty homemade bird feeders and dutifully covered lawn furniture outside.

I'm falling in love with you, he'd texted her. For her, he'd learned the technology.

I already fell, she'd texted him back, alert and swift on the keypad. What Oliver had yet to discover was the nature of her love. They had shared their histories, he had heard of the others in her past, but he could not discern the precise dimensions of her proclaimed love for him, the scale it represented in the grand scheme, the place he occupied in her assemblage. If her love were a pie graph . . . If she had to rank-order . . . If one love was the indisputable winner . . . She had declared it so easily, so early. While he was still falling under love's revered spell, into its cloistered chamber, she had already, she said, arrived. She looked at him as if he were the sun. She undressed as if her exquisite body embarrassed her. After sex she clung to him and wept, whereas at Wheatlands, which she managed, she had the reputation of a wisecracker, an even-keeled, efficient, unsentimental straight-shooting no-nonsense boss.

He kissed the part in her hair because she had a hard time meeting his eyes.

They drove away in their separate cars. They would meet here tomorrow. Oliver had held her at the door and experienced a strange light-headedness, as if she had somehow lifted him, relieved him of his body at a moment when he'd briefly left it. And then he was suddenly heavy again, with things to do. Unlike his wife, he had a day planner filled with appointments.

The last of these was the charity auction being held across the street. It had been a piece of luck that Roe and Roe and Roe were to host their party at the Hyatt, at the same general hour. The Sweetheart and the bakery she managed were catering the auction, a bakery that had been Oliver's most recent successful venture. It occupied an old car dealership in dying downtown; the picture windows now exposed ovens instead of Fords, a fleet of youthful staff wearing aprons rather than auto salesmen in cheap suits. At the thought of the Sweetheart in her Wheatlands apron, her hands powdered with flour, Oliver's heart suddenly began drumming. He relished the thrill of this sensation, the impending encounter. He wished to delay it, to revel in anticipation of it, let the snow continue to fall in its perfect way.

"You're whistling 'Here Comes Santa Claus,'" his wife informed him now. She was busy folding the paperwork Junior had returned to her to tuck it into her cocktail bag, discarding the envelope in the trash can before the bank of elevators. There in the container's rimmed lid full of sand was an ornate letter H. "Someone has to go around all day, putting H's in the trash-can sand," Catherine marveled. "You can't even smoke in here, and still there's an ashtray, with a cute cursive H." She glanced around before swirling her hand through the carefully raked golden sand.

"Brat," her husband said as the elevator arrived.

Inside, there they were once again, mirrored in golden tone on the ceiling. They both glanced up at their faces and elegant clothing. Was his tuxedo older than his wife? Oliver wondered, doing the math. Very nearly. The music continued in the elevator. "You want a drink before we meet up with the rest of the penguins?" he asked the reflection overhead.

"Sure."

"That kid, Joshua, I probably met him before. There was a kid at a party, years ago."

"Really?" *Rilly*, he heard; people were always saying it, uselessly.

"Yes, *really*. His parents used to throw parties, when I first moved to town. He might have been the one driving home the drunks one night, yours truly included, plus the wife."

"Which wife?"

"YaYa."

"That starter wife of yours. Will I never hear the end of her?"

"That one," he agreed. "And you asked."

They sat at the bar and admired themselves in *its* mirror, their faces among the array of beautiful bottles. The identical music played; in spite of himself, Oliver was impressed with the seamless sound system. This time it was Bing Crosby dreaming of a white Christmas. The bartender had some clever moves with the stemware. The walls were made of wood, the seats leather, and drinking, contained herein, could never seem a seedy pursuit.

"No television," Catherine noted; Oliver routinely asked that televisions be turned off; he didn't allow them in any of his own businesses. It was perhaps the only common ground he shared with his mother-in-law, a hatred of the television's omnipresence in the world.

"Just these outstanding carols."

"Although I am sort of enjoying watching the stuff about the BTK. You have to admit, that's pretty compelling stuff. I wasn't ever afraid of him, back when it was going on. Maybe if I'd been older, I would have been afraid? Isn't it strange, how immune I felt? Or maybe that's what being a teenager is all about."

Oliver wondered if her capacity for imagining her own death had been fully formed yet; for how long could she continue to charm with her girlish innocence? And was it the fact of the Sweetheart that brought it to his mind, her more legitimate claim to youth? He himself could not remember the day when his own demise had appeared to him, but once there, it never went away. "I always thought he was an amateur," he told Catherine, concerning the serial killer. "And you know my thoughts on amateurs. Plus, for all his ham-fisted idiocy, he still never got caught." The most salient emotion Oliver recalled from the first mention of those times was his irritation at the way the killer distracted the local population from the monkeyshines of their disgraced president. Nixon flew off the front page; onto it landed the not-yet-named BTK. Local trouble always trumped the national; you had to get used to it, living in a smallish city. "May I tell you just one more thing about YaYa?" he asked.

"If you must." She only pretended to not want to hear; Oliver knew that Catherine considered herself a winner, in the competition of his wives. She'd been one a little longer than either of the others.

"YaYa also had an encounter with a serial killer."

"I never said I encountered him. I said—"

"I know, I know. Yours is different. But listen." YaYa's claim was that she'd been driving to California from Kansas—

"A journey all Kansans have to make," Catherine interrupted. "They either return to Kansas, or they stay in California."

YaYa, Oliver told Catherine, had planned to be one of the latter, but en route, by herself, she had gotten lost in the desert. *Which one?* Oliver had asked, to which his first wife replied, *I don't know! I told you, I was lost!* There she'd run into a cop in an unmarked vehicle. Only the two of them, there in the unknown desert. The cop was incredibly polite, helpful; after several tries at verbal instructions, he'd written down the directions that would take her back to civilization. And then he offered to follow, to make sure YaYa, twenty-two-year-old Kansas naïf, didn't get lost.

"Hello?" said Catherine, incredulous.

"I know," Oliver agreed. *Why didn't he lead, and you follow?* She was twenty-two, YaYa explained; how was she to know such things? The cop's directions took her farther into the desert; eventually she was turning onto a dirt road. With every navigational choice she made, she consulted her rearview mirror, just to see the officer nodding approval behind her, raising his fist, thumb up like a turtle's eager head. Down the dirt road she traveled. Upward, toward dusty hills, the rocks pinging and thumping beneath her—Karmann Ghia, she'd interrupted herself, knowing Oliver would be curious—until she reached the final fork, one path that veered downward, a weaving steep route made and taken by thrill-seeking dune buggies, a sandy chute-like trail that YaYa could trace across the desert floor below her, the other a continuation of the road proper. The sign on it said Road Ends.

She did not hesitate in choosing the dune buggy trail, although the face in her rearview mirror frowned mightily. She flew down the winding path, hardly able to see, crying piteously, making promise after promise if only God would find her a highway, get her out of this mess. She would quit smoking, she would return to Kansas, she would start speaking to her father once more, she would go back to college. Behind her a cloud of dust, before her a careless snaking path that could very well have ended at the edge of a plateau or butte, this sloping lane designed like an amusement park ride, totally thrill, no destination, all of her unamused effort for naught, car plummeting over the cliff.

The cop's vehicle, she assured Oliver, was too large to take the dune buggy road. His big dumb American-made car, she said.

And God was listening, it appeared; she rode bumping and pitching, sailing and banging, winding through the desert for many digressing miles. Dark came on, she nearly ran out of gas, she was riding on at least two flat tires, ruining their rims, and her oil pan was drizzling from several punctures, but eventually she found the pavement. And on it she and her Karmann Ghia hobbled to a small town—no, she could not remember the name; it was a traumatic event, didn't Oliver understand *any*thing?—and went immediately to the tiny lighted police station. The officer there did not recognize the handwriting on the map and instructions the purported cop had provided. He didn't look as if he believed YaYa's story, although he did assist her in replacing her tires and oil pan, feeding her a sandwich, filling her gas tank. He found a genuine road map and drew a fat black line from where they were, here, to where she wanted to go, there, and sent her on her way.

"It wouldn't have been a story YaYa told if there weren't the two-weeks-later part," Oliver said. Two weeks later, the real cop called to say that the phony cop had been caught off in the hills. He'd lured many a woman out there, said the officer, lured, raped, killed, and buried. "YaYa was lucky to be alive. All her stories ended with her being the person nobody could pull a fast one on."

"You believed her?" Catherine asked, motioning for the bartender to bring her another drink.

Oliver shrugged, as if to suggest that he hadn't. But he had. He didn't any longer, but once he had. His passionate love for YaYa had overridden common sense. Now YaYa was merely his ex-wife the chronic liar, his fond nemesis, but back then she'd been his dearly beloved. He supposed that love still had that eclipsing power over him. How else to explain his current dilemma? He had fallen in love. It hadn't happened to him in a very long time, not since Catherine, but he couldn't deny that he was in its grip again. And he loved being in love. There wasn't any more salutary emotion, he genuinely believed this, than being in love. It was good for him. It improved his health, that valuable jewel he protected. He was sixty-nine years old, and he wouldn't scoff at an improvement in health.

In his right pocket he kept his public cell phone; in his left breast pocket his secret one. When it vibrated, with a message from the Sweetheart, he felt it near his heart. He was living two lives, which ran abreast of one another, and he could perform adroitly in each. He had his wife, with whom he'd spent eighteen very happy years, and he had his Sweetheart, with whom he had made love only three times now. Just the recent memory of that third encounter resulted in a surge in his chest, as if his heart were literally being worked. Amazing. Far preferable to pharmaceuticals, the extraordinary power of falling in love. Oliver felt certain he could become a triathlete, if he wished, now that he had this spare energy to burn, this reinvigorated muscle hardly contained by his rib cage.

As a young man, he'd taken for granted love. He'd believed he'd find it everywhere. He didn't take it for granted now. He found it rarely. He treasured it, and yet also treated it as if he could hardly believe in it, as you might a miracle, as you might a dream from which you did not want to wake.

He swallowed his drink, shot his cuff to glance at his watch. The Sweetheart, and her allure, was starting to seem like an imperative, something that could slip away if he didn't hurry. "We're going to miss the auction," he said. "Didn't you want to bid on a cruise?"

Catherine leaned over and laid her head on his shoulder. "We could stay here, just listen to crooners and badmouth your exes."

But there was the Sweetheart, waiting. He could feel her eyes anticipating his arrival, feel them even now turning toward the doors to monitor guests. Before he could make an argument for going across the street, his wife made it for him. She had met the Sweetheart, in her role as manager; she understood that the girl needed their support and presence, their parental beneficence at the ball. Reluctantly, she shook off the bartender's offer of another round, applied lipstick, put on her game face.

Oliver said to her as he draped her coat around her shoulders, "I think you'd rather hear about my inglorious youth than tell me about yours. This kid, this bizarre gift that came out of nowhere, this blast from the past. What's the story with that?"

CHAPTER 5

IT WAS A LONG TIME AGO," Catherine said. She and Oliver lay in bed now, in her bed and bedroom, neither able to sleep. Insomnia was something they had in common, tonight in combination with two nascent champagne headaches. Did he also see little streamers of light when he moved his head? Did his eyeballs also seem out of sync with their sockets? And why had they purchased yet another Oriental area rug at the auction? She'd thought they would sleep separately, Oliver usually worn out by extra social obligations, in need of his monkish solitude: the large hard bed in the unheated room. The earplugs plus the white noise machine. The window shades designed to obscure all light. And the sleep induced therein? Like hibernation.

But no. He'd joined Catherine in her room, in her quaint old bed that complained when you turned, that dumped you always in its center, a too-soft nest made of feathers. She called the room her study, but in fact it was more closet than anything else, occasional guest room. Location of her sentimental cache from childhood, those things her mother would have donated or thrown away when she'd had to move from the old house. Without meaning to, she'd made the room a replica of the one she'd grown up in, floral lamp, antique dolls, free-standing full-length mirror. Outside, weekend hooligans had begun abusing the holidays, spinning on ice after closing the bars or parties, their usual exuberance spiced by seasonal cheer. The police had their hands full, sirens whooping and bleating, unnerving the Desplaines' two dogs, who whimpered from their pads on the back porch downstairs, distressed about the helicopter overhead, about the fire engines and ambulances. If the disaster persisted (multicar pileup? house ablaze?), grew worse, her husband would reluctantly rise and "release the hounds!" allow them to come burrow beneath Catherine's bed. It was the only solution.

They were never allowed in Oliver's room.

"I guess I promised her," she said, of her old best friend. "I can't remember doing it, but I don't doubt that I would have. We were pretty close." They would have been drunk or high at the time, she did not say; her former self was a sometimes shaming secret, an undignified interlude—too like Oliver's delinquent daughter Miriam, who'd lived with them during her own bad time, who'd occupied this bedroom and stolen a few of its mementos. Moreover, Catherine sometimes worried that she herself hadn't let go of those days as thoroughly as she ought to have. She was in possession of all the markers of adulthood, was in every legal way entitled to claim the role, but still she was nagged by teenage unease. When she looked around her room she found the props from the past, the large oval mirror in which she'd studied herself for decades, a familiar wan wondering: When was that person looking back going to seem like somebody in charge?

She and her best friend had been among the holiday hooligans, back in her true adolescence, careless and careening. To realize how lucky she was to have survived her own incautious past always sent a shudder through Catherine—one run red light, one inexplicable pill, one bad man, one unforgivable decision, and everything would have turned out otherwise. Reckless they'd been, yet de-voted: apparently they had exchanged this promise with the same conviction they'd exchanged blood from pricked pinkies, secrets from stricken souls. Best friends, sworn, avowed. If any-thing should ever happen . . . But Catherine hadn't been close to her since high school—hadn't even seen her since college gradu-ation, when Catherine had been onstage, wearing a robe with the others, awaiting the subtle plucking of the tassel from one side of the mortarboard to the other, and her receding best friend had been out there in the wobbling heat-soaked sea that was the audience, a distant face stoned and grinning. Even then, twenty-some years ago, their friendship was on the wane. Cath-erine hadn't yet met her husband, but she'd been cultivating an affinity, finding him by dating his prototypes. These were not the same types her best friend dated. Certainly at graduation there'd been a man in the audience beside Catherine's best friend, somebody who'd supplied the cocaine or ecstasy, the hip flask, a drugged-up dropout just like her. Eventually that same type had materialized for long enough to father a child, then evaporated back into obscurity, perhaps only one among many, anonymous by virtue of ubiquity.

Come to think of it, wasn't it often the case that Catherine had been onstage, performing in choir or receiving an award, play-ing some ugly stepsister or second-string Jet, even as far back as seventh grade, glancing out at the crowd, her best friend's face there, down below, unheralded, unspecial, looking up, a slight smirk at the corner of the mouth that recognized the silly sham of it all? That lone skeptical observer, who seemed to penetrate with X-ray eyes.

"You know what I just realized?" Catherine said to her husband, blinking into the dark, newly alert. "When she spent the night, when we were in junior high and high school, we slept in this very same bed." Yet another emergency vehicle went screaming by beneath the window, bright red and blue illuminating for a succession of strobed moments the confines of the bed, its rosebud details cast along its iron rails, the shadows they made on the wall like the bars of a cell. Catherine had picked out the bed at an antique store when she was thirteen, her unlikely birthday gift that year from her parents; her friend had drolly accused her of being a future spinster. Since then, Catherine had painted it a few times, and, most recently, stripped the layers of paint to locate its original brass luster. "And not that many people have slept in this bed with me," she said now. The bed had stayed in her childhood home until she'd married and settled, waiting there safely with her parents until Catherine could be trusted with it.

Her bed gave Oliver back pain. Her bed made him sweaty and claustrophobic. He only rarely joined her there. Perhaps he was paying penance for being curt with her earlier; perhaps he wished to make love.

"Did you have a best friend?" She took his hand now as if he'd extended it at the last minute, over an abyss, into the deep. She was afraid of falling further into her memory, that unresolved reflection in the mirror that was her extended teenage life, its injury, its bottomlessness. She wanted a recollection of his to act as neutralizer.

"I don't think boys have best friends in the same way," he said. "We move in packs."

"You're not in a pack."

"You move in packs until you get married. Then you have a wife."

"Or a few wives."

"I lost my taste for the pack. Maybe you can't go back, once you've broken out."

"You're wolves, you're saying."

"Yes, wolves. Wolves, and dogs."

A second helicopter joined the first, rocking the house, and the actual dogs, though they'd tried, could not help barking, a terrific fit that made Catherine and Oliver laugh. He rose, filled his cheeks, and blew his elaborate bird-calling whistle, the song the dogs knew meant that help was on the way, and Catherine felt her heart thrill, as it always did when he indulged the rare pitying gesture. He had left the heartless pack to live with women, and they had domesticated him.

From the stairs he was addressing the animals. "Lads," he admonished. "What will the intruders think?" He bemoaned their neuteredness, blaming that for their lack of fortitude. In a less charitable mood, Catherine might note Oliver's neutered state; did he feel reduced? When the porch door was opened, the dogs ran thumping—like fat rabbits, with their long ears back—up the stairs toward Catherine, nosing clumsily beneath the bed, jamming themselves happily against the wall. They were brothers, two portly corgis two and a half years in age. Lacking children, Catherine had pleaded with her husband for dogs; her mother hadn't allowed her pets, she hadn't had siblings, there would be no babies—surely he could understand her desire? Their friends no doubt pitied their misplaced affection. This was the third pair of siblings they'd owned, first black Labs, next cocker spaniels, now the corgis—each set a slightly smaller breed. "We'll die with Chihuahuas," Catherine had once told Oliver.

"You'll die with Chihuahuas," he corrected her. "I'll die during the dachshunds." In the past, he had enjoyed pointing at the discrepancy in their ages, his future ghostliness that would haunt her. He didn't do that anymore.

"They've shredded their holiday bows," Oliver reported. "Total confetti all over the porch floor."

"They took heed when you told them to cowboy up."

"They still smell like they fell in the foo-foo." He climbed into bed again, toes icy from his brief errand.

"I like picking them up at the groomer's," Catherine said. "I enjoy their sniveling gratitude." She'd almost forgotten them there, today; yesterday's unexpected letter and its contents had derailed her, left her in a funny uneasy fog. Beneath the bed, she could feel the dogs nuzzling together, bumping against the box springs and slats. They were disallowed from Oliver's room, that immaculate cell. Solid as ottomans, willing to be thumped, cheerful and attentive, they were the only dogs she knew who made unabashed eye contact, who could in fact outstare you. Her profound love for them frightened her.

Her friends might be right to find her affection misplaced.

"If I had a best friend from high school," Oliver resumed, "it would have been Ogdoerf."

"Ogdoerf?"

"We went by last names. Linus Ogdoerf."

"Good God. Poor kid."

"And if I got notified, twenty-odd years later, that he'd died and left me his child, and had moreover named that child for me, well, I'd be just flat-out astonished. I'd be less surprised to win the lottery, which I don't even play."

"Oliver Ogdoerf," Catherine speculated. "Terrible! But you and Ogdoerf would never have spent the night in the same bed?"

"True. Same tent, but not the same bed."

"And I bet you didn't practice kissing each other, or inventing dance steps." Or discuss how best to purge meals, or pierce one another's ice-numbed upper ear rims using needles and corks, or carve into one another's shoulder, with a Zippo-flame-sterilized shoplifted pocket knife, an asterisk, to signify the idea of extra content, footnoted character not readily available to the average, casual eye. Still there, Catherine thought, touching hers briefly, a little star-shaped divot.

"No," he said, "we didn't do that, either."

"Still, it astonishes me, too," Catherine said. "The dying, that most. Besides my dad, I don't know very many dead people."

"You will," he said in that world-weary way he had. His family was entirely gone; he did not mourn the loss particularly, those people who'd not really understood him and wouldn't be around to trouble him now.

"Then the bequeathing and the naming, a whole other ball of wax." It was the fact of the name, she understood, that most intrigued. That for fifteen years there'd been plenty of general but only one other particular Catherine in the world. "She was never very happy with her own name," she recalled. "Misty." *Misty.* Into the telephone, in the high school halls—once it had been a name always on her lips, and now not for years. It carried with it the distinct sensation of regret. A turned back.

"Misty?" her husband said. "I never knew a Misty before. Dusty, yes, Misty, no. I know a Rusty and a Sandy and a Hunter, even a Rocky, but no Misty. What could that be short for?"

"Misdemeanor?" Catherine guessed. "I never thought about it. For all I know, she was named for that movie."

"She was already around when that movie came out," he said. "You have an abysmal sense of history."

"And math. And geography."

"Those, too." He said it gently, fondly, pleased once more with her silliness.

"We were Misty and Cat, back then, sometimes Foggy and Dog. She lived a totally different life from mine. She was what I guess you might call white trash, although we didn't call it that. My mom called her The Bad Influence. She got blamed for everything, even though some of it was my idea." Most of it? Catherine wondered. She'd been a sheltered child, brought up by idealists, good citizens; she'd been restless, however, even before meeting up with Misty, restless and sometimes naughty. Her own parents were teachers, voters, drinkers of milk, while Misty lived with her grandmother, in a ratty house where certain lights were never extinguished, like a convenience store, where there was always some vigilant wakeful presence, scheming, ready to greet anyone who came through the door, just as ready to phone the police and rat out that anyone. The old woman—not a jolly gray-haired grandma but a scrawny embittered alcoholic on whom everyone dumped what they no longer wanted, the odd pet or child or broken machine—the smell of her home, the nauseating gloom, the occasional creepy relative, moody malcontents always giving the impression that they'd been recently released from a state institution of one sort or another, always with the twitchy gestures and paranoid countenance of the confined. "My parents didn't approve, but they also were sworn liberals, so they were duty-bound to trust me with my decisions. Misty scared them. Which I must have liked about her. She was like a lesson I wanted them to learn. She'd been held back in grade school, so she was already driving a car by ninth grade. Her teeth looked like something out of the Soviet Union. The epitome of white trash: she had a car but not a dentist."

"The lure of the dark side," said her husband. "You met how?"

Catherine closed her eyes, trying to recall, sending herself into the dizzy void of memory, amplified by the evening's cocktails, but no inaugural event appeared. Misty in the driver's seat of the beat-up Buick, Misty waiting slouched against lockers outside classrooms, Misty flirting with a man holding a pool cue, underage at a bar, or falling into this very bed with her clothes on, even her shoes—those scruffy beloved moon boots, faux leather, peeling—the two of them head to head on a single pillow, rehashing their day and night. Misty's terrible teeth and worse haircuts, the products of poverty, her caustic laugh, her savage muttering cleverness, an odor of cigarettes and sour clothing, of concrete, as if she were preparing for homelessness. Tough as nails, Misty; had Catherine ever seen her cry? She opened her eyes against a sensation of the drunken spins, of drowning. No, not quite that. It was the sensation, perhaps, of having let someone else drown, of having let go. *Misty.* She said, "We would have seen each other in grade school, but it wasn't until junior high that we were friends. She was maybe one of those people who thought high school represented the apex of life." But that wasn't quite accurate, either, since that conjured star athletes and their fetching cheerleader counterparts, prom queen and quarterback, quickly pregnant and hastily married, sent into middling jobs and maternity, settled in the suburbs. Misty hadn't been popular, nor had she wanted or done those stereotypical (yet disappointingly true) things. Still, it was the past that now mattered, the past in which a pledge had apparently been made, remembered, and honored by at least one party to it.

Outside, the sirens had ceased, the helicopters had flown away. The silence had the quality of waiting, the trembling feel at the end of any sounded alarm. The air kind of vibrated. Catherine let loose her husband's hand just before he could let loose hers.

"I'm going to take a pill," he said. "I have too many things to do tomorrow." He rolled from the bed. "You want one?"

"Yes," she said. "Plus something else for the headache."

"Good idea."

After they took their capsules, sharing the water glass, kissing with cool damp lips, married couple committing to a mutual dulled slumber, Oliver decided to retire to his own room. Catherine curled away from him, her back to his departing back and the shutting door.

By habit, she reached to grasp the metal rosebud on the far side of the headboard. This had always been her side; she'd seen the bed's brass origins only because her worrying hand, over many years, had unearthed the shine by clasping in her palm the chilly ribbed rosebud. One hand on it, the other tracing the tiny six-pronged scar on her shoulder. Now she waited for the wave of narcotic and painkiller to wash over her. She did not want to lie awake revisiting any more of the past, where, beside her, Misty had lain. She wished Oliver had not left her here with that vacated space.

She could go to him, she thought, she could crawl into his bed the way she had her parents' bed as a child, seeking assurance of protection. She could also summon the dogs from their cave beneath her, merely whisper, "Boys," and pat the comforter, where they would land like logs and rest their chins upon her legs.

But instead she lay alone, in this bed where she and Misty had read pornography together, here where they'd suffered hangovers, where they'd laughed long into the night. Eventually they slept, but more often they were inexhaustibly conversant, buzzing and pleased, two teenage girls burning bright as neon in the dark.

CHAPTER 6

THE MAN IN JOANNE'S ATTIC came downstairs on the first day of the new year. Maybe it was his resolution. Two thousand and five: inaugurated the night before in Montpelier with gunshots and banging pans, just the way it was in Houston. Cattie had spent the evening wandering up the hill from Joanne's house, watching at the top in a bundled crowd as a meager display of fireworks was set off. The bright bursts of color in the sky reflected on the snowy hills. Everyone clapped and hooted every time, waving fizzling sparklers in their hands; small towns reminded Cattie of her public school events back in Houston, the insulated adoration and devotion of a very biased group. Both Joanne and Ito had gone home to New Hampshire for New Year's, having declined to visit there at Christmas. They weren't much alike, Ito and Joanne, one too happy, one too glum, but about their blended family they completely agreed: awful, and tolerable only with a sidekick along. Now it was just Cattie and the soldier in the attic. His name was Randall, but even Joanne, lax landlady, didn't know if it was his first or last. He paid rent in highly tangible cash; otherwise he comported himself like a ghost, drifting down when everyone else was asleep or away, leaving traces of himself that were nearly imperceptible, occasionally emitting a noise from his upstairs quarters, a strange bump or step, something that might be mistaken for the house itself, a rodent running over its roof, a blown tree limb banging at its siding.

Down, however, he came on New Year's Day morning, dressed in a uniform (the new camouflage, pixilated patches of tan and yellow, boots the color of gourmet mustard), carrying a razor and can of shaving cream. In the bathroom off the kitchen he filled the sink and scraped away at his face, having passed through the room without saying a word to Cattie. As if she were the ghost.

"I can make coffee," she said eventually. *So what?* she answered herself.

"Fine," he said. She delivered the cup to the lid of the toilet, where he stared at it briefly as if they'd had a misunderstanding. Maybe they had.

"I'm Cattie," she said, leaving the small room. *So what?* He had finished shaving and was peering into the mirror at different tipping angles, noting his own features curiously. Cattie knew the feeling. Avoid a mirror long enough, and you became a kind of curiosity to yourself, some internal idea going smash against the reality, and never in a good way. He was not much older than she, a fact that was made clearer when his cheeks were smooth, when his physique was obviously young—unfinished and still disproportionate—inside a uniform that did not quite fit. He could have been one of the students over at St. Sincere, if he were a photographed headshot rather than a person in motion. His evasive facial expressions and his jittery movements said he'd never been treated as a pampered or beloved child.

She and Ito had researched and discussed PTSD ad nauseum; this tenant appeared to be a textbook specimen.

"Randall," he said; she repeated her name in response. He

didn't seem an enthusiastic drinker of coffee but a resigned one, as if Cattie had ordered him to do it. If Ito were here, he would have begun a peppering assault on this man, querying him relentlessly, merrily: the uniform, the strange hours, the horrors of war—how did Randall feel concerning the Iraqis, and President Bush, and weaponry, and what did he think of conscientious objection? Did he hate those cowards? Ito never, ever ran out of questions. Cattie had some curiosity about Randall, but depended on conjecture rather than inquiry. She was an awkward inquisitor; the practice did not come naturally to her, reluctant as she was to reveal much about herself. About Randall she had decided the day before that it was foolish to be afraid of him. If he'd wanted to do something to her, last night would have been his chance. Her bedroom, that former little boy's room, had a simple eye-and-hook lock; he could have broken through it with one swift kick, so she'd not bothered to latch it. She didn't feel fatalistic, exactly, but was operating as if waiting for instructions that made sense to her. This period in her life was a lull, longer than the usual lulls she guided herself through (cavity-filling at the dentist; class periods that bored her; road trips during which she knew she'd be carsick). She'd gotten plenty of advice that didn't make sense to her, delivered to her daily on her cell phone's voice mail, but none, so far, that felt absolutely correct. The fact that somebody was paying her phone bill impressed her; if the service ceased, she supposed she might have a motive to step back into the world. That, or when she had spent all of her money.

Already Ito had suggested they drive to New York City to pull cash from an ATM there, just to throw off the authorities, those mysterious figures who would be waiting for just such an alert.

"You want to help me with something?" Randall asked suddenly. He still stared at the mirror, but Cattie assumed he must be speaking to her.

"Maybe." She had completed the crossword puzzle, something she had once made fun of her mother for caring about. These commemorative days, the seasonal lazy hush between Christmas and New Year's, could not help but summon up their earlier versions, Cattie and her mother in restaurants or their own home, lounging on the couch, exchanging gifts, toasting with a glass of ginger ale, suffering the few bites of black-eyed peas on New Year's Eve to assure the next year's good luck. A new year had begun—Cattie felt herself now poised atop a blank scrolling calendar, a lengthy furl made of shining blank aluminum, a blinding slide into the void. Time would launch her, and down she would fly.

Ito and Joanne weren't due back until nightfall.

"All right," she told Randall. They left the house on foot, Randall several yards ahead of Cattie. If she hastened to catch up, he raced forward once more, so she gave up and followed. In general, Cattie did not care what people made of her, so tagging along after a crazy hell-bent soldier on New Year's Day in Montpelier, Vermont, didn't bother her. Not the way it would appear to others, anyhow.

The East was different from the West, where Cattie had grown up, and one difference was that the woods seemed always nearby here. Clearly the town had been carved into them. There were no reassuring flat plains to consider, and the sky was frequently cloudy, so that navigating by the sun was also impossible. She'd not known which direction was north since arriving last August. She'd not known she'd cared which direction was north until then, either. She hadn't realized she actually possessed orientation until it was rendered opaque, and then she missed it, imagined her mind like a compass spinning aimlessly. But now Randall was leading her away from downtown and toward a forest. This wasn't necessarily frightening; the forest was everywhere, and for all she knew, there were houses inside that cluster of trees, a whole neighborhood or other little village, some civilized place from which they were going to pick up something he said he'd found yesterday. He couldn't bring it back alone, was the deal. "And damned if I can find a box," he complained about Joanne's. Nor a basket or wagon or wheelbarrow.

"How did you get here?" Cattie asked. He made the hitchhiker's fist, led by an extended thumb.

Under the train overpass they went, Randall storming ahead, Cattie trailing, past the last dilapidated wooden buildings, those places where derelicts and crack addicts would have lived, if they were in Houston, but where birds nested here, and then the two of them were in the sudden hush of the woods. A new quiet settled, more quiet than the quiet of the town in the holiday morning; the snow was clean, untouched. Now he waited for her to reach him. It seemed warmer among the trees, also darker. "I'm pretty sure it was right along here," he was saying under his breath, moving more tentatively now, and definitely speaking to himself. For a long time they made footprints in fresh snow; beneath it, pieces of the forest floor were slick with ice, and Cattie could hear Randall breathing, muttering random piloting information about his own route the day before. She had not been aware that he left the house for walks in the woods; was there a hatch on the roof from which he sprang like a jack-in-the-box? She might have shared with him her own passion for walking, especially walking at night, but sensed that he wouldn't necessarily welcome an interruption from her, nor mention of the ways they resembled one another. Resembling others might also remind him in a bad way of the military, the haircuts and outfits and those famous group marches. Like her, walking for him seemed to be a way of thinking, and today it was about retracing his steps.

She'd not brought a proper coat to the East Coast, and that fact was abundantly clear today. She'd not known how to imagine the

East, nor had her mother. They'd showed up shell-shocked, giving each other meaningful glances during orientation, sitting together at lunch making unkind remarks about Cattie's new peers and instructors, who went by Tutor instead of Teacher. Students were addressed by their last names. "If you don't like it, you can come home," her mother offered before driving away. "Right, Mueller?"

"Yeah," Cattie agreed. Her mother had often surprised Cattie with her ability to simplify a problem. At the mall, for instance, when the jeans wouldn't fit and Cattie was near tears, her mother had shrugged, sitting patiently on the dressing room bench. "There's a million pairs of jeans in this mall," she'd said. "Do you really think we can't find some for you? No big deal." That was her motto, in general: no big deal. When Cattie hadn't been invited to parties, her mother had said, "Most teenage girls are assholes. Why would you want to spend time with them?" And then they would go to a movie on a school day, or to an expensive restaurant on the roof of a skyscraper, or off to Austin to swim in the springs. "We have money," she explained. "If there wasn't money, it'd be different, believe me. A lot of this shit that is not a big deal would become an enormous deal. A royal pain in our ass." Her mother only worried when Cattie was without her. It seemed, then, that their separation was the only big deal, especially a separation in which Cattie could not be found.

One just like this, Cattie thought. Nobody knew where she was now. Her current flimsy connection to humanity, in the form of Ito and Joanne, had been effectively nullified when she stepped out the door behind Randall. Who would know to look in these woods, should the time come? At what point, she asked herself in her present cold, lulled mood, would she begin to worry about her own sanity? She was following a clearly unstable person into an obviously alien landscape. Woods were where dead bodies were found; the untouched snow suggested nobody came here very often. In general, she was neither so curious nor so dumb as to be reckless, so it wasn't for the adventure or out of idiocy that she was making this trek. And she wasn't suicidal, she told herself, although it also seemed to her that she couldn't see much point in carrying on. Not that she would end her own life, just that she would probably not offer much resistance if someone else saw fit. The instinct for survival, maybe, would have left her. That funhouse slide she imagined as the new year's commencement was a long chute into nowhere.

"Hear that?" Randall said, stopping abruptly, hands flapped backward as if Cattie were making a ruckus. Lost in her philosophizing, she bumped into him. She did hear; her mother's recollected words suddenly evaporated, Cattie refreshed to her profoundly silent surroundings. Faint frantic mewling; she looked up into the trees, certain the noise was made by birds. "Careful where you step," Randall ordered, forcing her gaze downward. He was gently testing the dusted surface of snow with his yellow boots before setting one after the other. And then there was a clearing, a sheltered needle-covered hollow beneath a pine tree, and in it a writhing black living form that became, upon closer inspection, upon proper focusing, a litter of puppies. "The bitch ran when she heard us," Randall said, squatting now. "See, they still got milk on their snouts. That's what happened yesterday. We just gotta sit till she comes back. She probably drug one of them with her, too." He counted the complaining puppies aloud. "I get seven." Cattie knelt on the other side of the squirming mess and made her own count.

"Me, too."

"Dumbass Mama definitely took one with. She'll be back. Don't touch 'em. Not yet." So they squatted on the frozen ground under a tree nearby and waited. It was excruciating, listening to the puppies cry and whimper. Had she known where they were going, and why, Cattie would have brought supplies.

She'd cared for small orphaned creatures many times before; it was a girl trademark.

Although had any of those orphans actually survived, now that she thought about it? And why, she wondered, had Randall felt the need to shave before coming to do this? It was something Ito would have asked as soon as they left the street and entered the woods.

"Some bastard body dumped her babies here," he confided to Cattie, leaning close so as to keep still. "My dad did it all the time, and the good bitches would find the spot. The good bitches would bust out of the basement and run, and not stop running, till they found their babies. It's not much a man that can't do better than that." Cattie offered no comment, storing away Randall's words for Ito, who would be ecstatic to hear them. Randall hailed from the South, she knew now, although a deeper and more rural one than her South. She would not have minded if he continued telling her about his home, offering the accidental sagaciousness of phrases like "some bastard body" or "the good bitches" or "not much a man" for her to ponder. Thinking was warming her up.

When the mama dog finally returned, her babies' whimpering had grown weak and without hope, and the eighth puppy was not with her, apparently having been stowed safely away elsewhere. Randall sighed. "Sheet," he said flatly. "She only got half her instincts working. If we weren't here, a coyote mighta eaten her others while she hid the one." He was slowly crawling toward the dog, moving to match her movements. "Course she wouldn't of left these if she hadn't heard us coming. And course she won't survive unless a human helps. Did we do you dogs a favor?" he asked the mama softly. "Did we really, when we made you our little whores?" As he neared her, he put his hand in one of his many uniform pockets, bringing out a hunk of white cheese. This he held patiently before himself, squatting like a child, forcing her now to breach the distance. The dog's hesitation was painful, accompanied as it was by the renewed cries of her puppies, not to mention her slack belly, vivid rib cage, and dangling teats. She looked like a farm dog, black-and-white mutt, ears laid flat in fear, starving out here, helpless and rattled. Randall simply waited on his skinny haunches, turning the graying cheese cube in his dirty fingers. He was a nailbiter, Cattie noted; his camouflage might have been useful in the desert, but he was utterly obvious here in forested verdant Vermont, place of Christmas trees and snowmen. When the dog finally stepped forward to nip the cheese away, he revealed a belt, whipped from another pocket like a magician's trick, and lassoed efficiently around her neck. She struggled, but she was not a large animal, and she was weakened, accustomed to people and the devices they used to control her, the commands they gave to which she unthinkingly responded. His desire to capture her was far larger than her desire to resist.

"Here," Randall said, holding the twisting dog by the belt with one hand, the other pulling a pillowcase from yet another pocket.

"No," Cattie said, shocked. She wasn't going to be party to a puppy execution, some rocks-in-the-bag river drowning. Was that what he'd meant, about his father's lack of manliness? That he wouldn't kill the babies, but merely abandon them to suffering starvation, go like a coward only halfway?

"I couldn't find a thing in that house," he said, reminding her of their futile search at Joanne's. "It's the only way I could think to bundle them together. You need two hands to carry them, or they'll get squashed. I'll do it, if you think you can—" The mother made a sudden feverish whirl at the end of the nooselike belt, shaking her head as if to break her own neck; she might have had the same fear Cattie had, that Randall meant her babies harm. Randall pulled up on the improvised lead, meanwhile using his foot to step on her hind feet. It was a training trick Cattie had seen her mother use, once upon a time.

"I'll carry them," Cattie said, taking the pillowcase and gently lifting the puppies, one by one. They were limp and warm, still sticky and with a faint bloody odor of being newly born, their eyes squinted, their faces indefinite, ugly. They started a fresh round of mewling when they found themselves together in a bag, and their mother struggled hard against Randall's tight hold on her. Dogs only understood a little of what you said to them; a sad fact, Cattie had always thought, incomplete knowledge. You might prefer utter ignorance. She clasped the squirming mess to her chest, terrified; what if she were responsible for one's death? For more than one's?

"We're gonna have to leave that other little guy, number eight, sacrificial lamb of the litter. Dumbass," he directed at the mother, although not unkindly. She was panting now over the choking tightness of the belt cinched around her throat. "Come on," he said, and they started out the way they'd come in, Cattie concentrating so hard on not squeezing or slipping or inadvertently asphyxiating anybody that she broke into a hot sweat.

Back at Joanne's house, returned once more to the kitchen, Cattie set the pillowcase carefully on the rug before the oven, repeating the mantra she'd been whispering to herself for the last hour: *Please let them all be alive.* She peeled open the sack, and there they were, smaller and blacker than they'd seemed in the woods, curled like tiny boxing gloves. Randall shut the room's doors to the porch, bathroom, and hall, and then loosened the belt from the mother's neck. She snarled at him, shook from head to tail, then barked once at Cattie as if to make sure Cattie understood she wasn't pardoned from being an accomplice. Cattie said, "Hey now," having ascertained that her work had been a success: seven beating hearts in those slack black pouches, those future independent beings. The bright kitchen, the warm air, the rag rug onto which they'd been set, had stunned them briefly, but soon enough the mewling started up once again. The mother then appeared to forget Randall and Cattie, and began a furious session of cleaning, her tongue so fierce as to knock her puppies over as they clamored at her feet. Randall lit a burner on the stovetop and then joined Cattie at the table. The room grew warm while they watched; outside, an early evening was falling. It would snow again, Cattie thought; the clouds were low and heavy. Eventually, when every puppy had been thoroughly tongued and mightily upset, the mother settled just off the rug, onto the linoleum as if to decline comfort, her back against the cupboard as if to prevent a surprise attack from behind, and her desperate babies finally plugged themselves in.

Cattie let out a breath. What an extraordinary length of time it seemed she'd been holding it. Then, to her complete mortification, she began to cry. It came like a storm, like an act of God, like a bomb. It was sobbing that would last for hours, uncontrollable, so much crying that her eyes would dry up and she'd have to wet them with her fingertips, licking them, then soothing her eyes. And still she would continue to cry, on and on. It was torrential, epic, explosive, and no less alarming to her than it was to poor Randall.

What the fuck?! his horrified thought balloon read. Cattie was thinking the same thing.

His capacity for human interaction had been seriously overtaxed by the simple request he'd made of her earlier. His conversation with her in the woods was the lengthiest he'd had in months. Her crying felt chaotic to him, as if it presaged other emotional havoc, episodes he had been avoiding and preempting with one hundred percent of his attention and time. At boot camp, he'd watched a fellow soldier drink himself to death on his twenty-first birthday. They'd passed out together, companionably enough, in the highest of spirits, and then his friend had not awoken the next morning. That was the last extreme feeling he'd allowed himself, that evening's high hilarity; it was a deadly indulgence, extreme feeling. To its credit, the army had seen that Randall required help. He was in the process of getting it when he discovered the gap between being dropped off for therapy and being picked up fifty-five minutes later. Into that gap he had fled. And here he had landed, a thousand miles north, hidden in an attic, not having any effect on any person, nothing he could be accused of or responsible for, the stakes of his existence blessedly bland. AWOL, and glad of it.

Attachments were dangerous; hadn't he just proved the point? Finding the dog had started the trouble. Not rescuing it meant living with what would become overwhelming guilt; rescuing it meant caring if its puppies died, risking his living situation with Joanne, who seemed like someone who might not have much use for pets. And now the girl was sobbing uncontrollably across the table from him, a girl who had appeared to be as interested in solitude and isolation and restrained interactions as he was, a girl whose dolefulness and privacy he had respected and felt indebted to. No game-playing for her. No attempts to bring him out of his shell. But now she would not stop emoting. If he put his hand on her shoulder, if he asked her what was wrong . . .

"It's okay," she kept saying to him, between bouts of tears, holding her hands up as if aware of his dilemma; she continued to impress him, despite his overarching alarm, despite his impulse once more to flee. "It's okay, really. My mom," she explained, "my mother . . . ," as if this more formal address might usher in more formal composure. But no. And later, in a hiccupping hush in which they could still hear the puppies sucking rhythmically, lustily, at the teats, she added, "I just remembered our *dog*. I don't know how"—she took shallow breaths, heaving and stuttering, pulling in air to plunge on—"I don't know how . . . I could possibly forget . . . about *Max*," she said, and burst into another round of inconsolable wailing.

CHAPTER 7

"Dude," his male employees and underlings had been greeting him all day as he made the rounds from one outpost to another. "*Señor!*" Clapping their youthful palms against his shoulders, or holding them up like starfish for him to slap in return, or making fists for him to bump with his own fist, these ritual admiring greetings, behavior bestowed by the apes, passed on via apish organizations such as football teams. Sometimes it seemed they meant to knock him down, clap him with enough gusto to illustrate their superior masculinity, the modern version of the bone-crushing handshake. Oliver Desplaines had known he would appear in the New Year's Day edition of the *Wichita Eagle-Beacon* as one of the city's ten Wichitans to Watch. He'd purposely not spread the news in advance, looking forward to hearing from people who would assure him he was a modest guy, a deserving hero; especially anticipating the Sweetheart's exuberant elation: her new love, a celebrity.

"I'm making my rounds," he'd said to Catherine before she'd risen from her bed or encountered the paper, bending down to kiss her forehead before she opened her eyes. A year ago, before the Sweetheart, it would have been her response he saved for last, after he'd been publicly heralded.

Did a life seem longer if you were leading two of them? Maybe. Since finding the Sweetheart, Oliver felt as if he were getting away with something, as if he'd happened upon a secret that others had missed, like a hidden chamber or a magic power. He'd stumbled upon this secret before. The two lives could happily coexist for a while but not forever. YaYa, for example, meant to kill him when she discovered his affair with Leslie, when the private had overwhelmed the public life. Certainly she'd begun hating him as fiercely as she'd loved him, some logical proportional relationship, love to hate. Leslie, on the other hand, upon discovering his affair with Catherine, had seemed to wish to wilt and vanish, tired flower out of season, perhaps deserving of her punishment.

Simpler if his ex-wives were both dead, he considered. Or maybe not dead, exactly, but something like dead. Oliver had obligations to both of those women today. January 1 was the date agreed upon, long ago, on which he exchanged artwork with YaYa, the paintings they'd not been able to divide when they themselves had done so, that outrageously melodramatic separation. YaYa might have suggested literally cutting the contested paintings in half, severing and thereby ruining every single one. She lived at high volume, a lusty operatic figure at the mercy of her strong feelings, always acting before thinking, very Old Testament. The first thing she'd done was destroy their wedding photographs while their daughter Mary, fourteen years old, stood wailing as helpless witness. Cutting, ripping, burning. Next, YaYa had exhorted the girl to despise him, to make a team of two against him.

It wasn't fair, Oliver always thought. He hadn't betrayed his daughter, after all. He hadn't quit loving *her*.

Mary was a painter, and the work he and YaYa traded back

and forth was hers, her early precocious self-portraiture, the paint-ings that made sense of the whole collection, the recognizable girl wrought in a variety of settings—Mary in the sunlit flowers, Mary in the brutal night, the side of her that was demure, the side of her that was demonic. Eight altogether; the four that Oliver hadn't seen since the year before were what allowed him to crate up the rest every January 1. He couldn't have the girl, but he could have her art.

He had looked forward to wrapping his news, in the form of newspapers, around the small frames, slipping them in their crate, and shipping his honor to YaYa as if accidentally. And she would perhaps grudgingly pass along the information to the daughter they had in common, who also lived in San Francisco. It was Mary whose opinion mattered most to Oliver, she who had not forgiven him. Should her mother YaYa die, perhaps Mary would feel an urge to renew acquaintance with her father. He felt he might trade YaYa's life for a fresh start with their daughter.

Did he love Mary because she refused to love him? Her paint-ings of herself created in him a special ache; he visited her recent work on Web sites, proud and mystified.

He'd anticipated his day in the public eye; however, when it dawned, and he spread the paper on the table, glasses cleaned and perched on his nose, the front-page spread struck him with a sudden wash of heat and dread, the sensation of a riptide or excruciating faux pas. All over town it was being digested; he realized he would have to accept the congratulations with a sar-donic rather than genuine grin. What he'd not known was that he would share his place among nine other Wichitans to Watch with the likes of the local rediscovered serial killer. The real es-tate mogul named Bunny he could abide; the fellow who planned to erect a brass statue commemorating the Korean War with a dozen looming soldiers (his photo showing him with the tiny model bearing flags that would eventually be the size of bill-boards), okay. Commerce, patriotism, his own entrepreneurial gifts, the grant-grubbing preschool teacher, the eighty-year-old minister who ran the soup kitchen, hell or high water. But an unknown killer? In place of a picture, this figure was a dark anonymous silhouette, a graphic white question mark coiling from his head down his brain stem and throat to a white dot on the chest. Oliver was not unaccustomed to ironies such as these; but he had let down his guard, he realized, when he discovered that it hurt his pride. He did not want to be lumped into a group that included a serial killer. He'd allowed himself to think the honor meant something, falling into a sentimental civic pride in his own abilities, only too obliging to pose at Wheatlands, his most recent successful venture, with his grin-ning apprentices there, wearing an apron over his customary black turtleneck, teeth bared.

The Sweetheart, its manager, there beside him, his arm thrown brazenly, avuncularly, over her shoulder. He had been looking forward to imagining her staring at that picture, her eye drawn, as his was, to the absence of space between them there on the front page. A plausible couple, Oliver had been thinking. People in love. Out in the open yet utterly hidden.

Now when his employees were slapping his back, he felt he might buckle, his footing unsure rather than confident and fancy. He skated, he danced, he sidestepped; he worked very hard not to stumble. It was as if he were being sent back to childhood, demoted and undone, back to Lawton, Oklahoma. He went by Oliver, but that had been his own invention, derived from his middle name, which was, simply: O. Tribute to his Okie father's best friend, O, the blacksmith with missing teeth and digits on all four extremities (frostbite, drunkenness, carelessness in the presence of sharp tools), a man whose name was also miss-ing parts, a circle of emptiness, a name that stood for nothing, a zero on a sign, on a birth certificate. Oliver's natural tendency toward hiding himself—renaming, re-origining—began early. First he discovered that he must hide his sensitivity, his troubling propensity toward tears. ("You should have been a girl," his mother once told him, attempting to console him.) Later, he had to hide the barbed persona he'd erected to shield the earlier model, his constant sarcasm and criticism, the eye-rolling, scathing scoffing that in high school had garnered nothing but illiterate ill will, brutal daily beatings, and universal contempt: voted Most Likely to Never Come Back. Upon moving to Wichita, he'd reassigned himself: not Billy O, but Oliver; not an Okie but a New Yorker—he'd spent a few years there, after all, acquiring tastes. Never mind that the place had eventually frightened him, the way it could absorb him without noticing him. The way he was, in a city that size, not just anonymous but redundant, his type everywhere, and therefore unnecessary, invisible. In Wichita, he was unique. Here, he had become cosmopolitan and avant garde, humble, even, in some small way, an asset to the community, a person praised for not moving away and taking his talents with him. These were, he reminded himself (and would be reminded by others), vaguely flimsy distinctions, and could be eroded. He might teeter off his pedestal. What, besides a point of view, would separate his poise from pretentiousness?

"Saw you in the paper, man," said yet another of his young admirers, this time accompanied by a wink along with the pervasive high-five hand. Oliver braced himself so as not to sway under its impact, felt the smack as if its germy content were the fateful coup de grâce.

Now he thought the award had the smell of prank on it. Somebody had known the serial killer would be included. Somebody, somewhere, wished to quite particularly humiliate him. Somebody who knew how precisely to insert this blade, a very thin and fine knife, more like a surgical laser, leaving results but no discernible sign of entry.

Paranoid! he scolded himself, exiting the celebration at Wheatlands (the Sweetheart never making eye contact, demure and blushing; they'd first embraced in the cold chill of the walk-in refrigerator, wordless, crucial, the scent of fermenting yeast surrounding them; now he could not know what she was thinking; he would find out later, when she got off work, when he reached the end of this taxing day).

He headed for the celebration at Kansa Karma. He had rescued the business by vetoing Spa-Licious and N-est-ce Spa, although he'd been too late to save them from unfortunate puns on their early marketing materials, lyrics from the odious and infectious "Karma Chameleon," and often found himself whistling the tune when he walked through the spa's otherwise tranquil space. His second wife had permitted this; she ran the spa with their daughter, Miriam. With these two women, unlike YaYa and Mary, he had an ongoing nearly daily relationship. Leslie was the most reasonable of his three wives, as well as the most dull. Because of the chaotic extravagance of his first wife, YaYa—the woman who demanded all the attention in the room, the elaborate liar, the promiscuous drunk, the insanely jealous— he'd somehow known he'd needed an earnest antidote, a woman who wouldn't question his every comment, looking for a double entendre or a joke or a veiled insult. If YaYa lived in Wichita, if YaYa cared enough to keep up with local politics, if YaYa had any kind of pull in this city, it might have been she who'd make him a Wichitan to Watch alongside a murderer. That would have been right up her very vengeful, extravagant alley. It would have amused her no end.

It was she who'd ruined whistling for him, she whose parting shot had been, "Here's some advice, Mid-Life Loser: you whistle like my grandpa Earl."

He would wrap the paintings in bubble wrap.

The women in his life, past and present, would ask themselves and one another how he was going to handle turning seventy next summer. His birthday: a future embarrassment, not completely separate from the one today. A person being offered salutations at some ambiguous accolade. They would worry not about whether to throw a party (no one would risk that), but about whether to mention the day at all, or if so, to note his having rolled over into another decade, closer yet to the inevitable end.

To his sweetheart, he'd lied, told her his birthday was in December instead of July. His sweetheart: he'd not been able to guess her mood at the bakery. For all the months they'd openly flirted before they began sleeping together, each now acted in public as if the other were not present. His secret phone was in the glove compartment; there, his need for it to buzz might make it happen. This was the magical thinking of illicit love. Of love, period.

He decided he would test his theory about the newspaper by gauging Leslie's response: he would know whether or not to be distressed by how she behaved. If she was proud of him, he would be proud. Or, if she were horrified on his behalf, horrified he would be. There wasn't a paranoid bone in Leslie's body. And what if she seemed pitying? How dispiriting and revolting to be pitied, and for even milquetoast Leslie to be savvy enough to see it. With her, he also could not simply brush off the honor as a joke. Leslie wasn't versed in joke, although he'd mistaken her quick smile for teasing, once upon a time—her pointed upper incisors suggested impishness, a complete misrepresentation. But that was before he'd discovered that she was just like the beverages she ordered at bars, virgin versions of the ones that carried the poison and punch of alcohol. Leslie: her innocence had eventually elicited in him a viciousness he'd not known he was capable of, a bullying creature who'd finally, mercifully, been rescued by finding a new love. And he'd been able to divorce poor Leslie, divorce her before killing her with his cruel sarcasm, with his cutting scorn toward everything she fervently believed holy.

Like this perfectly fine business she'd managed to make a success. Oliver parked in its full lot and was pleased. It was he who'd kept it from contemporary flaky kitsch, he who'd recruited and trained her fleet of professional help, yet Leslie who'd bestowed the place with absolute unwavering goodwill.

She wouldn't hurt his feelings, and that was a relief. "Hello, my friend," she said when he came through the door, putting her dewy cheek next to his. He had the same brief realization he always did at her customary greeting: it was exactly the way his current wife addressed their dogs, *Hello, my friends*, and he could never be certain that Catherine wasn't having a little joke at Leslie's expense.

But now she didn't mention the award at all. Quite possibly she'd neglected to look at the paper; she was persistently untutored on local or national or international news; she'd often forgotten to vote, come fall. She was fifty-seven but could pass for forty, her body tiny, her hair clipped like a French waif's, her skin unmarred by sun or stress, her black linen outfit so utterly neutral, so thoroughly practical, as to be outside the realm of fashion, invisible like a mime's, liberating like a martial artist's, timeless as the sci-fi character clothed from some purely utilitarian future. Kansa Karma smelled always of flowers, not the sickly thick concentration of perfume or incense but the scent of fresh flowers, held just a few inches from the nose, and with a gentle breeze ready to further attenuate their presence, leaving you following their odor rather than turning away. It was she who'd given his current mother-in-law wind chimes to hang over the heat vent at the nursing home, a sweet tinkling sound, soothing; once upon a time, Leslie had taken classes with Dr. Harding, lugged around for a few semesters the massive anthology with its composite of stern suffragette faces on the cover. Further cross-pollination had occurred between this wife and the present one when Miriam had needed teenage counseling, and Catherine was recruited to provide it. More recently, Catherine had spent a few months here at Leslie's spa, placid behind the desk, making appointments, filling water jugs, answering the silently ringing phone, welcoming clients with a murmur and a smile. She still came in occasionally, working when someone was ill, trading her services for the services of the spa, pedicure, massage, facial. Oliver wondered why it did not bother him to think of his ex-wife's hands on his current wife's body, his daughter working at Catherine's face. Had he grown inured to the coincidences and ironic overlap of living in a town the size of Wichita? After all, Catherine's mother had been Leslie's favorite professor, a mentor; might he not be more bothered that Dr. Harding had had some early meddling influence during Leslie's formative years? Wasn't that, in fact, a far more insidious intimacy?

Maybe Dr. Harding hadn't had enough of an influence.

When Leslie forgot to tell him to take off his shoes, Oliver caught the first hint of something awry. "What's wrong?"

"Miriam," she said, leaning close and speaking lower than usual. "She brought somebody here last night."

He sighed. Miriam was thirty-two years old; her adolescent hijinks should have ended more than a decade earlier. "And?"

"He's still here." Motioning with her hand, she indicated that he should follow. What was supposed to be an obligatory gift-receiving session under hot stones (Leslie's promised Christmas present, a gift Oliver had not particularly wanted, yet did not have the energy to decline) was now turning into an all-too-familiar episode in the continuing saga of Miriam's arrested development.

Leslie padded along duck-footed, looking from the back like a Ninja, leading him through several whispering panels that all glided smoothly on their oiled tracks. They tiptoed past toweled women on benches, cubbies full of boots, wooden pegs holding a row of hooded white bathrobes like a soldierly line of ghosts. Always so quiet here in the spa, the dripping water, the flowering air, light filtering through the endless rooms of rice-paper doors, walls that slid away to reveal other rooms, fountains, clear beverages in which floated lemons and cucumbers, here a bowl of raw almonds, there a pump bottle of sandalwood oil. The light was autumnal, all year; clocks were disallowed.

Leslie pulled open the final rice-paper door separating one small lounge area from the pedicure room. In the leather massage seat with his eyes shut and his feet in a tub of water rested a naked man.

"Jesus Christ," Oliver said. "He's breathing?"

Leslie nodded.

"Where's Miriam?"

"Doing an exfoliation. As you might have noticed, that Mom's Day of Beauty idea was really popular." This had been Oliver's most recent brainstorm, a Christmas stocking-stuffer coupon for clueless husbands and their exhausted wives.

"What did she say about him?"

"She met him at an NA meeting."

"And?"

"Then they got drunk?" Leslie shrugged helplessly. She'd done everything she could for Miriam: helped her through school (Miriam's business card named her Esthetician), put her on the payroll, invited her back into her old bedroom at the house. But she'd never understood her daughter's naughty habits. She'd not been that kind of girl, herself; Oliver supposed Miriam had inherited her taste for danger from him.

At least *his* secret life was secret.

"If it weren't for the tattoo, he'd look like a frat boy," he said. The man was carelessly handsome, beautiful by virtue of youth, his blond hair messy, his slackness more like something sculpted than something abandoned, his mouth open and his youthful white teeth showing. But the vivid colorful narrative covering his upper arms and continuing down along his wrists bespoke some other life. His hands hung slack—squared knuckles, a large silver skull ring big as a drawer pull on his pinkie—and framed his flaccid penis as if to present it. His knees splayed open and his feet rested in the electronic bucket used to clean and soothe toes. Its motor was running, a filmy gray surface of scum burbling away.

"I wonder how many times this kind of thing has happened, and we didn't find out about it?" Oliver said. He already knew about ones that Leslie, innocent Leslie, had not discovered.

"He can't stay here," she said. "I have clients. And he smells terrible." He did, some sour combination of alcohol, smoke, sweat, and general male carelessness. Leslie's nose was tiny and very sensitive. She wished to dispose of this creature the way she would any dirty object fouling her sanctuary.

Oliver looked around the room. "No clothes?"

"No. Nothing. No car, no clothes, no wallet. It's like he crawled out of the walls."

Or was sent from above, Adonis. Or from below, some devilish counterpart.

"And Miriam has nothing to say?" Oliver shook his head. Miriam. Was it his fault she did things like this? Was he to blame for her bad instincts with men? Early on she'd made wrong assumptions about her own father. She was sure he would prefer being called by his name rather than something as potentially sentimental or enfeebling as *Dad*. She liked to think of him and her in collusion, sometimes against Leslie, Miriam having also inherited some of his skepticism, his sharp tongue. His large head and skeletal thinness.

Leslie said, "I'm sorry, Oliver, but can you do something?"

"Of course." In fact, it was sort of a pleasure to have something other than the newspaper to think about. "Okay. Grab a robe and some slippers. I'm going to pull the car around back."

The man breathed peacefully through the awkward and unsavory process of dressing and moving him. Leslie had provided sterile gloves for Oliver, knowing very well his squeamishness concerning touching other people. In a terry-cloth robe and scuffs, his tattoos hidden, the sleeping man looked more like a model, someone on the edge of a swimming pool at the Playboy mansion.

"What was she thinking?" Leslie asked her ex-husband in the back alley by the garbage cans, genuinely perplexed. "What was she thinking bringing a stranger here, letting him . . ." She couldn't say. It would pain her to have to learn the terrifying possibilities. This had always been her problem, behavior she herself would never perform being unimaginable to her, her own daughter welcoming into her life and body the unseemly and careless, the strangely dangerous.

Now that the man was in Oliver's car, she breathed a sigh of relief, clasping her hands before her, beaming at him, so pleased and relieved to have removed this ripe disaster from her heavenly spa. The blue vein in her forehead was visible as it always was when she felt something incontrovertibly positive. She stood like a former ballerina, feet pointed out, spine erect. She probably weighed ninety-nine pounds. Catherine said that she always felt like a cow around Leslie, bovine, thick.

"Healthy," Oliver had corrected Catherine, savoring, then, those large breasts, remembering Leslie's nearly nonexistent ones.

"That's what all the well-intentioned say about girls like me," his wife had replied.

But now it was the Sweetheart's body Oliver compared with

Leslie's, her swiftness and efficiency of movement, her practical thinking clear in her actions, her long dark hair that she was incessantly shoving out of her way. A brunette swatch of which had lain on his arm, in the newspaper photo, for all the world to see. The spill of it, on the pillow; the bound length of it grasped in his hand

"I'll take him to the ER. I'll tell anybody who asks that we found him out here in the alley, that we worried about an overdose, hypothermia, something like that. Don't worry."

"You're a genius!"

Leslie's praise was always excessive, saccharine; there'd been years when Miriam wouldn't speak to her, so outraged was she by her mother's unbridled, oblivious effusiveness. Maybe the spa clients liked it, Oliver thought, when Leslie thanked them for letting her spend an hour or more tending to their minor aches and pains and vanities, massaging their buttocks and skulls, breathing heavily over their knotted shoulders and crepey necks while they lay supine, inert, blissfully salved. "Thank you," she would say, like a martyr, bending in a respectful bow.

Now she said, "I'm so blessed to have you to call upon."

"Well," he said, and then instructed himself to stop there, to bite his tongue before it did something awful.

But maybe that was why he'd really come here in the first place, to be thanked by a martyr instead of feeling paranoid, to put his prank theory on brief hold. "You packed up the paintings yet?" Leslie asked now, smiling benignly as if the comatose stranger weren't still right there before them, head lolling on a headrest.

He gave her a half smile as he opened his door. "You never forget anything." On a good day, it might look like selflessness; on a bad day, it seemed like somebody hoping so passionately to give the impression of selflessness that she manically displayed her ability to recite everything, absolutely everything, that was going on with those who surrounded her, as if she were being tested. It wasn't nosiness, Oliver thought, and it wasn't actually concern. It was the habit of a person who had nothing better with which to occupy her thoughts. Leslie did not read books, did not enjoy films or politics or shopping or gossip or competition or collecting or researching or imbibing or ingesting or any other of the myriad ways her fellow human beings filled their time and conversation and obsessive self-doubting. She occupied herself with other people, recalling their birthdays, learning how to address their superficial rather than existential troubles, anticipating their need for a glass of water or a bite of protein just moments before they noticed the need themselves. She settled them in rooms that resembled nothing more closely than the womb, a comforting, mindless space.

"Already started wrapping them up," Oliver said, of the paintings.

"I always liked the even-numbered years best," Leslie said.

"You like landscapes. You like seasons and trees and clouds. You prefer flowers." He stopped himself from one further remark, because she would interpret it as criticism, which, to be honest, *was* criticism: *You would rather die than deal with conflict.*

"Much better than those monsters." She shuddered her shoulders, blinked as a kind of mental exorcism of the very thought of the odd-year paintings. She meant the abstracts, in which she— and she alone—had seen devils and dark alleys and menace, modern art as Rorschach. It was true that Oliver and YaYa had an eclectic collection, somewhat manic-depressive, young nude figure demure in a bucolic hilly vista one minute, then suddenly obscured in a moody black-streaked murkiness the next. In their annual exchanges, the atmosphere in either house was abruptly switched.

"Better go," Oliver said, nudging his head toward his passenger.

"Come back later for the hot stones?" she asked. "Please? Just thirty minutes? It would make me so happy to do that for you." She was ready to pretend that Miriam's latest mistake not only hadn't happened but wouldn't be repeated. Rinse out the foot bath, sponge off the chair. Switch on the ceiling fan, spritz some kind of floral spray, kill the man's odor.

Oliver waved noncommittally, slamming the Saab door and studying his passenger. He wasn't going to deliver him to the ER. As he pulled out into the street, he opened the passenger window to let cold air do its work. He took Adonis onto the overpass, just to get up some speed, exited onto the belt loop, then circled for a few miles. He could drop the guy at the recently shuttered amusement park, Joyland, that bizarre place with the rickety wooden roller coaster, the maniacal larger-than-life clown who pounded on the Wurlitzer organ, the general queasy atmosphere of things that too closely resembled menace, cotton candy like fiberglass insulation, rides designed to mimic the heart-stopping physical fears of falling or crashing.

Here you go, Mr. Tattooed Man. Joyland.

Oliver took the Kellogg exit too swiftly, which brought a flicker of consciousness from his passenger, his head wobbling forward, then knocking back against the headrest. By the time they'd gotten up to speed heading west, the guy had roused himself fully, blinking and popping his lips. He woke without surprise.

"You related to that cunt?" he asked at last.

Oliver turned sharply, the word making his knuckles whiten against the steering wheel.

"Muriel?" the man guessed, his eyes narrowing to recall. "Marian?"

"Is there somebody you want to call?" Oliver asked, locking the passenger window open just as the guy was reaching to close it. "I'll dial any number you want." The man looked down at his bright white bathrobe, lifted his half-covered feet, gazed at the car's interior and then at the billboards rushing by outside. Oliver motioned toward the strip malls, the airport when it went by. "Anywhere you want me to stop?"

The guy sighed angrily. Oliver would never ask Miriam whether it was NA where she'd found him, or why she'd brought him to the spa, nor what she'd done with him there. It was behavior that bespoke a sick appetite, an insatiability, a public disregard; it made Oliver nauseated to consider it. He might have had to vomit if the window were closed, if there weren't frozen air cleansing the atmosphere. They drove in that windy silence for a few more miles, away from the city.

"There," the man finally said, motioning toward a motel sign across from the cemetery. It was a place Oliver himself had noticed before, a place he'd thought about as a possible rendezvous spot, once the grandparents returned to town and he and the Sweetheart had to find somewhere else to play out their passion. He was attracted to the old-fashioned sign, the black and white tipped top hat, the unrenovated sleazy aspect that said the motel proprietor would rent by the hour, would take cash, would understand the idea of parking in the back. Like Joyland, the motel was a fading piece of the former city. For Oliver, this imagined seedy locale was part and parcel of his second life, that simultaneous existence that was a lurid undercurrent beneath the one on top, the nocturnal answer to the broad and reputable daylight.

This tattooed creature was the kind of lodger who'd be in the room next door while he and the Sweetheart made love.

"She won't always get off so easy," he said when they'd stopped outside the motel office. "Someday somebody's gonna be sick enough of her shit." With this he slammed the door, taking with him the two twenties Oliver had offered, and shuffled off in his scuffs to the main office. The clerk, there behind bulletproof glass, looked up without surprise. Eleven a.m. on New Year's Day. A handsome youth in a bathrobe. Yes, there was a vacancy.

Oliver now declined to retrieve his secret cell phone to read his Sweetheart's text. *I am kissing our photo*, that message might say, alluding to the newspaper. On his public phone, he called Leslie to leave a message about her unwelcome visitor, that mess he had so easily disposed of. He considered leaving a message for Miriam, but then could not fashion a sensible straightforward admonition. She was an adult; he had failed her as a father; she was injuring her mother; her life was in danger. The enormity of her trouble—its duration and repercussions, its scariness—was daunting. And enervating.

After a few mindless turns down one empty street and another, Oliver decided to head home to Catherine. The day had started badly and only gotten worse. There at their house she would be waiting, she who would still be in her own bathrobe, drinking Irish coffee, smiling wryly, treating the newspaper accolade with kind and sardonic indulgence.

"My husband, the Wichitan to Watch," she would say. "You and the BTK," holding up two entwined fingers.

CHAPTER 8

IT WAS NOT legally binding. The expression itself interested Catherine. Legally. Binding.

One trademark of the serial killer's methods was binding. Drawstrings, extension cords, scarves, pantyhose—whatever, it seemed, was at hand. Catherine lay in bed letting her thoughts circle and knot (*neckties, jump ropes, leashes . . .*) while Oliver prepared for his workday.

He often reminded her that she was impetuous. Allowing this strange girl into their house would be, maybe, an example of that. He had had an operation after his second accidental child, with his second incorrect wife. Catherine had become a stepmother to those girls: Mary, whose artwork hung around her house yet whom she'd never met, and Miriam, of whom she had always been terrified. Thirteen years old when Oliver divorced her mother to marry Catherine, the girl was inordinately attentive to her young stepmother. She made Catherine nervous; no girl was supposed to love her stepmother. Everybody knew that. It was the presence of Miriam that eventually precluded the idea of adoption. There were enough of those apocryphal tales circulating among their group of friends, the damaged goods they'd invited unwittingly into their homes, gene pools contaminated by ignorance, addiction, desperation, and simple bad luck.

Miriam herself had seemed a cautionary tale, seemed so still. Once, she would have told Catherine any- and everything: her delinquencies and exploits, offered up in a child's enthusiastic bragging manner, begging for Catherine to reply with her own confessions—like a big sister, perhaps. The girl had been so happy to spite her Pollyanna mother, to act as if she and Catherine were naughty cohorts. But Catherine had been attending to becoming a wife, not a sister, not a mother. Now Miriam skulked around the spa wearing the approved uniform but nonetheless looking anything but healthy, her skin sallow, her hair unwashed, an emaciated and angry and distracted girl, eyes dilated, thoughts uncharitable. She would never not be Catherine's stepdaughter, Oliver's daughter, that child they had failed.

"*You,*" Oliver would sometimes say, disciplining the dogs, "we can put down."

That was the thing about choice, Catherine noted now: you could have too much of it. As an unready person, she'd had two abortions before marrying; when she found her husband, he was finished conceiving children.

"We should meet her before we say no," Catherine said from the bed, Oliver's large firm bed, its tight sheets, her voice still croaky. "Little Catherine, I mean." She said it to see how her husband would react; because they'd had sex the night before, this was as charitable a mood she would ever find him in. On one hand could she count the serious disagreements in their marriage.

"That seems reasonable until you push the scenario a step further," Oliver answered from his position at the ironing board; he licked his finger and tested the iron's heat, a petite sizzle. "We meet her, and then we say no?" Last evening, fully in his cups at a dinner party, he'd presented the situation as conversation fodder. People had different responses. Some said they'd accept without thinking twice; others said they'd decline with the same haste. And a few, people like Catherine, had a provisional inclination. *If*, they said . . .

But if what?

"She's a complete stranger." Oliver stated this obvious fact for at least the tenth time, although he probably didn't realize that. He stepped into his warm pants, folded up the ironing board, and opened the bedroom blinds behind him. There were moments he seemed to be making a physical point to Catherine, illustrating that he could move like a much younger man. He did this now. "Still winter," he notified her.

"She's not *exactly* a stranger," Catherine said. There was Misty Mueller's face, her perpetual sleepy expression, her lazy smile and crooked teeth. One of Catherine's later boyfriends, during college, had said Misty reminded him of a basset hound, droopy, mournful, and resigned, preparing to emit a baying complaint. Catherine had laughed; she and her best friend had already begun, by then, to grow apart.

"Call Houston," Oliver advised. "Get details. Maximum input." This was how he handled all potential projects, asking for further information, waiting until everything was spelled out to him.

"I already have as much information as exists," Catherine said. "There just isn't any." Over the phone she'd befriended the Houston State Farm insurance provider, Dick Little, who was fascinated by the girl's absence, and the tragedy of the mother's death. His first assurance to Catherine, before Catherine had had any notion to ask, was that his office was not treating the accident as a suicide.

"What if it *was* a suicide?" Catherine had asked.

Dick Little paused, perhaps suddenly aware that he had possibly overstepped his authority, had opened his big mouth when discretion was called for, then explained to Catherine that the insurance payout was significantly different in the instance of intentional death.

"Oh," said Catherine. Of course. But how was it she hadn't known about this? How had she gotten to be as old as she was without catching on to such a perfectly obvious clause as this? The sensation was not an infrequent one; it seemed others had come with their practical minds better prepared, or perhaps put into practice more often, challenged by the world at regular intervals. She could blame her bossy mother, she could blame her older husband, those loving protectors who'd apparently always simply handed her the fish rather than teaching her how to catch her own.

And it occurred to Catherine that Misty had also been one of those protectors, the less apparent yet necessary one in between, who'd shepherded Catherine from her childish life in her mother's care to, eventually, her adult life in her husband's hands.

It was Dick Little in Houston from whom Catherine learned that Misty had been a real estate agent.

"Real estate?" Catherine had said, surprised. But what job wouldn't have surprised her? Misty had been adept at a great many things—hustling pool, scoring weed, forging signatures—but none of them easily translated into a viable grown-up career. They'd gone through high school getting teenage jobs together, then getting fired together—thieves at worst; insolent, irreverent, and careless, at best. For a single evening, they'd been professional babysitters at the eastside Holiday Inn, called to take care of the children of visiting strangers. Misty hadn't known how to quiet the infant she'd been handed; her response was to put it screaming in the bathtub, shut the door, and turn up the television. When Catherine came from her own charges—three siblings two floors away—appalled at the scene, Misty had shrugged. She'd grown up without a mother, without a childhood of tenderness or spoiling, without even dolls on which to practice such things.

The baby had been rolling side to side in the tub, its large bald head bumping as it shrieked, hot, soiled, red. Damaged, Catherine feared, holding it fearfully to her pounding chest, soothing it, while Misty watched *Saturday Night Live*. Misty hadn't understood why Catherine insisted they abandon the babysitting business.

Yet it was Misty who'd become an actual mother, finally, not Catherine. Catherine hadn't even been an adequate stepmother, poor Miriam still a lost soul, sleeping with strangers, taking risks that terrified everyone around her. Sometimes it seemed she did the things she did in order to keep her family on alert. She'd not outgrown that teenage girl's perverse pleasure.

Visiting the real estate company's Web site, Catherine didn't at first recognize her old friend smiling there among the others, her eyes skipping right over that coiffed lady in search of the person she knew. Then she repeated the process, seeking to penetrate the camouflage of the ordinary. And there she was: Misty's hair streaked blond now, kept shorter, buoyed, curled at her temple and ears. Catherine leaned close to the lit computer screen, squinting into the cheerful face with Misty Mueller's name below it. Her teeth had been repaired, and it was obvious that she was comfortable showing them, as she had never been before; she also wore glasses, frameless things that might have hidden the dark circles Catherine remembered. She'd grown older, had Misty, but it seemed that gravity had worked on her features in reverse, lifting and lightening what had been her previous expression. No one viewing this photograph would have been reminded of a basset hound. Furthermore, she had a long list of citations beneath her photo and had been what her company proudly named a "Harris County top producer" for the last decade.

This woman wouldn't have put an infant in the tub and drowned out her cries with the sound of a television laugh track.

So there was that official information, and more like it. Then there was the much briefer résumé of her daughter, young Catherine who quite plausibly had been named for elder Catherine, guardian. The private school in Vermont continued to assure her that they were as concerned as she was about locating the girl, meanwhile never failing to mention that they were in no way responsible for her disappearance, that the code of conduct—contractual, it seemed—at St. Christopher's strictly outlined the student's willingness to obey it. They had this in writing, and would be happy to provide Catherine with a copy. "No thanks," Catherine told the head of school. She conceived of a bias against the woman, merely from her tone of voice.

The police in both Texas and Vermont had been notified. The girl was a teenage runaway; it was an epidemic group. Her mother Misty had been one, once upon a time. Catherine had been her accomplice. They had an elaborate code for Misty's collect phone calls from the road, different names given by Misty to indicate different locations or dilemmas; alternate responses, from Catherine, to signal the mood at home. Ludicrous convolutedness. Catherine had driven Misty to the Greyhound station in Misty's car, and then parked the Buick back at East High. What had been the reason for her odyssey? Catherine could not recall. Might she have suggested it, herself, an adventure for Misty that would arouse her negligent grandma into action? Catherine had been invited along, and may even have feigned some temptation. But push coming to shove, she would never have gone. She'd have sent Misty, in her stead, to see what such a thing would become, her experimental surrogate, her guinea pig.

Her own version of scaring the grown-ups.

When the grandmother finally noticed Misty wasn't home,

when the school security patrol had finally tagged Misty's automobile for the third day, that's when the alarm was finally sounded. And then everybody suddenly realized that Misty was eighteen, and could not be officially designated as a minor. She became a missing person. And then she rode the Greyhound home, where nothing had changed except that she was further behind than usual in her classes, and there was a giant orange sticker on her windshield that wouldn't come off. It stayed there for years, fading and shredding and peeling.

"Agenda?" Oliver asked Catherine, eyeing her from his bathed and ready position while she lay still rumpled in bed.

"Doctors, waiting rooms, bad magazines, insipid conversation." *The annual humiliation*, her mother had named the day, long ago. Physical, bloodwork, pap smear, mammogram, colonoscopy: all scheduled in a row, one long day of undressing, probing, stirrups, plates, tubes. Catherine was her chaperone and driver.

Oliver offered his wife a Valium, then said, "I admire her optimism."

"Meaning?"

He glanced over the pill bottle he'd extended to her. She could see him manufacturing a more diplomatic explanation than the true one: Why bother, he'd meant; a seventy-four-year-old invalid woman might just as well let nature take its course, rust or rot have its way with her like any old thing, untroubled by intervention.

"I don't like it when you seem cold," Catherine said; his postcoital cheer had gone. He withdrew the Valium. To distract her from his coldness, he bent over the bed and embraced her—aftershave, mouthwash, starch—and then he was overly solicitous of the dogs, encouraging them to see him to the back door, to follow his progress outside from inside as he walked to the front of the house, and then turning to trill his special whistle for them, the mockingbird run he could execute perfectly, knowing they would be watching from the glass front door, their nub tails twitching, their vocal cords gargling. This was all designed to endear him to Catherine.

Now she rose. Normally she would visit Oliver's businesses, check in with his managers, catch up on the continuing human drama of his employees. To her he'd offered a few of those managerial jobs, restaurant or day spa or art gallery or martini bar, but Catherine preferred being his ambassador while he was off looking into the next venture. He not only made loans to the men and women who launched these projects, he trained the employees who would work there, his army of chic service industry drones. Catherine had been one herself, long ago. She'd been very good at it; it's what she'd done after college, breaking her mother's heart when she announced she had no intention of going to graduate school, she was done with book learning. She wanted, she must have argued, "real life experience." She'd been raised by teachers, she'd been in school for as long as she could remember, she'd majored in education. Enough! Catherine had left the college dorm, rented an apartment, and gone to work for Oliver alongside his other devotees; from that institution she'd taken what she considered highest honors, graduating to become its guru's wife.

His trophy, her mother had disagreed. His plaything. His unserious living doll.

The newspaper headline reported yet another dispatch from the serial killer. He was ready to claim yet another victim, offering as evidence of his authenticity the medallion she had been wearing when he killed her. The dead woman's fingerprints were on it. He'd not been credited with this murder, now thirteen years a cold case, because he'd not bound her. Nonetheless, she was his, his letter said. Braggart, Catherine thought.

The BLT, she and Misty had named the killer, that minor

character in the saga of her youth, that mad jokester who punctuated and titillated the dark age of her sexual awakening. Recently, Miriam had exhibited rare enthusiasm when she asked Catherine about the guy; she'd printed up a guide of his kill sites, a kind of lurid Map to the Stars for their town.

"I'd probably recognize him if I met him," Miriam claimed. What alarmed Catherine was that she thought it might be true.

She sought out the Valium Oliver had offered, but could not find it. She actually did not know where he kept his pills or what, exactly, he took them for. They appeared every morning in a colorful little pile beside his wheat toast as if fairies delivered them. No arsenal of orange bottles on their bedside table or kitchen windowsill. Only when her mother's body had become unavoidably available to Catherine had it occurred to her to wonder about her husband's health. He was young for his age, everybody would agree; still, wasn't it strange not to have a clue about what that clutter of medication held at bay? She could see that he wasn't overweight, didn't overindulge, and spent a lot of his day walking. As a profile, his was utterly public. The only detail she alone knew for a fact was that he had no trouble getting an erection.

Plus: he was fanatical as a surgeon about hand-washing.

"Want to come with?" Catherine asked the dogs. Unlike Oliver, they never said no to coming with.

And they were such emissaries of goodwill, such reliable ice-breakers, the two of them crowding through the nursing-home doors and greeting all the lounge chair occupants, sending those lazy kitty cats fleeing down the halls. Professor Harding was waiting, standing with her walker before her, wearing a wool dress and hose. Zippers, buttons, shoes with laces. Catherine sighed, helping her with her coat and hat. Her mother despised the Day-Glo tennis balls that had been attached to her walker, and Catherine removed them as she loaded the device into her car trunk, tossing them into the back seat with the dogs. Her mother flinched as the animals scrabbled and bumped against her seat. It was going to be a long day.

But Catherine had brought with her Miriam's map of where the BTK's victims had lived. And died. Since she was driving all over town anyway, she might as well drive past these infamous locales. Her mother couldn't object. It wasn't the sort of thing her mother would ever have wanted to do, but for how many years had Catherine been the one whose desires went unconsulted? Had she wanted to take piano lessons? Attend lectures by visiting scholars? Spend every Saturday morning at the public library?

First, phlebotomy. And Catherine geared herself for the role she would have to play: demanding interrogator, on her mother's behalf, of the professionals. They naturally assumed that it was she who doubted their abilities. "This is what I do," the man taking blood informed her, cutting her off. "You do not have to tell me my business." Later, as he jabbed for the third time into her mother's desiccated arm, he complained about her rolling veins. Catherine sighed. "I was trying to explain before. Her veins roll."

"She should drink water," he replied. Professor Harding's eyes shot daggers at them both.

On the way from bloodletting to the GP, Catherine took a detour through a neighborhood where a tornado had touched down not too long ago. When she slowed the car in front of the decrepit little white house, the dogs leaped to look out the back windows. Her mother studied her crookedly, her right eye these days lower than her left. "This is one of the victim's houses," Catherine explained. "It doesn't look like anybody lives here, does it?" Not a soul appeared on the street; the only sign of life was the parade of rolling trash bins that had been pulled to the curb. He had locked the woman's three children in the bathroom and savaged their mother in the room next door. They'd stood on the toilet and watched through a transom, the eldest boy all of six or eight. Catherine tried to imagine their faces in the dirty window, tricycles in the yard, broken plastic swimming pool. "He showed one of the boys a picture," she told her mother, pulling away from the place. "Supposedly he was looking for his dog."

In between the GP and the imaging center, they visited two other victims' addresses. The second of these structures no longer existed, the house by the university razed in the eighties. At each, Catherine said what she knew, the woman's name and the way she had died. The unexpected brother of one, a witness like the three small children, yet left with bullets in his face, brain damage. Her mother said nothing, but the silence was acquiring an interesting texture. Her mother had been annoyed, at first, probably at Catherine's unsurprising and disappointing interest in things tawdry or ordinary. But now Dr. Harding seemed to be trying to make Catherine's pilgrimage into a more edifying preoccupation. This was her mother's way, abstracting the individual into some larger paradigm. When Catherine had been socked in the face by a black girl in junior high, her mother had insisted that Catherine not hold the girl herself responsible; history had led to this confrontation, shameful history. While her mother tried to lecture away the hurt—the literal bruise, the more profound wounded feelings—her father had handed Catherine a frozen bag of lima beans to hold to her temple.

"I wonder if the people who buy these places know what happened in them?" Her old friend Misty, real estate agent, might have had an answer.

This year, for the first time, the assistant to the anesthesiologist asked, in one long rehearsed impersonal rush, if Professor Harding had an advanced directive or living will, if she was an organ donor, and what faith she practiced. As if the answers did not involve flesh, blood, sentiment, sacrifice. Catherine had never been more grateful that her mother could no longer give lectures. The girl didn't look up from her clipboard, so she missed Dr. Harding's steely glare. Catherine affirmed the will and organ parts, declined to name a religious preference.

"Everybody's getting so sensitive to litigation these days," Catherine explained after the girl had gone. "I'm sure it's some new formality, just official ass-covering. You're going to be fine."

Her mother shook her head in annoyance. *Atheist*, Catherine understood finally, as they reached the smaller waiting room, the hard expression on her mother's face having been summoned as if by rope from the depths of a well, spilled uselessly here for Catherine's benefit. As if Catherine didn't already know all about it.

"Remember, it's the day of humiliation," she told her mother, hoping they could retain, or resuscitate, the thin veneer of humor about the day. Her father had been more naturally ironic; missing him came upon her suddenly, a surprising pain, a quick pinch, that always resulted in tears. The colonoscopy was the last procedure; Catherine's head ached from mediating: at each office she had to delicately balance her mother's silent demand to be accorded respect, in the form of mind-bendingly thorough information, against the doctor's or nurse's or receptionist's or technician's indifference and/or irritation concerning this particular patient's not-very-unique situation. If Catherine didn't fully explain her mother's worries (the same every year, identical in every way to what she'd noted many times before), her mother would fume in the car afterward, yank her arm out of reach, labor dangerously to pull herself from the vehicle, or attempt to fill in the endless paperwork with her functioning left, wrong, slow, sloppy hand.

Her former physicians had been of the old type: friends with Grace Harding, Wichitans who'd come of age as professional peers, people whose circles of acquaintances weren't exactly the same but whose orbital revolutions brought them into contact every now and then outside the office, wearing nice clothes. There was overlap, a colleague married to a partner, a son or daughter who'd taken a class, a mutual acquaintance whose recent symphony performance had impressed, so that medical appointments were more like social visits, pleasantries first, ailments discussed as secondary business, handshaking and fond wishes all around. Now the physicians were one or even two generations younger than Grace Harding, indistinguishable from each other in their multicolored scrubs, and her inability to speak allowed them to pretend that she had nothing to say. They were either solicitous (as if dealing with a child or foreigner, loud and simplistic and smiling) or brusque (as if encountering another in a long line of widgets on a tiresome conveyor belt); Catherine preferred the former, her mother the latter. All day long, from one depressing strip-mall office to the next, Catherine had to endure her mother's furious eyes, those fiery blue peepholes, those stormy portholes behind which a furnace raged.

Better rage than despair, she supposed. The Weeping Woman, she recalled. The woman chanting the children's book text like a sound track to a horror movie. Far better to rage.

Before her father died, before her mother had been ruined by stroke, they'd taken each other on these excursions, trading at playing patient and caretaker, passenger and driver. His death was shocking, her perfectly fine-seeming father picked off as if by a sniper, struck by that expedient aneurysm, still sitting upright in his reading chair when his wife had returned home from an afternoon seminar.

Catherine's familiar fantasy appeared in her head, her mother in her adjoining reading chair, hand clasped in her husband's, the lightning bolt hitting him, its sizzle pulsing down his arm to include her.

Orphan, Catherine thought. Her husband would die before her, too. And so would the dogs . . .

"Hardy?" called the girl with the roll sheet.

"Harding," Catherine corrected.

"Right," the girl said, snapping her gum, shuffling along in what looked like bedroom slippers, pushing open the door before them and passing through without holding it. Because there was anesthesia involved, because the procedure demanded that Grace Harding be absolutely removed from her own oversight, because it required total relinquishment of control, this was by far the worst of today's indignities. Her mother had never happily handed over control; she refused to fly on planes, always tartly replying when told of the statistically proven safety that if she were behind the wheel, she would always be able to judge the wisdom of continuing or jettisoning the trip. She did not trust that others would be so scrupulous in their considerations.

Catherine would have happily turned over control. She was a very contented passenger; she never chose to drive if someone else offered. "If I could," she told her mother, "I would go through this for you." It was heartfelt, but her mother's response was an impatient whiff of air. How had she earned such a dim sentimental daughter? "There you go off to Cloud Cuckooland again," she had used to say when Catherine came up with an idea Dr. Harding found especially preposterous and therefore infuriating. Her mother's disappointment could still derail her, still hurt her feelings in the lip-trembling way of a small child. And now there was no longer the solace of her sympathetic father, who had many times come to commiserate, nod knowingly, offer his patient platitudes. Catherine took a more firm than necessary hold of her mother's arm and guided her down the hall to the chamber where she would undress her, again, and slip her into yet another soft hospital gown opening in the back, ties flapping uselessly. And when this was accomplished, she would come along as far as the procedure room itself, always reassuring her mother that she would be right here, on the other side of the door, waiting.

All day, waiting.

Into the silent fury her mother now generated like heat, Catherine posed a sudden question. "Mom, do you remember my friend Misty?"

Her mother blinked, annoyance subsumed by confusion. Catherine could practically see the recalibration, like watching a jukebox mechanism remove one little spinning platter to replace it with another. Her eyes said yes, she remembered Misty. Misty and all her baggage. Misty the bad girl. Misty the friend who would not do what powerful Dr. Harding wished and disappear.

"She died recently," Catherine said, watching her mother's disapproval now shift to surprise, perhaps shaded by shame at having felt anything negative. Her mother had been an unusual woman for her time, but she was still a product of her generation and geography, and those rules said that one did not speak ill of the dead. "In a single-car accident, although I don't think it was suicide. In Colorado." Her mother looked curious now. It was with Catherine's family that Misty had traveled to Colorado one summer. Until then, she'd never been out of the state of Kansas; Catherine could still remember her parents taking in this news, it being the deciding fact on their agreeing to Misty's joining them. They could never resist broadening somebody's horizons; their own daughter had been to many states, and a few foreign countries. And the summer trip had softened their opinion of Misty. She was a girl who might know how to roll her own cigarettes or change the oil of an American-made car, but Catherine's parents had been pleased to teach her the difference between mountain and standard time, to identify raptors by their wingspan, to witness her appreciation of the short stories they read aloud while rolling along the highway.

The four of them had visited the old mining towns, staying at former brothels, panning for gold, riding a narrow-gauge train, hiking to the tops of mountains. Misty was the willing rube newly exposed to room service, to artichokes, to word games in the car and card games in the hotel. The photographs from that trip filled an album, one that was shelved in Grace's room at the home, its label reading 1976, the bicentennial. On the Fourth of July, there'd been a morning parade in Ouray, thrilling military jets buzzing the crowd, then fireworks later in Crested Butte. Catherine and Misty had spent the day sneaking drinks and carving their names in whatever surface they could find. The highway Misty had fatally driven off had been on their Colorado tour, not far from Telluride, where they'd crept out during their overnight stay there and met up with some local boys, skateboarders happy to share their beer and cocaine. "The thing is," Catherine went on to her mother, "it seems she has a daughter. A fifteen-year-old girl. And for whatever reason—I really cannot guess what reason, it is truly baffling—she named me as guardian." Her mother's lips had parted, as they did when she wasn't vigilant, and her entire face appeared to melt. The effect was to immediately soften her aspect, make her vulnerability paramount, frightening, as if she might topple right over, as if the melting were general. Catherine pursed her own lips to alert her, and her mother quickly clamped her jaw back into place, blinking, taking in the news.

Now a rap came on the antechamber door. "I'll tell you the rest later," Catherine said, hoping this would prove sufficient distraction for her mother's final hurdle in this day of humiliation. What would she be thinking as she slipped under the anesthesia, long-forgotten (good riddance, bad rubbish) Misty Mueller back in her head, reconfigured now as a person in the past tense (bless her heart, poor thing)? Misty on their Colorado tour, roughly the same age then as Misty's daughter was now, and Misty dead, arriving there in advance of Dr. Harding, out of sequence?

Catherine pondered the connections, pins on a map, coincidences and repetitions, tenuous links, Catherine the fifteen-year-old girl: herself then, and someone else now.

It reminded her of the way she and Misty had met another group of boys, a group here in Wichita. The two of them had been on the telephone, Misty in her grandmother's garage on the greasy wall-hung model, Catherine in the upstairs hall outside her bedroom, lounging on her back with her feet up the wall. Her mother had a special frustration with those black heel smudges. The girls talked; they'd been talking all day, passing notes, sharing lunch, meeting between classes at their next-door lockers, riding home from school in Misty's car, then not an hour later, armed with snacks and a beverage, were back in contact. "What can you possibly have to say?" her mother would complain. "Can you conceive of no better way to spend your time?"

"Shhh!" Misty had interrupted Catherine one day. "Listen." And Catherine could hear another conversation, very faintly, two men talking and laughing. The girls began shouting into their phones, yelling at those men busy with their own call, screaming until the men finally heard and understood. They shouted back; numbers were exchanged. Other calls were made. And hence began Catherine and Misty's long and crooked association with Lyle Skinner and his gang of locally grown cohorts. Of course such an alliance would begin with crossed wires.

She had not thought of Lyle in years. A meeting was arranged after that first conversation. Lyle. He was a slacker, a loser, a complete disaster. Yet Catherine and Misty couldn't have been convinced of that, chirpily arriving at the appointed time and place, that spring evening at the 7-Eleven. He was better for having been found over the phone line, faint voice in the distance like the murmuring of the devil. To that voice they attended. Later met his dope-smoking friends, men who hadn't finished high school and certainly weren't going to college. Eventually, they would find jobs, shave their scraggly beards, quit selling weed and start selling, say, weedkiller, down at the Ace. But for then, they were the girls' dark secret, their attractive nuisances. Those men believed Catherine and Misty were already in college. They believed they were of age. They believed, no doubt, that the girls were idiots for thinking so highly of them, as no girl their own age would give them the time of day.

Catherine and Misty began to join them every weekend at the grungy college bar called Lucky's, across from the U, flashing their fake IDs. This bar was a couple of miles from Catherine's house, a place where you threw your peanut shells on the floor, markered witticisms on the bathroom stalls, left deafened from the overloud live bands, and where Catherine insisted Misty park around back, since Professor Harding's students lived in the neighborhood.

Also in that neighborhood was the victim whose house was plowed under, the absent address Catherine had just today driven past. Once a place in view of the bar's parking lot. The BTK could easily have been among the lone men who were always drinking away their afternoons at Lucky's, slumped there, waiting for dark; when he taunted the media, after the woman's death, he claimed that he'd first spotted her picking up her mail, and he could have done that from the Lucky's parking lot.

Again Catherine experienced the sensation she had for months now, the strange dreamy memory of the past, something that she had not really revisited in many years. That period of time when she and Misty had been friends, when the killer had been out there occasionally making an appearance in their world, and also Misty's rights to the initial killings since he'd picked her neighbors to begin his campaign. Later, Catherine had been able to brag that it was Yasmin Keene whose class he had to have attended. Hints, threats, arrogance and menace. Together the girls were proud of his obviously having wandered the Lucky's terrain, no doubt glancing at the two of them some evening, weighing their worth as future victims. Why hadn't this truly scared Catherine, back then? Why hadn't she wondered if the killer were Lyle, or one of his hopeless friends, those unsavory men whose ratty apartments and trailers she and Misty had so mindlessly visited? Perhaps the girls had been too far habituated to their own dramatizing and fictionalizing and exaggerating. Their conversations always escalated into wild speculations about their teachers and family members and classmates—they told themselves that the algebra teacher was sleeping with a cheerleader, that Misty's parents were actually alive, that Catherine's mother was a lesbian and loved her colleague Yasmin. Dr. Keene: they snickered helplessly about her and her horrible black walking stick. Was this how they'd been so cavalier concerning the serial killer? His extremity merely another wild tale to be told? Or was it the fact of their friendship, the two of them, unalone in the world, and somehow thereby impervious? Protected?

But maybe everyone in town felt some peculiar affinity with him? Certainly her stepdaughter Miriam was obsessed.

Catherine sat with others in the recovery area of the clinic, in a plastic seat near a bed, behind a curtain. This waiting was a living purgatory, its passage unregulated by the ordinary measure of minutes. They stretched, they expanded, they went backward. She felt her own tremendous solitude connect with that of the other waiters, her depressed boredom commingle with theirs. For her private entertainment, she imagined it was Oliver who was lying on the table in a flimsy nightgown, the tubular apparatus en route to his bony backside, prepared to make its snaking trek inside him. "I admire your optimism," she could say later, blandly, when he came home woozy and sore, surely feeling thoroughly defiled.

Soon her mother would be wheeled to this makeshift stall, lifted to the bed, coming slowly out from under anesthesia while Catherine watched. Her mother was the only one to whom she could speak about Misty as a girl, yet even her mother had not known Misty, not really. She'd seen what a mother would see: her daughter's unfortunate best friend, a casualty of many circumstances, including poverty, orphaning, and simple neglect. Genetically, she'd be inclined to addiction; socially, toward unenlightened attitudes. Her mother's sympathy would not be for the girl herself, but for the larger doomed demographic the girl represented. Professor Harding, had she language, would announce to Catherine that it didn't surprise her to hear of Misty's end. She'd say, if she could, that it was upsetting but not unpredictable.

"Mom," Catherine said, when the double doors flew open to reveal her on the wheeled bed. She was still asleep, her features pale and slack as death. Catherine recalled her father, his body at the mortuary covered by a sheet, leaving his head floating there; her mother looked just like that.

"She did fine," the orderly pushing the bed claimed. But how would he know?

The last place Catherine wished to visit was the site of the first killings. Her mother sedated in the passenger seat, Catherine parked in front of the house where Misty had lived. She'd driven by here often without actually thinking of Misty. How could that be? The house and the neighborhood had been here, faithfully, reliably, for all these years, and yet she could not recall the last time she'd looked with intention at what she passed through.

This was a route to a branch of the public library where she occasionally drove her mother, to the organic meat market Oliver had bankrolled, to the bungalow of Yasmin Keene. The grown-up habit of taking this street had erased the adolescent one, the former destination had become a place she passed by without thinking.

The first victims were a family; the only multiple killings. Misty's home, the little drab pair of boxes (formerly the gray-green of cement block), had been painted cream, trimmed in burgundy, reroofed in black. At the curb, two black posts with lights, a motif of colonialism. Somebody was reclaiming this neighborhood, one home at a time, accessorizing and trimming, hanging window boxes and filling them with flowers, erecting short ornamental fences that would keep in or out nothing. At Misty's, there was now an official driveway instead of the muddy patch that had slopped into the yard and up to the door. The place no longer resembled the encampment that it had twenty-five years ago, a site best approached wearing work boots. When Catherine had visited that home, there had been sometimes furniture in the yard and car engines in the kitchen, inside-out, outside-in, one of Misty's uncles or cousins or honorary relations either reclining out front with a beer or dressed in a grimy jumpsuit, armed with a wrench, twisting something greasy and mechanical at the dining table. The family ate carryout; the refrigerator was full of beer and live bait. The photo albums featured dead elk, rows of rainbow trout, vehicles covered in mud, evidence of exploits out in mother nature, not a human face anywhere to be found, only their bloody tools to illustrate scale.

Hatchet, shotgun, hunting knife.

The dogs pressed their noses against the car windows, optimistic; there was a park here now. "No, my friends," Catherine told them. "Sorry, just looking." Young trees were tethered to the ground, waiting to grow thick enough to withstand the Kansas wind. She shivered and turned up the car's heater, aware that the chill running through her was not about the weather. This park was named the same thing as the school that had once stood here, the elementary school where Misty and Catherine had met those many years ago. The school was utterly gone, deemed too expensive to repair, too inefficient to replace, too shabby to convert. Catherine had driven by here when the wrecking ball and earthmovers were in action. It was a job that took only a few days. Now there was a swimming pool and a rec center, a parking lot and these brave little sticks, future shade trees. All of it prettily corralled inside a loop of sidewalk. Not a single person in sight—a few geese poking at the fence surrounding the empty pool; ahead there was a yellow street sign especially for the birds, a crosswalk warning. Misty's family would have shot such a sign full of holes; Misty's family might have shot the geese themselves.

When the old elementary school had been there, Misty attended because she was in its district, within spitting distance. Out her front door she would have run every morning, crossing the street and entering the building thirty seconds after exiting her own house. Catherine, however, had been imported, bussed over from five miles away because she was bright, designated "Accelerated," and this was where the program sent her. Her, and fifty-nine other "Accelerated" students, fourth-, fifth-, and sixth-grade children who stood quivering at their various bus stops, a daily commute of thirty halting minutes each way, a plan meant to fill the emptying classrooms, the school's neighborhood aging, its former parents now grandparents or ghosts, its small children grown and gone, its older ones delinquent.

Misty hadn't been in the Accelerated program; she and Catherine had been enemies, generally, back then, the Regulars versus the Accelerateds. For the three years of Catherine's gifted education, she and her cohorts suffered the taunts and jeers of the neighborhood children. Onto the buses they clomped each afternoon, taking their elevated seats, watching from their Accelerated windows as the Regular gangs dispersed below into the small houses, or through the canal where fetid water ran, into the great cement drainpipes to smoke cigarettes and draw pictures of purported sexual acts and shout foul echoing words. On Fridays, if you happened to be in sixth grade, you could take yourself to Pizza Hut for lunch, and there the Accelerateds would suffer the thrown crusts from the Regular tables, the savage wrath of the average children, and the stifled anxiety of the freakish ones, the ones designated special. No adult, either customer or employee, ever felt like identifying with the Accelerateds, standing up for them or quelling the abuse. Catherine remembered that, the aggrieved expression her group encountered: they were stuck up, sissies, pussies, pathetic. In some other food chain, they would be cut from the herd. Small consolations were offered at home; their parents might routinely promise that adult life would be different, when the tables would naturally turn.

In junior high, a year later, Catherine herself had begun to disdain the Accelerateds. They were an awfully unadventurous group, timid from their time with bullies, soft from having been sheltered, now let loose into the festering depths of junior high school. She was one of only a few who splintered off; the others remained a quaking group, taking Honors classes, huddling together at lunchtime, joining chess and debate clubs. Her mother had been horrified when Catherine declared her break from this tribe. Why would Catherine renounce a better education, a more enlightened group of friends, the lucky advantage that was hers? "They're dorks," Catherine had explained.

She'd smoked her first cigarette at the table with Misty's grandmother, who considered smoking a natural juncture of life, akin to the loss of molars or acquisition of a driver's license. At age fifteen, Misty had been smoking long enough to be trying to quit. Every third house in the neighborhood was the same, a development pattern from two generations past.

Her mother, roused from her sedated nap, blinked blankly. Catherine said, "That family? The first victims? Their floor plan was exactly the same as Misty's." She recalled Misty's ownership of the story. The way it could have been anyone on the block, it could have been Misty's own grandmother that maniac had encountered, bound and tortured and killed; instead of that other girl it could have been Misty left dangling from the basement plumbing, semen on her socks. The murderer had stolen the family's car and left it in a grocery store parking lot, the very same grocery store where Misty's grandmother shopped, where they themselves—Catherine and Misty, Accelerated and Regular, enemies, then, had bought candy after their Pizza Hut Fridays of sixth grade. The photographs appeared on the six o'clock news of the parking lot, the station wagon sitting in that familiar place.

They'd been avowed enemies in grade school, but it might have been that day in the junior high school cafeteria, Misty holding forth about the scandal, Catherine thought now as she pulled away from the curb, when she and Misty had first become allies, when they'd started on the road to being best friends.

CHAPTER 9

IT DOESN'T MATTER if you don't have a license!" Ito assured Cattie. "*I* don't even have insurance!" They were drinking sweet coffee in the sunshine, watching Montpelier's teenagers take their Friday lunch break. He was endorsing a road trip; it was right up his alley, half the continent out there waiting, packed full of interesting strangers to meet. "Plus I'm not supposed to own that car anyway. Registering it cost more than I paid." He'd bought it for ten dollars from a neighbor widow in New Hampshire, a woman the police threatened to incarcerate if she didn't stop driving; they'd taken her keys but she had extras. It wasn't hard to imagine that Ito was the old woman's only friend; he might have been many people's only friend. He was Cattie's, for instance.

"I don't know how to drive," she explained. "It's not just the license, it's the skill."

"Boo? Any fool can drive." He swept his bangled arm and nail-painted hand toward the intersection, where, it was true, a four-way stop had resulted in a cluster of confusion and waving fists and screeching tires.

"My mother . . . ," Cattie began, and Ito understood at once, slapped his hands over his mouth: her mother had died in a car accident. It wasn't natural for Cattie to want to drive, not just to Texas but to anywhere, ever. Ito had offered his car without thinking. But a bus would suffice. She even knew where the stops were, both here and in Houston. And nobody paid any attention to who purchased a bus ticket. Whack-jobs and runaways and outlaws always rode the bus, in perfect anonymity.

But Cattie sighed. "I just get so carsick in the bus." As did others, the odor, or threat, of vomit just one of its regrettable trademarks.

"The bus is dis*gust*ing," Ito agreed. They sat on a brick ledge outside the coffee shop, out there with the rest of Montpelier, soaking up the rare bright sun, giddy and distracted, perhaps blinded by it at the now-clogged intersection. Cattie and Ito mutually concocted Bus in their imaginations: the foul endemic atmosphere—along with vomit, the odors of diesel fuel, urine, French fries—not to mention the swaying boatlike movement. "Oh oh oh!—that grease from people's hair on the windows!" Ito recollected.

"The Jesus freak."

"The guy with BO."

"Plural, *guys*. Plus the drunk skinheads."

"Who are *armed*. With weapons. And the screaming baby."

"I don't mind the screaming baby," Cattie said, considering. "I would even hold the screaming baby, if the mom would let me."

"So. *Cute!*" Ito said, squeezing her shoulder in congratulations.

"I was a babysitter. I was kind of good at it. I guess I could stand the bus if it didn't take forever. If there actually *was* a screaming baby. If I didn't have to sit next to a pervert. If I had a book to read. If I bought Dramamine . . ." Cattie sighed. "I miss Houston," she said.

"Yo, don't cry!" Ito hugged her again, his own eyes now wet, smiling feverishly. "You want a muffin? Latte?" He jumped up to retrieve these, to distract her. Cattie agreed in order to make him happy. In his absence, she imagined herself stepping off the bus in Houston, into the lush humid clemency of her city. Such a relief to know precisely where she was, the known city spreading around her for miles and miles, mapped without gaps. To breathe the polluted soggy air of home, I-45 overhead carrying its endless roaring traffic, the clouds yet higher still, moving as always with incredible speed, sometimes breaking around the city's tallest buildings, moisture either falling or about to, and those ubiquitous black clattering birds. The audacious heckling grackles. Staring at Montpelier's populace, she imagined the walk home among Houston's, tacking south and west all the way from downtown to Montrose, over the light rail tracks, under Highway 59, across the Blue Bird parking lot, through the St. Thomas campus, right to her own street with its odd knitted stop sign sleeve. The mysterious Montrose knitter, who had, for the last few years, covered with colorful yarn cozies all manner of outdoor objects, poles and door handles and hydrants. Cattie had walked this route before, not from the Greyhound station but from a Vietnamese restaurant close by. At her house, she would cut across the neighbor's yard, duck beneath and climb over the live oak limbs, fish her lone key from her backpack, unlock the carport door, step into her back porch. And then what?

She had no idea. Her imagination led her that far and no further. As if the door now opened upon a deep sinkhole that had sucked everything beyond it into the earth.

Ito returned with muffins and scones, laid them out on wax paper for Cattie to choose, his eyes pleading for her to be happy. "Would you let Randall drive your car to Texas?" she asked him, selecting randomly among the pastries.

"*Ran*dall?"

Cattie chewed on her scone, thinking of a trip with Randall. Terrible motels, for starters; him sleeping in one bed, her lying in the other wearing her clothes, twitching restlessly under the bad bedspread all night. This, too, was not quite fully imaginable. Then she remembered the dogs—the complete cast and scenario of Dogs: the rescue, Joanne's ominous declaration that she did not want dogs in her house, Randall's more frequent downstairs visits, and of course the poor runty puppy that had died, limp black rag beside the back door one morning—and now she vaguely brightened. "Me and Randall," Cattie said. "We've been talking." They hadn't been talking, she and Randall, but they'd been seeing each other, engaged in their mutual project, feeding the living, and burying the tiny dead dog out back in Joanne's desolate junky yard, each working to prevent Joanne's wrath, the litter staying in Cattie's little room with her, the mother taken daily by Randall for long walks. "And the dogs, actually. They'd have to come, I think. Joanne won't keep them." Down the bad motel bedspread went to the bad motel carpet, where the dogs would make a warm pile. A pile between the bad motel beds holding Randall and Cattie, there like a moat.

"God*damn*, I want to go with you!" Ito cried. "That sounds so awesome! Road trip with *puppies*?"

Now Cattie put Ito's sedan in her Houston driveway, herself at the carport door once again, this time with Randall following, dressed in his military uniform and his Dijon-mustard-colored boots, carrying the puppies in their box, pulling their mother on her belt leash. Now Cattie could go further, into the kitchen where Max's bowls were, one for water, one for kibble, both empty, of course. The bag of dog food, there in the utility closet, now probably stale and soggy, but did dogs care about freshness? And the sink faucet, which she'd have to run for a while to clear rust from the pipes. It wouldn't have been turned on for months now. When she set down the water and food bowls, the dogs would fall over themselves, roll into the containers, knock them over, slip in the mess. Randall meanwhile would require the bathroom, which would mean leading him down the hall, to her bathroom, and then most naturally she would enter her bedroom, directly across from there. Randall would eventually exit the bathroom, and then her imagination clouded. In the hallway the two of them stood, her perhaps adjusting the thermostat to ventilate the place—that momentary throat-clearing noise that the compressor made, and then the roar of air in the vents—Randall frozen, uncertain what to do, where to go next. The only other bed in the house was Cattie's mother's, and she couldn't imagine allowing Randall to sleep in it.

As far as she knew, there'd never been a man in that bed.

Where was Max? she wondered, not for the first time. This question pressed more fully upon her than others, such as: What had her mother been doing in Colorado? Was she drunk when her car went off the road? In not one of the messages collecting on her phone had anybody said a single word about the dog. And now another scenario suddenly popped up: Max dead in the house, lying there on the kitchen floor like a sack of bones, a bigger version of the dead puppy she'd just encountered yesterday morning. Or lying at the front door, whose wood surface would be deeply scarred from her futile attempts to escape. Or on her mother's bed, curled tightly between the pillows, perfect taxidermy. Cattie's eyes filled.

"What?" Ito said. "What's wrong?"

"I can't figure out where Max is," she said. "What the *fuck*?"

"Your mom would have left her with a friend." But this reassurance came from somebody who took the idea and reality of friends for granted, he who had them, who readily made them, and who expected a reciprocal exchange of favors with them, a harmonious unending network built on smiles and guileless, boundless curiosity and tolerance. This was not Misty's way. It wasn't Cattie's way, either. Ito read her face and tried again. "Don't get grossed out, but listen: if the dog had actually been left in the house? If it had died? The neighbors would have smelled it. It wouldn't still be there."

Cattie nodded thoughtfully. "True," she said—the old busy-body next door, the mailman, the endless parade of children selling worthless crap, or the yardman. Dick Little, insurance snoop. "Thanks," she added. Ito was like that, helpful. He'd gone online to find the accident report from Colorado. Single-car, at least a week before it was found, one victim, from out of state. Out of state: that was the whole problem—going out of their state. They'd been fine when they stayed in Texas. Cattie felt the onus of her own responsibility for the mess her life had become. If she'd managed to get through high school in Houston, she'd never have been shipped east. And her mother wouldn't have sojourned to Colorado; it wouldn't have been possible, if Cattie were still at home instead of *out of state*.

Home. Now she put herself and Randall back in the hallway, toilet chuckling from his recent flush. *She'd* sleep in her mother's bed. He could have her room. He would probably enjoy the mural on the ceiling, although some of her bumper stickers would probably offend a war veteran. And then there came the stray mother dog, sniffing crazily at the baseboard and carpet, followed by her puppies, all six of them running pell-mell around the living room, locating Max's toys, the stuffed weasel, the weasel hut, the tennis ball, the leather men's shoe Misty had designated fair game. Max had never mistaken any of Cattie's or Misty's shoes for ones she could chew, just this nasty leather loafer, one she'd found in the street. She was a smart animal, Max.

And the puppies would pee on the carpet, and Cattie would have to find newspapers (in the recycling bin, there by the back door, *Houston Chronicles* dated from September), and also the doggy door gates, which were down in the cellar, leaning alongside some rejected artwork and old school projects on poster board just outside the sump pump pit, and then every other tangible part of her house came upon her suddenly and overwhelmingly, all the things she needed to do. Immediately.

"Dude, I am so going with you!" Ito said. "Fuck school! Fuck the fashion show!"

But Cattie couldn't put Ito in the picture. She tried, for a moment: Randall now lowering his duffel onto the desktop in Cattie's room, Cattie making a nest on her mother's bed for the puppies, closing the closet door so as not to see her mother's work outfits hanging there, refusing to investigate the medicine cabinet or clothes hamper or any other receptacle that too much contained that gone person, next ordering pizza, checking the refrigerator for soda, showing the new dogs the old dog's entry-way, the rubber flap that allowed access in and out of the house to the fenced backyard. Despite the busy workings of the house, filled now in her imagination with strangers both human and canine, Cattie couldn't make room for Ito among them.

"Randall will bring back your car." She had no idea if this could be true. Why would Randall play along with any of what she had just invented? He might not even be able to drive; he hadn't driven to Vermont. Maybe he'd been driving in Iraq when he acquired his PTSD. If he had PTSD. If it was Iraq where he'd been.

"I don't give a shit about the car," said Ito. "I just don't want to miss the party! It's going to be excellent!"

"You have to stay," she said. "If you leave, they'll figure out how to find me. Why fuck up your senior year? You have to graduate and get the hell out of here for real. I'll send postcards to Joanne's. I'll call you from pay phones." Who, she wondered, was receiving the cell phone bill? Who was staring at the blank monthly page that described her current lack of action, her refusal to dial out? And mostly: Who continued to finance that mute receiver of messages?

"Thanks for the food product," she said to Ito, dropping down from the ledge on which they'd been sitting. "Let's go find Randall."

CHAPTER 10

OLIVER PROMISED HE WOULD GO to the nursing home every day, but surely the day that Catherine drove away didn't count? Who would ever find out? Nobody paid any attention to the guest registry; Grace Harding couldn't speak. Moreover, she didn't like him well enough to complain even if she could.

So the day his wife went to Houston, Oliver hosted the Sweetheart at his house. He was sensitive to the first-person plural and didn't use it. "My dogs," he said. All but one of his windows could be covered. But through that one, should somebody choose to crawl across the garden and fight away the prickly pyracantha to glimpse, his reckless indiscretion would be on display. Oliver could not deny the heedless thrill of such a thing. He peeled from her sweating body the Sweetheart's running clothes as if that, too, were part of her exercise routine, on a clock, cardiovascular.

"Your dogs are watching us," she said, beneath him, cheek pressed to the floor, ponytail wound round his fist.

"They're very discreet."

For a second he imagined the possibility of Catherine's not coming home. Her dedication to the mystery of the strange girl—

both the one from the past, who had died, and the one in some possible future—seemed nearly providential. In a flash he relocated the Sweetheart to this house, saw her sleeping head beside his, felt her bare feet on his calves. Another chapter. A new life. He could fall back upon this fantasy at any moment, spool it out beneath his real life like an ongoing film or dream in which he played the lead. How was it that anyone could be satisfied with only one story? With the surface, and nothing beneath it? With the familiar and repetitive, routine equaling the death of any plausible adventure?

It was still daylight when the Sweetheart left, so Oliver decided to fulfill his promise to Catherine. He brought with him to the nursing home a new computer; he'd already ascertained building-wide Internet access. This was a kindness. It was also a project with a tangible series of time-killing steps, and an outcome he could report to his wife. Proof of many things about himself that he felt he needed to prove in maintaining his non-fantasy life.

"You're the one who said I should gather information," Catherine told him as she packed for her trip. "You're the one who said find out all the facts." True, but he hadn't said she should go to Houston.

"I hate 'you're the one' prologues. And I can't be responsible for another child," he added. Pathetic.

Catherine had stared at him calmly. "But I can't just ignore her, can I? I mean, really?" It was while she was arranging her toiletries that she added, "And how responsible, actually, are you for those other two?" Touché, Oliver supposed. Hauling Miriam's trashy companion out of her life hardly qualified as parental triumph.

Moreover, he was arguing against the trip only because he relished the freedom it provided him.

"Is this your brother perhaps?" pandered the Haitian nurse at the home. Her teeth were blindingly white. "Come to see you, Miss Grace?" Neither Oliver nor his mother-in-law corrected her; the question wasn't the sort that either of them bothered acknowledging, tedious noise meant to be flattering. And how difficult it had always been for Professor Harding to say those words "son-in-law," even when she could speak.

Not friends, not strangers, not blood relations. Yet also not mere acquaintances. What did you name this thing they shared? She might be his enemy, Oliver decided, another one like his first wife YaYa, an adversary so entrenched he nearly could respect her. Nearly.

His mother-in-law's room held various pieces of her old life: a desk, bookcase, reading chair, lamp, and on the walls, where others would have hung studio photos of grandchildren and weddings and pets, Dr. Harding had hung her academic degrees. B.A., M.A., Ph.D.: all from institutions far away and highly celebrated. "It's like she's criticizing me," Catherine would lament. "Me, with just my lousy old one degree." Her bachelor's was from the local institution where her mother had taught; Catherine claimed that her mother was saying something to her without saying anything. But Oliver could understand wanting to display her pedigree. She'd been unusual, for her time. Minus the bed, the room would have looked a lot like Dr. Harding's old office at the university. As if she still held office hours.

Oliver set down the computer he'd brought; it was as advertised: light and portable as a notebook. Grace's PC was an antique; she'd worked on it for so long there were rubbed-away letters on the keyboard. Oliver had mastered technology as a hedge against growing obsolescent himself. On only one previous occasion had he tried to convince his mother-in-law that she would enjoy the Internet, information-hound that she was. This was before the stroke; loudly she'd disdained the Internet as faddish, yet another juvenile gesture that Oliver himself would, soon enough, get over. Her attitude toward him had always been like that: scornful of, vaguely superior to, the old man trying to be young. The lech, the vain person who required a pedestal, not unlike a few of her male university colleagues, those men who left women their own age in favor of younger, simpler girls, students and acolytes. She looked at him as if to shake a scolding finger: *You ought to know better.* Sometimes at holiday gatherings she would reference the decades that preceded her daughter. "You'll remember this," she'd begin, addressing Oliver.

Their first president had been FDR. Catherine's was JFK.

Catherine's father had been much more polite and forgiving than his wife. It was as if he were embarrassed for being Oliver's age, instead of expecting Oliver to suffer the awkwardness. Had it been he, and not Grace Harding, who had ended up at Green Acres, Oliver could imagine stopping by regularly, gladly. They would do what any father- and son-in-law did, sit in companionable silence watching sports on television. That, or take long drives into the country to look for wildlife. Catherine's father had enjoyed doing that, and Kansas was surprisingly full of creatures.

"That nurse is the type to always be telling you to smile, isn't she?" he said now.

Grace lifted her head, a weary nod.

He explained what he was doing as he did it, moving aside her monstrosity of a machine to unfold the new laptop, using terminology as a weapon, a foreign language to her ears, and his agility as a way of separating himself from her enfeeblement. She and he finally sat beside one another at her desk, the screen brightening before them.

"Voilà!"

What he did not bargain for was her inability to operate a mouse. How had he not anticipated that? Her signature gesture these days was lifting one hand with the other, right with left. She was competent on the keyboard—in a one-handed sort of way—but she'd never had reason to figure out a mouse, let alone learn it now with her wrong hand. Clearly she enjoyed seeing what Oliver made pop open before her eyes on the monitor, but also clearly she would never manage to make this happen by herself. Well, he would settle for less, then. They would sit like this during his visits, he guiding the cursor to sites she might be interested in, waiting for a nod, him reading aloud or enlarging as she indicated. He took her, like a child, to Houston, Texas, on Google Earth, so that she could imagine Catherine there. Then, when they were back in outer space, looking down at the blue planet and breathing in disconcerting tandem, she typed in *Italy*. And then *Rome*.

Professor Harding's first sabbatical. Rome in 1968. Except Oliver had only ever heard about it from Catherine, whose memories were a child's. She was seven that year; everything she could recall were set pieces: her at the local pizzeria amusing the employees by nonsensically chanting *si* or *no* to their questions; Catherine raising a goldfish in the sink of the apartment's second bath; Catherine wandering the ship deck either crossing over or coming home, thrilled by the monkeys on Gibraltar; Catherine at the Trevi Fountain, wishing she could toss off her shoes and splash around with the local urchins for the tourist coins. "Like in *La Dolce Vita*," Oliver had commented, and she'd looked at him blankly: *Huh?*

His mother-in-law typed in a street name, and then a number. The image pulled short at about a hundred feet above it. She stared intently at the screen. The shadows of pedestrians could be seen from the air. Oliver asked, "Do you recognize the roof?"

She turned to him. It was as near to her as he had been since dancing with her at his wedding reception eighteen years ago (waltzing: they'd grown up having had lessons, unlike his young wife, who simply hung limp on his shoulders, the slow dance of disco-era prom). Grace's pale blue eyes were filled with tears. Affirmation, he supposed; this was the place.

For the next hour they watched videos on YouTube of home movies and political footage, art shows and tourist ads, any- and everything late-sixties Italian. Eventually Grace retrieved a photo album from her bookcase and showed Oliver pictures of the family in Rome that year. He had not seen these photos be- fore. In them, Grace Harding was the slender young woman in the chic clothing, and Catherine was a little girl. Here was Cath- erine, sitting on an Italian street curb, eating a gelato with her legs heedlessly splayed, while her modish mother stood behind in a striped dress and sunglasses, smiling condescendingly. An Italian man, caught on the photo's edge, was giving Grace an ap- preciative once-over while striding by. Mr. Harding must have enjoyed that, his stylish intellectual wife, his cute daughter. Oli- ver would have given the woman the same look, he was sure; the little girl he would have ignored, if he'd noticed her at all. He'd have noted and approved the woman's keeping her figure, post- childbirth.

Maybe that's all Grace Harding had ever wanted: to have turned Oliver's head. Her misgivings concerning him might be more interestingly messy than he'd previously believed.

"I was in Rome not too long before this," he told her. "Nine- teen sixty-one." He and YaYa. Their daughter Mary had probably been conceived there, YaYa somehow neglecting to pack birth control. YaYa who'd hauled two laundry baskets full of clothing to the airport because she couldn't decide what to pack until the last possible minute. They'd fought the whole two weeks they were abroad, YaYa unhappier than usual when out of a familiar ele- ment. She thought the Italians were talking about her and ex- pected Oliver to know what to do about it. To this day, he could not imagine what that would have been: Pick fights? Suddenly, magically, understand Italian? She had been an impossible woman.

"Did I ever tell you about my first wife?" he asked Grace now. When she shook her head, he told her all about YaYa. He hadn't seen her in more than a decade; she, like him, was only a few years younger than Grace. The only time they had contact was when they exchanged paintings every January. From his daughter Mary, that child conceived accidentally in Rome, he heard nothing. He told Grace that, as well. He Googled his daughter in order to display her work, three galleries' worth of the massive abstract canvases, their prices astonishingly high.

To whom could he ever fully explain his pride in her, the strange intimacy he felt with this daughter who seemed closest to him precisely because she'd declined to remain attached? He said to his mother-in-law, "I don't really know her, but when I see her paintings, it seems like we're in touch."

While he talked and clicked and scrolled, he realized he was inviting, or perhaps merely allowing, his mother-in-law to pity him. This was not his usual tack—not with her, not with anyone. Catherine always said it was easier, ironically enough, to be with her mother now that she couldn't speak. She wouldn't have wished this disability on her, this one or any other, but an element of strain had lifted from their relationship. Oliver was grateful today for that same feeling. Perhaps he should be quiet more often himself; into his mother-in-law's attentive silence he poured a narrative he had not spoken in many years, maybe ever, illustrated by artwork that only heightened the mystery. They sometimes frightened him, he told Grace. "I might have lost her anyway," he speculated aloud. "But it didn't help to divorce her mother just when she was hitting high school. I've done that twice, you know. I always thought it was better to stick around until they were through being little kids, but I'm not sure that's kind."

Grace still had the Italy photo book open on her lap, her left hand clutching one side, her limp right hand inert as a paperweight on the other. Catherine with sunglasses. Catherine standing dwarfed by the Colosseum. Catherine at a sidewalk café, scowling at a plate of food. But always her more striking mother in the foreground, the true subject of the photos, Catherine as afterthought. That's how Oliver had felt about his wives and children, when he loved one and tolerated the other. It was last generation's regard of offspring: better seen than heard. And perhaps only from the point of view of the person taking the photograph, in this instance: the husband.

If Oliver and Catherine had had a child, if they'd produced yet another in the line of daughters, she could be the adolescent age he described. It would be just about time for him to move on.

And there would be the Sweetheart, waiting in the wings.

"I have to go," he told his mother-in-law abruptly. "I'll come back tomorrow. We'll check out France, how about that? Or maybe Turkey." Her mouth hinged open in surprise, but she swiftly clamped it shut.

Outside in the parking lot he sat for a few minutes, staring at the ugly building he'd just left. Originally, he had planned to meet up with the Sweetheart again, this time at her grandparents' house. She'd said he could bring the dogs; a sleepover, a dive into his fantasy life while his other one ran steadily forward in his absence. But he did not open the glove box to consult his secret cell phone. He would invent something that had detained him; he was a very adroit liar.

Instead, he drove home, turned up the heat, washed his hands, poured himself a glass of red wine, switched on the local news, lay back on the couch with the two dogs, one fat foxy face on either leg, and phoned his wife.

"I've been thinking about you," he said honestly. She offered the same words, but he didn't believe they were heartfelt. That was okay; marriage was like that, two people trading turns at sincerity and gratitude, the other allowed indifference or neglect. Give and take, teeter-totter. "Guess what your mother and I did today?"

"Oh, I dunno. Scrapbooked? Made divinity?" she said. "Had sex?"

He surprised himself by laughing. "Went on a virtual trip to Rome."

"Do tell."

He elaborated on the visit. He told Catherine about the pictures of herself in the album, ones he'd not been treated to before.

"My father didn't like that haircut," she told him. "He was furious with my mother for taking me and getting it shorn like that. But my mother didn't know enough Italian to describe what she wanted. The guy just cut it like all the kids' hair. A low-maintenance pixie. Something easy to pick nits out of."

"Very fetching."

"Like Mia Farrow, in *Rosemary's Baby*."

"Your mother was quite the looker, back then."

"What?"

"I said, your mother was hot, in her day. Where are you? What's all the clatter?"

"Somebody dropped a tray. I'm killing time, waiting for the insurance guy to get off work. Don't laugh, but he's called Dick Little."

"I'll just be pleased he's not called Dick Big."

"Why do you sound so surprised when you say my mother was good-looking?" And why, furthermore, was it the rule that others could not insult the mother that you yourself could insult?

"I think I might get her on the information superhighway after all."

"We should bet on it."

"You always bet a blow job, and then you never pay up."

"That sounds just like me, all right. This is a good bar, you'd like it." She was speaking loudly, around laughter and conversation. "It's going for a kind of British pub motif. Except with ice in the g and t's, thank the lord. Waitresses in knee socks and little kilty things. No television, best of all."

"That reminds me, your serial killer has sent the paper some insane puzzle, some horrible scrambled word thing and other paraphernalia. Big excitement here in River City. They keep showing only partial clips, just in case some civilian out in the audience might solve it before the cops can."

"Say again?" she said. He repeated himself. The killer had made a puzzle, letters and numbers as in a Seek-and-Find, Sunday-comic-style exercise. On the one hand, it was hard to take him seriously; on the other, it was impossible not to.

"Your man's a moron," said Oliver. "But the fact that he has to keep prodding everybody is getting embarrassing."

"I thought about him a lot on my drive down today. The way he sort of kept popping up all those years. And the way he just vanished." Conventional wisdom held that he'd come back because the newspaper had featured a story last January, anniversary of his first crime, still unsolved three decades later. Wrongheaded speculation about his demise had apparently forced him to set the record straight: alive, intact, authentic, at large. Winning the game he was playing with the city. Catherine paused. "It's hard to imagine my mother on the Internet. Also hard to imagine you and she spending time together in that place. The smell alone . . ."

"You warned me, and I still forgot the VapoRub. But actually, it was fine."

"There's a woman there who does nothing but cry, all day long. And another who reads the same line from the same children's book. 'Jesus *loves* the little children. Jesus *loves* the little children.' Listen long enough, and you think that she's going to inflect differently, sooner or later, 'Jesus loves the *little* children.' This other lady always asks if I've heard from her sister. Every time, 'Have you heard from Moira?' How could you live like that?"

"I couldn't." He'd already told her, years ago, that he'd kill himself first. The question was, would you remember what you wished for, when the time came? If the weeping woman, for example, wanted to kill herself, how would she pull it off now? How would her old self redress the situation of her new self?

"Thank you," she said. "I know you hate going there, and I appreciate—"

From his end, the dogs suddenly began barking. "Must go, the lads are having a fit." He didn't like to be thanked. His second wife, the martyr, had ruined gratitude for him. It was very difficult to make him hear it. They hung up. Catherine consulted the phone to see how many minutes they'd spoken. Only four. She was quite certain that he'd prodded the dogs into their frenzy. If you took them to the deck door and gestured toward the railing, they would assume defensive positions in anticipation of squirrels, cats, possums.

And then she asked herself: Why hadn't she brought the dogs with her? How had she forgotten to bring them on her sojourn?

The short-skirted waitress who'd earlier brought her a drink now delivered Catherine her dinner. "Sole in Its Coffin," she said. "We like to say it's to die for."

"Thanks."

Houston was not at all what Catherine had expected, although she couldn't quite pin down what she *had* expected. Astronauts? Oil rigs? Ten-gallon hats? It was moist, filled with trees, houses that reminded her of ones in Wichita. When she arrived, she'd parked in Misty Mueller's bungalow driveway and studied the front porch. Yellow brick, cream-colored trim, a flower bed and porch swing. Frogs, crickets, birds: the rhythmic noise of creatures and nature, the atmosphere pleasantly sodden. She'd decided then to cancel her hotel reservation, to stay at Misty's.

When she returned to the house, after dinner, she sat on the porch swing and creaked it back and forth. Dick Little was late, but she didn't mind. Pleasant, this place. The sound of traffic, at a distance, and the restless animals in the jungly undergrowth up close. The nighttime city sky, pink and lacking stars. Some sweet balmy odor reminiscent of spring rather than January, which made time seem strangely upended. From down the block came a single light, wobbling. An overweight man on a bicycle appeared, ringing a bell that sounded like an old-fashioned telephone. "I apologize, I apologize!" he was calling. Dick Little was large yet graceful, appearing to embrace and flaunt his size the way one would a parade float, the way Santa might behave, navigating magically up the drive and off the comically small bike in one smooth motion. He approached with outstretched hands, the Venus flytrap shake, helmet tucked between elbow and ribs.

"Come in, come in! Isn't this a sweet place? I've been checking in on it, making sure nothing says 'Unoccupied, welcome crack hos, come on in, gangbangers.'" He was flipping on lights, igniting one room after another. "Someone else has a key," he called out, "probably from her office, somebody who emptied the fridge before the food could rot. Thank God I didn't have to do that! AC! AC!" he trilled, disappearing down a hall.

Catherine looked around, wondering anew at what she did not know about Misty Mueller. They'd parted ways almost exactly half her lifetime ago; this was what had happened next.

The place was clean, its air stale and damp, its separate spaces appointed as if adhering to the designs of dollhouses: living room with a fireplace, dining room with a long empty table and candlesticks, two bedrooms, two bathrooms, a kitchen with all the compulsory appliances. Misty had not grown up with this clarity and order, this protected museum atmosphere. To see it here on display made Catherine's chest hurt.

Her uncle with his red-eyed ferrets. The Lava soap rough as sandstone in the kitchen sink. Toolbox packed with greasy instruments instead of sideboard filled with silver. A deer carcass hung upside down in the garage, blood drained in the horse tank, offal thrown in the alley.

"Without a dog around, any old thing could walk in," Dick Little was saying, indicating the small plastic opening in the larger back door. Around its edges a dark oily stain, where the dog had rubbed coming and going. "Couldn't leave that open." He'd duct-taped the thing shut.

"I was just thinking that I should have brought my dogs." Catherine described the corgis, her adventurers and companions.

"I have a bichon frise," Dick Little said. "He has asthma, just like me!"

He was florid, freckled, grinning, ginger-haired, a man holding on to his health with a tentative grip, socially robust but succumbing to something larger than asthma. His fingers and cheeks trembled, an illness or drug reaction, and it took him a moment to steady his breath. From their phone conversations, Catherine knew she would like him, as she did most fallible or frail people who gallantly tried to hide those things, to laugh rather than whine. Now he produced hand sanitizer from his pocket and offered Catherine a squirt.

"I hadn't seen Misty in twenty-three years," Catherine said, not for the first time. "But when we were in eighth grade, we stole a dog once. This jerk of a guy owned it, and we saw him beating it in his yard. Yelling at it. Every day we walked home from junior high past his house, and finally we just decided to take his dog." To prove him evil, they'd returned a few days later, pretending to look for a lost cat. He'd snarled menacingly at them, sworn that some asshole had stolen his dog, then slammed his front door in their faces. Vindicated, they kept his dog, that servile, flinching animal. It went between their houses, each girl claiming that the other owned it, that it was just visiting. At Misty's, it lived in the backyard in the mud, in a box; at Catherine's it stayed in her closet, undiscovered by her mother, who would have objected. Her mother objected to anything that hadn't been her idea.

"I'm a dog person," Catherine said.

"Me, too," agreed Dick Little.

That dirty animal stain ringing the dog flap was the first thing that made Misty seem real to Catherine. Real in the way of sensing her, imagining Misty making a mental note to someday scrub away that mess. Imagining the dog's head coming in, its tail going out. Familiar, a dog who, in Catherine's mind, looked like that long-ago rescued creature.

Young Catherine surely must wonder what had become of that dirty dog. An empty kennel had been found in the wrecked car.

"Not to speak ill of the dead?" Dick Little said, "but I was very sad to see that." He indicated with a wagging finger the pretty half-empty bottle of citron vodka centered on the kitchen table. "We were AA buds. She was going on sixteen years sober."

"Maybe she threw a party?"

He shook his head knowingly.

"She drank vodka when I knew her," Catherine admitted. "We liked it with orange juice." She shuddered to remember the flavor—healthy breakfast beverage made toxic by alcohol.

"You just hate to see sixteen years gone."

"Yeah." Catherine put together the information. "She stopped when she got pregnant."

Dick Little tilted his head, rolling out his lower lip. "You're right, that's probably it. And then her girl goes away, and so what's the point? Higher power: AWOL."

"But she was keeping everything together," Catherine said, indicating the home. "I mean, bills were being paid, right? Mortgage, utilities?" Why did she feel a need to defend a virtual stranger, a person who'd been, in fact, indisputably headed toward disaster when last Catherine had seen her?

"Direct deposit," Dick Little said. "For a while, the cleaning service was still coming once a week." The vodka on the table, the car off the cliff in Colorado: this was evidence contrary to "keeping things together."

Before he left, Dick Little turned the thermostat to 75, fiddled with the television remote, flushed a toilet, provided Catherine with young Catherine's cell phone number ("I leave messages. It's still receiving calls, but be prepared for the greeting: whew!"), then took his leave. "I'm fascinated to know what is up with that child," he said, strapping on his helmet. "Gimme a shout?"

"Of course." Catherine thanked him, closed the door, and stood in the center of Misty's living room. Eventually she poured herself a glass of that pricey, lemon-infused vodka. Then she sat on the couch and sipped at it. From where she sat she could see a photograph of the girl, her namesake and goddaughter. In her unsmiling face Catherine attempted to make out the father. Could it have been any of those boys she'd once also known? Not for the first time today, she followed the twisty path of her and Misty's attachment to those boys and men. The path that had diverged, eventually, she going one way, Misty another.

She'd had a meditative day in the car, remembering them.

First had been Lyle Skinner, who for starters had a real beard. Not mere wisps or patches, not the soft facial hair that some high school boys (not to mention some high school teachers) seemed not to have even noticed on their own faces, but a beard that was busy at all hours growing, surging anew every morning scratchy and rough, perfectly shaped to hold his features, lips, nose, chin. Brown red blond: the girls stared at his face in the early dawning light of a night spent with him, each admiring how, when he lifted his chin to most efficiently inhale the last hit of cocaine, his new beard sparkled like bits of glass on the beach.

She and Misty had found him on the telephone, haunting their call like a poltergeist. Whomever he'd been speaking to, he'd not brought with him to meet them.

He liked to talk to Misty, but he liked to look at Catherine. Maybe this was why, for a while, the three of them were enough. Misty could match him, drink for drink, smoke for smoke, drug for drug, all night long. Catherine tended to pass out, or to pretend to pass out, which gave Lyle somewhere to rest his eyes. She curled into a beanbag chair between the couch and the television, a spot Lyle let his gaze settle on while comparing notes with Misty about relatives and prison sentences. Like a man, Misty's conversation style was of one-upmanship. In response to the news that Lyle's father was in Leavenworth for desertion, she notified him hers had died in a local jail awaiting extradition. "Attempted murder," she explained. Of her mother. While her mother was pregnant. With Misty.

Liar, Catherine would think, amused, opening her eyes to see Lyle caressing her with his stoned focus. She might shift her slightly plump shoulder, hunch it beneath her chin, chilly in the vinyl chair. She could have covered herself, but she liked to imagine the way her body snuggled into itself, her hands up at her throat, crossed at the wrists, like a child napping, knees drawn to elbows, the hemline of her shorts cutting into her thighs: all under his adoring eyes. Her bare feet, like her hands, folded into one another, a person elegantly compacted, as if put in a package. Say, an eggshell or pouch, a satin nest perhaps.

"And rehab?" Misty would be saying. "Don't get me started." She drank beer and enjoyed it, not like most girls, who drank only to get drunk, their faces pursed in distaste. She carried stick matches and lit them with her thumbnail. She shook her no-color hair out of her face like a boy. She wore Levis and work boots and work shirts, undershirt and no bra. She had a mole on her jaw, a few hairs growing unplucked from it. Her eyes sloped depressingly down, but her mouth was loose, lazy, likely to grin, which exposed her crooked teeth. She wasn't stupid, but she looked it. She wasn't morose, but she seemed to be. She would have made a better man than woman, but she wasn't lucky enough to have been born one.

She looked like someone with bad luck.

"You guys lesbians?" Lyle had asked the girls, their first night together, the first time he'd watched Catherine slip into her dreamy silence, the first occasion on which he and Misty had yakked away the hours, each staring in blurry fascination at the pretty sight Catherine had arranged of herself before them. His question led the two of them, Misty and him, to sex. Catherine roused at the query, which Misty had felt obliged to answer, like a man, with action rather than words, as if he'd challenged her rather than merely announced his curiosity. And still Catherine knew Lyle watched her as he and Misty fucked on the couch. Catherine's mouth was shaped as if to say, "What?" and she could feel his focus on her parted lips, on the welcoming curious kiss they seemed to form.

But she was frightened of Lyle. When they went somewhere in his truck, he often insisted that Misty drive so he could arrange himself in the middle, put his right thigh up close to Catherine's left one. Against the door she nudged herself, resisting. Meanwhile, Misty would shift aggressively, throwing the knob into third and fifth just so she could run her palm over his knee. Again, he would watch Catherine while Misty touched him.

Catherine staring out at the Kansas landscape, fields and cows and flashes of lightning in the distance. Bored summer, bottles of beer and vodka hidden beneath the dash, some hair metal band on the radio.

Eventually he had to invite friends. Ron and Don Kovich, twin brothers. "Meet the Twinkies," he said one night when Misty's Buick had rumbled into his trailer's drive. The girls had hung back, seeing two other cars there, the car ticking like their own hesitation. Catherine was made nervous by men; she flinched when she visited Misty's house, the uncles and cousins and neighbors and coworkers who did not greet visitors, who sat unmoving like volcanoes, simmering. They drank as if to quench that heat inside. They stared at Catherine as if assessing merchandise. Misty they treated like one of them. Catherine always felt childish in their midst, ignorant, innocent, pampered, irrelevant. Representative of a group these men wished to avenge themselves upon. She'd been brought up by people who asked how you were, what you wished to eat, where you were going when you left. Parents, in short. Misty lived among a different set of adults. They sent her on errands because they were too wasted to perform them themselves. They did not indulge girlish novelties like privacy or squeamishness, a diary or a fear of mice. Misty slept in a sleeping bag, like everyone else. Her earnings, from the Dairy Queen where she and Catherine both worked, went into the community pot.

Catherine's paychecks went directly to a savings account. When she had enough in it, she planned to buy a velvet chaise longue she'd put down a deposit on at a thrift store. Purple. It would go with her antique bed.

Like Lyle, Misty's relatives also studied Catherine's prettiness. Her flesh, her polished toenails, her hair in its ponytail, the thick mascara on her lashes, her peace symbol earrings. She hung around Misty, but she wasn't like Misty. She did not wish to be one of the guys. When she got drunk, before she passed out, she would begin to assert herself, her funny opinions, her quaint notions. She would tell them about the book she was reading, or about a party her parents had thrown, or about a place she'd visited as a child. Alaska. Italy. New York City. Drunk, she quit worrying that she was bragging or offending or being pretentious. Why shouldn't she let them know who she was, what she liked, how she spent her time when she wasn't wasting it with them?

"Asparagus makes your pee stink," she informed them once; no one else in the room had ever tasted asparagus, let alone known what its effect was on urine. Sly minx, she thought of herself.

On the evening she and Misty were introduced to Ron and Don, the Twinkies, she discovered a mix of cocaine and vodka that allowed her to both stay awake and converse without inhibition all night long. Adding two men to their original threesome somehow served the purpose of liberating Catherine's tongue. Now she had a real audience; she and Misty weren't subtly competing for the attention of Lyle—an attention Catherine feared even as she coveted it, rebuffed even as he insisted on bestowing it—instead, they were negotiating a complicated set of attractions. Which man was most desirable? Which girl? A hierarchy developed where none had been before. It was practically geometry. Lyle, in the face of this, grew possessive. These were *his* girls, the one he nervously adored and the one he casually fucked. He didn't understand how pleased he'd been with the situation until the Twinkies showed up and ruined it.

Catherine staggered to the trailer's bathroom, and the four others all shifted on their seats, adjusting, clearing their throats, passing cigarettes and waiting as if at intermission in the drama of their evening. Without Catherine, the performance would not continue. Misty's presence did not make it a party.

And Misty was fine with that, actually. She was accustomed

to it. Her gratitude in having company, the company of another girl, that was enough. More than enough. She had been alone with men her whole life. Her grandmother, like Misty herself, might just as well have been a man, tough, irritable, aggrieved by unending hardship: mouths to feed, bonds to post, fights to quash. That Catherine seemed to find Misty amusing, that Catherine consented to accompanying her here, and elsewhere, made Misty newly amazed and thankful every single day. That she could provide these men with the likes of Catherine meant she was necessary, a linchpin in their fun plan. The bathroom door opened, and they could all hear the toilet's suctioning recovery, Catherine coming unsteadily back, the trailer sensitive to all motion in it, all lurching and bumping. Into the beanbag chair she fell, skin squeaking on the vinyl. And another screwdriver handed her, each one stronger than the last. At Lyle's, there was far more vodka than orange juice in the refrigerator.

One man led to the next man. Through Lyle the girls met the Twinkies, and they each chose one of them, Catherine taking the shyer of the two—he wouldn't have been the shy one in another situation, but everything of course was relative—and Misty took the other. Which? Catherine would not be able to recall, twenty-five years later. After the Twinkies, because of the Twinkies, they met two other men, at a bar. From that bar, they were invited to another bar, the F.O.P. bar, where they were often the only girls. Underage among cops; could anything have been more satisfying? The cops they selected—first Catherine, then Misty—led them to their next men. Misty chose, or was perhaps chosen by, a mean cop. Catherine went with a gentle, older man. He did not allow her to drink when they were together. Tommy, he was named. And so began the de-escalation of Catherine's wild phase. She was, it seemed, not so feral or fargone as she might have believed. Tommy gave her a wise, kind smile and recommended books. He watched birds and kept a record of what he'd seen. They met without Misty, which had never happened before. They went to movies and shared popcorn, Pepsi, Junior Mints. He wasn't old enough to be her father, but he was old enough to be her protective elder brother, her still-hip, fuckup young uncle, her teacher, her friend. The night the F.O.P. bar was raided, Tommy made sure Catherine wasn't there.

"You have to go to college," he told her. "You don't want to regret that. College is the best part. I promise, you'll love it." Her parents had been saying the same thing, but it was him she listened to. Tommy, who could only have sex if she lay facedown on the bed, his body uniquely fierce and nearly violent against her back, almost as if he were ashamed to let her see him that way.

Misty wasn't going to college. If Misty didn't get her act together, she wouldn't graduate from high school.

She must have finally received her GED, Catherine thought; Misty surely had turned around that slide she'd been on those days, gotten traction somewhere, somehow, and climbed out. After Tommy, Catherine had dated one of her professors—a colleague of her mother, somebody in between the sanctioned and the un-. He was another wizened soul, protector and admirer. Western civilization. Philosophy. Alcoholic, pothead, but educated, pensive. Slowly she was emerging from the debauched place she'd resided for those few years with Misty Mueller.

And Misty? The men whose hands she'd been passed through had also shared traits. But she'd opted for more danger, more brutality, selecting, it seemed, against safety, or maybe simply selecting what seemed familiar, familial. The girls had begun with twins, Ron and Don, who were identical, nearly indistinguishable (which one of them blushed more easily? Because that was the one to whom Catherine had been drawn, the one who felt some small degree of shame, a modicum of alarm), and then they'd parted ways, each choice leading each girl further from the other. Three men later, and they were no longer best friends. Misty's boyfriend rode a motorcycle, carried a knife, and had a parole officer. Catherine's was pale and slender, holder of a Ph.D., a man who wore sandals to walk to work at the university.

With him, she'd gotten pregnant twice; he'd come with her to the abortions, apologetic and kind, unstinting in his aftercare. Who had fathered Misty's child? Catherine wondered. And how surprising it was to think that it was Misty, in the end, who'd become a mother, and not Catherine. Dr. Harding would never have predicted that.

Nor would Catherine, she admitted to herself, seeing again that red-faced hysterical infant, that stranger's child squalling in the hotel room bathtub, Misty unmoved on the bed before the TV.

The photos on the walls of this tidy bungalow were of Misty, her little girl, and their dog. The daughter resembled Misty to such a degree that Catherine felt returned to high school. The basset hound look, the half-lifted lip. The heaviness and apparent torpor in her posture. Slow-moving and methodical. Unflappable. Her eyes straightforward and challenging. Catherine had liked that about Misty, too. This was why she had been drawn in. Misty wouldn't lie, she wouldn't pretend, she wouldn't veer. She would not buckle to parents or teachers or men at bars. She was fearless, loyal, in love with intoxication, adventure, a challenge, prepared to always say yes. This girl in the photos might as well have been Misty, Catherine's best friend.

CHAPTER 11

I DON'T LIKE to spend money," said Randall on the first day of their trip to Houston.

"Me, either," Cattie agreed. So far, so good. Ito's car got twelve miles to the gallon; by her calculations, the remaining three hundred dollars she had saved, plus the two hundred Ito provided, would barely suffice. She had packed the trunk full of single-serving-size potato chip bags, Joanne's contribution to the journey.

"I mean, I *have* money," he went on, "but I don't like to *spend* money."

"Okay."

"It's the principle of the thing."

What thing? Cattie wondered.

They left during a snowstorm, which probably accounted for why the gas station attendant failed to notice that they hadn't paid for the tank of gas. That, and Randall's military fatigues. Everyone seemed either enthusiastic—handshakes, a nod of gratitude—or embarrassed—averted gaze, muttered greeting—when he made his appearance. It was interesting to be his companion. People probably thought she was his girlfriend or wife, somebody who could be either happy to have him back, or sad to see him going.

The litter of puppies only made the whole situation more adorable. At McDonald's, the teenager in the drive-thru provided six free Happy Meals. Randall wouldn't let Cattie give the dogs any of them. "Beef and wheat and potatoes are unhealthy for dogs," he told her. "That cow milk's no good, either, but probably the bitch needs some calcium." He kept disturbing the wholesome impression of their entourage by casually referring to the mother dog as "Bitch," as if it were her name. The word never failed to make Cattie balk. That he used it without thinking made him seem a little criminal.

He preferred driving at night, so Cattie and the dogs slept then. At daybreak, he looked for large chain hotels that always had a breakfast bar, do-it-yourself waffle machine or pile of bagels, free coffee, free juice, free bananas. Powdered doughnuts, if they were lucky. They parked in the back of the building, then wandered around to the front, young soldier and his wife, hungry for their complimentary food, friendly with the day clerk. Later in the morning, Randall stopped at restaurants with booths, then stretched out on one side and took a nap while Cattie drank coffee on the other side. As far as she could tell, this was all that boarding school had taught her: to drink coffee. To know the difference between gourmet and diner types of it. To fill it with sugar and cream and sprinkle nutmeg on top if somebody offered.

When he roused himself, Randall washed in the restrooms, shaved, and applied deodorant. His fatigues were designed for inconvenient durations of wear. Moreover, a napping man in a uniform didn't have to explain a thing. The coffee was always on the house. Someone would invariably offer to pick up Cattie's tab, and she packed away leftovers for Randall—pancakes, hash browns, piles of bacon. A piece of pie for later. A cheese sandwich for the little lady.

"When did you first adopt this no-money policy?" Cattie asked him on the third day. She'd surreptitiously paid for the last tank of gas, not wanting to attract undue attention. He had a talent for finding the station that allowed you to fill up before paying, the aged mom-and-pop, on-its-last-legs place where the local farmers trafficked, a place where, if you lollygagged long enough at the counter, fingering souvenirs or car parts or nicotine products, they might forget you'd gotten gas at all an hour or so ago. The routine was to pull in and for Cattie to take the dogs two at a time to try to train them to pee outside while Randall used the pump. Then he'd move the vehicle to the parking slot by the front door. They'd ask for water for the dogs, a bathroom for Cattie, directions to a motel (where they'd never stop for the night), and the name of a friend of Randall's who'd mentioned the town once in a tent or foxhole or other faraway frightening place. "Jared Peabody," he'd say. "Brandon Del Mar." Soldiers he'd known. A boy who'd died or had his legs blown off or his mind messed up. The locals would shake their heads, speculate on what other nearby town he might have mistaken, what soldier boy of their own he might be meaning. It was a wonder to behold.

Her mother would have liked this about Randall, Cattie thought. Her mother enjoyed getting away with things. Riding with him, fooling people this way—this principled bit of amusement—made her imagine her mother watching them, approving or at least being entertained by it. Plus, Cattie was heading home. Surely her mother would have been in favor of that.

Even when they got caught—the unpaid bill at a station in Ohio—the fellow who chased them down on foot (catching up at the first stoplight) apologized when he reminded them they hadn't paid. "I'm so sorry!" Cattie cried, from the passenger's seat, a blush rising on its own to her cheeks. "I'm so sorry, I forgot!" and whipped out her wallet to hand the guy two twenties.

Randall had sat stony-faced, staring out the windshield with his chin quivering and his right eye twitching, for all the world as if he planned to sock Cattie in the mouth the minute they drove away. The gas clerk was frightened, seeing that expression on the soldier's face. He was probably exactly between their ages, Randall's and Cattie's; he probably had a girlfriend like her, neither beautiful nor ugly, merely average, invisible. Forgetful, careless, a little slow. And he himself was most likely always worried about what was the right thing to do. His glance at Cattie said that he believed he'd made a grave mistake and that he was very sorry.

"Can't always win," Randall said mildly when the light changed.

"You win a lot," she said. "I'm shocked."

"People are dumb."

"Or maybe just nice." Both, she thought. And also clever and scared and cruel and distracted. And also so involved in their own lives that they often didn't quite pay attention to others'. Didn't notice when others weren't doing the expected thing. In part, it seemed that Randall was fascinated by discovering just that about them, as if he'd been sent out to test the routines they'd allowed themselves to fall into. To shake them out of those.

They traveled south, but it never got warmer. Instead, it got flatter, bleaker, more desolate. Plains: they were very plain. Nothing but road and fields, wind and snow, heaps on the horizon that never turned out to be substantial mountains but only mere clouds, harbinger of further cold. These were the same states she and her mother had driven through last summer, going the opposite direction, Max riding in the back seat in her kennel. They'd taken the interstate, stayed in luxury hotels, ordered room service, visited famous sites and judged most of them overrated. When no dogs were allowed, they enjoyed sneaking Max in, breaking the rules, getting away with it.

Like this money thing with Randall, there'd been no point to it except being naughty. Just for the sake of naughtiness.

Randall made sure the dogs were comfortable. He never forgot to give them water, check their eyes, probe their fleshy bellies, poke at their meager stools. It was he who'd known to provide worming meds back in Montpelier. When the newspaper lining their box in the back seat was wet or soiled, he changed it immediately. He stroked the mother dog, who now was in the habit of holding her face against his leg, leaning into him while he ran a hand over her flank. She could not get enough attention. Randall did not begrudge her need. "Good bitch," he would murmur; sometimes he had to remind her to get back to her babies. His tenderness was what Cattie trusted, more than any other thing about him, his large fingers gently twiddling the dog's ear, the vague tremor in his hand irrelevant, just then. It was what permitted her to fall asleep slack and unguarded against the window on the passenger side, or, later, when her neck grew tired from jerking constantly upright, to lie down with her head almost touching his thigh as he drove through the night.

When they landed in the ditch, it all fit very precisely into her dream. How rapidly the mind made a story. In her dream she was flying a plane, skimming over the Rockies; the crash was into a peak obscured by clouds.

"Blowout," said the person in the pilot's seat. Was it an order, Cattie wondered? Would blowing out help relieve the tightness in her throat? Before she could ask, he was gone. From the back came a chorus of high squealing. Cattie's actual circumstance surged through her. She liberated herself from the seat belt— source of pain—and cracked her door to ignite the dome light.

The puppies' box had dumped onto the rear floorboard, and they were underneath it, their mother in the adjacent foot space, nudging at the overturned cardboard. When Cattie lifted the box, she discovered one of the six puppies missing. "Goddamn," she said. They kept dying on her. She was afraid to stick her hand under the seat.

The trunk suddenly shook. Randall appeared at her door. "You okay?"

"A puppy is missing."

He reached through her legs, his face suddenly there at her knees, looking up at her. "Here," he said, pulling the poor thing out. "Not dead," he added, so that Cattie would open her eyes. "Also, no spare tire. It's a witch's tit out here, I'll tell you what." He swung shut Cattie's door, leaving her in a brief span of dark, then came around to climb back behind the wheel. Light, then dark, then the sound of his palms bouncing on the dash. Behind Cattie, she could feel the dogs resettling themselves, pushing against the seat, mewling as their mother adjusted for this new nest. "Let me think," Randall said, although she'd already known better than to ask what now. She was grateful to be unharmed, the image of the mountain peak still flashing before her eyes. She'd been convinced the end was upon her, in her dream. Despite never having been in Colorado, never approaching a mountaintop in a plane, she was certain she'd experienced an authentic scenario.

Dreams were useful, that way. You could figure out how you felt, having something right in your face. Since her mother's death, Cattie had broached the topic of her own more than once, guessing that she was indifferent to the prospect. But the plane crash notified her otherwise. She'd been terrified and sorry to think it was the end; apparently she did not want to die.

"What you want to bet those other three tires is just as dry and pitiful as the one that went?" Randall said. This was a rhetorical question, so Cattie didn't respond. He went on with other nonanswerable queries, the heels of his hands now bouncing on the steering wheel. Cattie wanted to ask where they were and what time it was, but held back, arguing to herself that it couldn't much matter, really. There had been not one other car on this road since she'd tuned in to their situation, not a single other set of headlights. What did that mean? The wind rocked the vehicle every few minutes. Snow blew up from the ground, although the sky was clear.

"When my mother's car wouldn't start, she called AA and joined over the phone. They came and towed her right then."

"Three A's," said Randall. "And you best have a credit card, for that."

Her mother was also in that other club of A's, the double one. She'd quit drinking when she realized she was pregnant with Cattie. "You saved my ass," she'd told her cheerfully, heading off to a meeting every now and then.

And then there was that disturbing drunk phone message in the middle of the night last fall.

Cattie flipped open her cell to listen to her mother's other voice, the saved sober message from summer. The screen claimed to be seeking service; it must have been doing that for a while, because the battery was nearly depleted, the device hot in her hand. Poor thing, she thought, switching off the power. "We can just buy new tires," she told Randall. "How much do tires cost?" When he didn't respond, Cattie began to feel frightened of him. She couldn't see his expression, and maybe he'd had just about enough of her nonsense, silly girl stating the obvious beside him in a car in a ditch. Where, he was probably longing to shout at her, did she think they were going to find a tire store in the middle of the night in the middle of nowhere on a road with no other traffic? Idiot, he was probably thinking. Fucking dumbshit girl.

Wait a minute, Cattie thought. Why weren't there any cars on this road? "Are we lost?" she asked aloud, one fear overriding another.

"Maybe," he said.

"Why?"

"I like back roads," he said. "I like the scenic route."

"But . . ." She didn't continue. They both knew she shouldn't nitpick about "scenic" things that could not be seen in the dark.

People assumed Randall had been to war, and he let them assume it; *vet* was the best person he'd ever been, the one that required the fewest explanations. But Ito's vehicle worried him—he didn't trust that grinning fag's eager urgency to send him and Cattie off in it, as if there were a trick involved. He'd been working on paranoia with his psychologist, back at camp, but maybe they'd not made particular progress. Moreover, the car's paperwork seemed quite sketchy, and there were no dated stickers on New Hampshire plates; he'd spread mud over the first digits back there. He had wisely chosen small roads, blue highways, and locally owned gas stations. There'd been no cameras at most of the places where they'd eaten. But now the tires were going to explode, one after the other, and they were on a county road somewhere in Missouri. It was extremely cold, and only three thirty a.m., so there were hours more of cold before them. He genuinely appreciated Cattie's seeming calm. She was not going to lose her shit, which most other girls would have done. Crying: how he hated it.

"It's not that scenic, in the dark," he finally acknowledged. "Here's what we're going to do. We're going to wait until it gets light, and then I'm gonna start walking toward Seymour. You're gonna wait here with the bitch." He would find somebody to sell him tires. That same somebody would give him a ride back to the car. Cattie would be fine. There were provisions (chips, dog chow, brown bananas soft as baby food). She could switch on the car heater every now and then; she could listen to the radio; she could take comfort in the presence of the dogs.

Cattie stretched out along the front bench while Randall took the back, with the animals. In the absolutely silent dark and cold of their night half-on, half-off the road, Randall said, "I don't like it when I feel responsible."

"What do you mean?"

"I mean, I worry when I'm in charge."

Cattie blinked, knowing from a long history with a reticent person that you had only to wait silently. You would learn. And so, eventually, Randall told her about his friend at boot camp.

"I woke up, and he was dead," he said into the black interior of the car. "I never been so scared in all my life."

Cattie listened, feeling suspended in time. Randall and his friend had been celebrating a twenty-first birthday; the friend had drunk every drink anyone had bought him, one after another. They'd somehow wound up back in their quarters, one waking in the morning, one not.

Some other person might have asked him to compare the experience of war casualties with the experience of a single death, but Cattie wasn't that person. And Randall was grateful not to have to lie and pretend. "I don't feel like I react the way other people do," he confessed to her. "I never have."

"Me either," she said.

"That'll cost you," he said. She let these last words run through her head, over and over, without responding. They must have slept, Cattie later realized, because it surprised her to see the world outside the window when she woke, Randall already up and out there with it, his back to her as he peed. Steam rose in a delicate plume.

She wished it was possible to stand behind him and lay her head between his shoulder blades. She wanted to touch him without forcing him to respond.

And then he was gone, walking down the road like an advertisement for the army, his fatigues still shipshape, his stride purposeful, the ground sparkling with reflected light on ice. His back said to her he was embarrassed to have revealed his secret grief, his confusion about his friend. The sunlight warmed the car's interior, and Cattie studied the U.S. Atlas. Seymour, he had said. He guessed they were between ten and twenty miles from it. He believed it'd be no more than eight hours before he would be back, with tire or tires, depending. He'd taken two hundred of her remaining four-hundred-some dollars for the purpose. He instructed her to lock the doors and to be glad that Bitch would bark her head off if anyone approached.

"I'm sorry," he said gruffly.

"It's not your fault the tire blew."

By nightfall, she was wondering if his apology had to do with abandoning her. Now she regretted having passed up the two offers of help that had come her way during the long day. The two boys on their ATVs; the farmer in his pickup. From the radio she'd learned it was Friday. From the atlas she'd discovered she was still a long way from Houston. When she studied the car, standing in the ear-aching wind, she saw that it wasn't one but two tires that were no longer functional, the car's front end slanted decidedly downward as if disappointed or exhausted, resting on its chin. The day had alternated between sunny and cloudy, and her mood had shifted as dramatically as the clouds above. Optimism, despair. A funny story for Ito, later, or the beginning of a terrible nightmare, as yet to unfold. She'd walked a few hundred yards in both directions on the road, testing her cell phone reception. The boys on the ATVs had smirked in a very familiar, debilitating way, and that had sent her back to the locked car. "Sic 'em," she practiced on Bitch, whom she discovered she could goad into growling.

The car was redolent of dog.

In the dark she grew angry. What sort of fools made a road that only two or three or four or five people drove on in a twenty-four-hour period? How goddamn useful was a road like that?

Was it even officially a road if nobody fucking drove on it? Where was asshole Randall? Had he gotten lost? Or had he just decided to hell with her, and taken off with her money?

No, she realized, all of a sudden, interrupting her own inner rant. He wouldn't leave the dogs. He might have left Cattie in this mess, Cattie and the embarrassed confession he'd made to her, but he wouldn't have intentionally abandoned Bitch and the puppies. It felt comforting, to Cattie, to know something so surely. With the passenger-side door open, she oversaw yet another series of peeing with the slight animals, slighter still in the enormous plain and its relentless weather, one at a time in the hard ruts of the frozen roadway shoulder, their hindquarters shivering, their slitty little eyes squeezing out tiny beads of tears.

The same farmer drove up in the same truck the next morning and blew his horn. This time he had a woman in the front seat beside him. "I called the highway patrol," he told Cattie when she stepped out of the car. "They're backed up with the jack-knifed big rigs on the interstate, so I brought my wife."

He was lifting tires from the bed of his truck. The woman sat inside the truck, not looking at Cattie. It seemed it might have been better for the farmer to have come alone. "She's shy," he explained, dropping the first tire onto the ground beside Ito's car. It spun for a long while before settling flat. "You go on and get in the cab. I'll be done in a jiff."

"I can help," Cattie said.

He looked her over, then toward his truck. "She doesn't bite. That's just her natural expression."

This turned out to be true. The wife scowled. She moved her jaw as if shifting something from one side of her mouth to the other, an object her molars worked at. She reminded Cattie of the Looney Tunes Tasmanian Devil, barrelish and monosyllabic. Her hairline seemed very low.

"My boyfriend walked to Seymour," Cattie told the woman.

"Yeah," said the woman, as if somebody had already fed her this ridiculous line.

"He's in the army," Cattie went on, "just back from Iraq." Once more the molars went round, grinding, the woman staring out at her husband, whose arm was seesawing away at a jack, lifting Ito's car.

It was a relief when he finished, bringing with him the frozen outer air, and the sound of recognizable words. "You drive this, Mama," he said. To Cattie, he said, "I'll make sure your alignment isn't catty-wampus."

"There's dogs in the back," Cattie told him, wishing she could ride with him instead. "Sometimes the puppies crawl under the pedals." Catty-wampus indeed, she thought. Wampus might be her middle name.

They rode not far on the empty blacktop, turning in at the mailbox that said "Kinderknechts" on it. A trailer sat all alone in the middle of a large flat piece of fenced land. What did the fence hold in? Or out? There were tires on the trailer's roof, which may have been where the ones on the car came from, and a large American flag whipping bravely in the cold wind over the front door. In the time it took to drive to the Kinderknechts' home, Cattie realized she would have to claim to know how to operate a motor vehicle. She was going to have to drive away from Missouri in Ito's car. The last time she'd tried to drive had been in a cemetery in Houston, her mother's logic being that everybody there was already dead. That had been last summer, on a Saturday so hot and demoralizing that the two of them had designed six different activities in air conditioning. Driving lessons came in between an action movie downtown and dinner at the café around the block from their house.

Cattie tried to imagine driving Ito's car into the Houston driveway. That didn't seem impossible. But her imagination refused to accommodate the patchwork of states she was fairly sure existed between Missouri and Texas, never mind the very intimidating knotted network of freeways that made Houston, on the map, look like something strangled by a bundle of multicolored wires.

"Let's put those pups in the lav," said Mr. Kinderknecht, watching as Cattie led Bitch from the car. "We've raised us a couple litters in a bathtub, haven't we, Mama?"

The Tasmanian Devil snorted.

The farmer studied Cattie's face. Now that he'd solved the most obvious, first, problems, what came next? "Let's all get out of the cold. And then I'll park your car out by the road. That way your soldier boy'll see it when he comes back." Like his wife, the farmer didn't seem to believe Cattie's story about this alleged driver who'd left her in the ditch. Maybe she wouldn't have believed it, either.

Without Randall there, Cattie thought it best to put Bitch on a leash.

Their home was warm, cluttered, close. The ceiling seemed too low, the furniture too large, the heat too high. Cattie sank into a leather couch and accepted a hot microwaved plate of leftovers from Mama the Tasmanian Devil. It was a huge serving, enough for two or three people, yet Cattie found herself eating everything. She could hardly keep her eyes open when she finished; what if they'd drugged her, laced the gravy with whatever . . . "Just lay down," said the Devil, taking the empty plate. Her voice was deep, like a man's, and slow. She provided a brightly colored afghan, "Go on, lay down. I'm giving your dogs some scraps."

Randall would have objected, Cattie thought blearily; beef, he'd said, was not good for dogs.

She woke only because someone had sat down on the other end of the couch, sending up a poof beneath her. She'd slept all day with her feet on the floor, her top half folded over on the sofa. Just as if she were still in Ito's car, and Randall was driving.

But it was Mama Devil on the end of the couch, in the driver's seat. The evening news was playing. Her hosts were arranged on either side of her, Mrs. on the couch, Mr. in the oversize leather chair that had been jammed into this too-small space.

Just before a commercial break, there was a story about the serial killer next door in the state of Kansas. The killer had been sending messages for nearly a year now; his most recent some kind of word game, the one before a package in a Wichita park. "My mother lived next door to his first victims," Cattie said, sitting up, rubbing at a crease in her face from the couch. Her hosts turned—like salt and pepper shakers, Cattie thought, opposites that fit together. The package contained the driver's license of one of his victims, something stolen from the crime scene. It also held a doll. On the screen appeared a naked dark-haired Barbie, hands and feet secured with panty hose, a plastic bag tied over its head.

"Lord have mercy," murmured Mr. Kinderknecht. His wife said, "Hmm," in a skeptical tone, as if she'd seen worse treatment of toys.

Just then, the house of the first victims appeared on the screen. A simple structure, not unlike the houses Cattie had drawn in the first grade: two rectangles resting against each other, one upright, one lying down. The slats of siding, the sloped roof, windows with curtains tied back, a chimney, a single tree centered in front. Her mother's home hadn't actually been next door but three doors down. Still, same floor plan. Same basic first-grade assurance of lines and planes and angles and slope. Smoke wafting from that chimney. At first, every man in the neighborhood had been a suspect, her mother once told Cattie. A community suddenly suspicious of itself, turned inward with doubt and watchfulness. "Especially the deadbeats at my grandma's. I come from a long line of bad seeds, baby. Be thankful you never knew them." For a while, whenever anyone returned home to the grandmother's house, they'd first pick up the baseball bat just inside the door, then the telephone receiver to be assured of a buzzing connection. The killer had cut the lines at the house down the block.

Cattie and the Kinderknechts stared at the small white house on the screen. Despite the fact that the house next door was not her mother's, Cattie found herself tilting her head as if to look beyond the photo on the screen, to see that place nearby, the unremarkable structure where her mother had grown up.

CHAPTER 12

CATHERINE HAD CHOSEN to sleep in the girl's bedroom instead of the woman's. Misty's bedroom oppressed her, its tidiness, its hotel-room esthetic, the needle-stitched motto overhanging the bed about God granting serenity, and the bed itself—overloaded with small tasseled pillows, ornamental flammable spread, navy blue silk throw carefully draped at its foot. The effort it took to make and maintain this every morning, this stuff that then had to be tossed onto the floor, come night. Catherine felt the same enervating regret she had when she faced Misty's photograph online: that something neutralizing and ultimately disappointing had happened to the girl she'd known. It wasn't as if Misty's life had seemed ideal, back in high school; it had been, in fact, a frightening specter, grubby and violent. A life Catherine had been allowed to visit, and then leave, like a privileged tourist dunked briefly into the third world but in possession of a round-trip ticket out. Misty did not have that luxury. She'd been a native to the place, suffered its hardships, carried its scars. For instance, as a toddler she'd fallen from an open car window and cracked her skull. The great-uncle who was in charge had neglected to either strap her in or take her with him inside the liquor store. Onto the pavement she'd tumbled; the uncle later complained of the inconvenience of having to haul her to the ER. You wouldn't wish such a thing upon a child; would Catherine really have preferred discovering that Misty was still living like that?

No. Yet it seemed that that life, and the girl who lived it, had been *real*. Misty had had a personality unlike anyone else's, peculiar and earned, her own. This bedroom, these recent professional photographs, had the feel of borrowed identity—that wasn't an actual bridge they were standing on, it traversed only the floor of a photographer's studio. The sky behind was made of paper. Throughout the house, there seemed to be a great deal of useless adornment—seashells gathered around the sink spigot and toilet bowl lid. Random hardback books—sold by the yard! Catherine knew, having seen ads in decorating journals—placed on shelves, the various pairs of bookends—statues, geodes, snow globes—on either side the true focal point. Business garments hung in dry-cleaning bags, matching low-heeled pumps the colors of sherbet lined up below.

She had shoved aside those plastic bags and shiny shoes, plowing through Misty's closet for any sign of a current secret life, some hidden message from the past one. But Misty either didn't possess such a thing as a secret life, or knew better than to hide its evidence at home. She lived, after all, with that most persistent and gifted detecting snoop, a teenage girl.

And that teenage girl's room was a welcome mess, in Catherine's opinion. Here she found the detritus of a recognizable person—messy, but genuine. A person who'd made her bedroom into her proclamation of self, that riot of likes and dislikes and righteous opinions and laughable lapses, the walls festooned with bumper stickers and pins and posters and graffiti, the shelves and drawers and closet overspilling with many seasons' worth of beloved trinkets and gear, disguises and embellishments. On the ceiling, an unfinished mural starring red skeletons apparently at a party for the dead: smoking cigarettes, clutching bottles, throwing back their skulls and dropping open their jaws in laughter, a couple in the corner with their various leg and arms bones entwined in what might become skeleton sex. Misty's daughter, she and her friends, had painted those characters. Stood on chairs and desk, brushes in hand, faces tilted up using paint the color of blood. Misty had allowed it, and that cheered Catherine.

Or maybe this had been done without permission, girls stoned and nihilistic, and there'd been an argument later, and lingering resentment, smoldering ill will. *My house!* the mother would roar; *My room!* the girl would counter. Catherine could remember being sustained by feelings like that toward her mother, the fuel of injustice simmering, ever-ready to erupt.

Catherine laundered the bedsheets she found beneath the skeletons. She slept in this girl's crowded den. The room was so full of what *was* there, under the red, nimbly dead figures on the ceiling, that its missing objects didn't immediately strike her. But there were no photographs—not of friends or pets or relatives, not of young Catherine herself. And no mirrors. No opportunity, in here, to examine and loathe the always imperfect adolescent face and body. Catherine ran her eyes over the exclamations on the walls, contradiction everywhere—gleeful cheer next to fatalistic gloom—the piles of books and DVDs and stuffed toys on the floor, this warehouse of excess and life being constantly, desperately revised, layered upon. A life coming clear to Catherine, or at least growing more specific, intriguing. And also heartbreaking for its feverish casting about: Boy bands! Political causes! Three different high school pennants! *I heart mutts. Buck Fush! Gaze long into an abyss, and the abyss will gaze back into you.* Catherine was old enough to be this girl's mother, yet the sensation the bedroom brought up in her felt distinctly un-adult. Maybe a person never ceased seeking her niche. In here, books meant for reading rather than decorating. Books about damaged children and their heroic helpers. Books about true crime. Books assigned in English classes that some students, some girls, this girl, would keep forever.

Attending the skeleton party overhead, one dog guest. Sitting at the foot of a lone figure in the corner. The person's skull was tilted, one hand's many bones stretched toward the dog's up-tipped skeleton snout.

That red figure was Cattie, Catherine understood. Spectator. And most likely she had painted the ceiling by herself. Not with friends. Maybe with her mother.

She could almost see them, the two of them standing on the desktop, bucket of red paint, two small brushes, stretching up and creating a party on the ceiling. It was something Catherine and Misty would have done themselves, once upon a time.

The house's air conditioner went on and off at intervals. Every time it ceased there were two heaving final breaths, like an exhausted monster sighing in the cellar. The girl would have thought that, too, Catherine thought. She and Misty would have an inside joke about it.

She listened to the messages on the answering machine. Queries about missed meetings, a reminder from dental associates, vote-getting messages from the Democratic Party, other solicitations, hang-ups, the public library concerning an overdue audio book, and three from a company called PetSafe. Catherine backed up the machine and noted the number. They were calling about a chipped dog; she used the same service for her own.

"This notification is nine days old," the woman at headquarters chastised Catherine. "Just after New Year's, in fact." What sort of responsible owner waited more than a week to respond? Why bother with a microchip if you didn't have the time to follow through?

"It's complicated," Catherine said. This was Oliver's way of defusing a person who was about to offer unsolicited advice.

"Nevertheless, an attempt was made to contact you," the woman said. "We stand by our commitment to returning every pet to its proper home, but the owner has to meet us halfway."

"I'm not the owner," Catherine said. "It wasn't me you were trying to contact. The owner died."

A silence fell upon the line. When the owner died, so much became frayed in an otherwise flawless system. The car had not only gone off the road but was then unfound for a while; the bereaved daughter was still at large; the executrix heir had a married name and forwarding address; and now the dog—incarcerated two states away! In Arizona at a shelter, the woman at PetSafe reported. She recited a phone number and hung up without saying good-bye.

"We hold them for five days, if they're chipped," the next woman told Catherine. "Three days if not."

"And after five days?"

"Adopted out or put down," she said. The general odds, it seemed. Max, the dog was named. Inscribed on the ceramic water bowl in the kitchen. In the family portrait by the phone dock in the hallway, a black-and-brown-mottled creature that looked like a coyote or hyena, wilder and leaner than Catherine's chunky bred animals, smiling nonetheless between the two people on the fake bridge, in front of a false blue sky, some plastic shrubbery. Misty and Cattie, two versions of the same girl.

How had their dog gotten from Colorado to Arizona, anyway?

"I hope it was adopted," Catherine said.

"It's always good to hope that," agreed the woman on the phone.

Later that afternoon the doorbell rang just as Catherine had fallen asleep on the couch. She had made a mistake in coming to

Houston over the weekend; it was the kind of error she was prone to, not thinking far enough ahead. Not until Monday could she visit the law office to sign paperwork. On the other hand, she was telling herself as she began to drift away, perhaps these extra days had allowed her to choose to sign those papers. Staying in Misty's house was what would convince her to . . .

The woman at the door came bearing a Christmas gift bag and introduced herself as the next-door neighbor. "When Misty left town, she asked me to collect her mail and her newspapers."

"Come in."

"This is the mail. I saved everything, you never know."

"Yes, that's smart." You never did know, Catherine thought, remembering the lawyer's letter that had almost gotten away from her, the one that started everything.

"Did you want the newspapers?" The woman feigned panic that she might have done the wrong thing, recycling the daily local paper. "I didn't think to save those."

"No, no." This was yet another type that her husband loathed: the person who has to be assured of her proper behavior. *Thank you*, is all she ever wanted to hear.

"And then I saw about the accident. Terrible!" The woman made a face as if she'd encountered an odor, trying to settle the bag of mail on the coffee table, where it kept falling over, finally giving up and letting it spill. "So I just kept picking up the mail, what else was I going to do? Bless her heart. And what in the world has become of poor Cattie?" The woman settled into the center of the sofa, looking around the room in a way that let Catherine know she'd not been welcomed inside the house before, or at least not lately.

"Yeah, I don't know," Catherine said. "Thank you," she added, for good measure. She took a chair on the other side of the table. The woman looked at her expectantly, chin and brows lifted, entitled to know how it was Catherine was in possession of a key. And Catherine would have been willing to tell some other kind of neighbor, divulge the strange circumstance that had brought her here. But not this neighbor.

"Beverage?" she finally asked. "Tea? Coffee?" Vodka, she might have offered, had it been somebody else.

"If there's a pot made . . ." She followed Catherine into the kitchen. It was neither of their homes, and each had a different claim to it. Come Monday, it would be Catherine's property, hers to oversee. The neighbor, meanwhile, informed Catherine that her grandson had lived with her ten years earlier and been little Cattie's best friend. She and Misty had shared a gardener, Ernesto, who was keeping up Misty's yard still.

"Does Misty owe him money?"

"Oh, I've been covering it."

"So she owes *you* money." The woman was exhausting. But retrieving a checkbook from her purse and writing out the amount due permitted Catherine a way to turn their encounter into something recognizable, services rendered, exchange made, coffee drunk, visit over. "Thank you," she said a half dozen more times, the last words as the woman disappeared behind the closing front door.

And in the bag of mail, the life Catherine had assumed must exist, the one she'd been seeking, finally arrived.

Misty Mueller had a pen pal in prison, a man whose correspondence came religiously, his seven-digit identification penciled on each envelope's upper left corner, the Huntsville imprint dated every week for the months of October and November. The final letter, dated December 8, was addressed instead to "Whom Remains."

This was the letter Catherine felt entitled to open.

I am sorry I did not know Miss Mueller had passed so I hope you will forgive this man if you saw what I wrote before. Please destroy those previous letters, I plead of you. Miss Mueller was a friend to me and time after time she would say to me I should wait til I know the facts before making hastie judgements. I did it again about her I cannot believe I did. It is true that I have learned nothing from experience (she would say that to me too!) Her passing away makes me more alone then you can know. In the paper it says a daughter is her survivor. If this is you, her daughter, whom remains from her, I want to say that your mother wrote to me so often to relive my solitude I looked for her mail to me and felt like I had a kindred spirit in the world. Someday if not today you will understand that a kindred spirit is like a light that is shining in a room of a house you can remember where you were happy with somebody a long time in the past. Its corny (believe me I can hear your mom saying that to me) but she was that light in a far away place and I cant believe its gone. I will keep this simple and say goodbye. And please if you are forgiving you will not judge me from those other letters.

It was signed "Ohell." The envelopes he regretted sending lay stacked on the table. Catherine was tempted to open them— the use of the pencil instead of pen already had given the man some kind of childish appeal, to her, his smudged earnestness, the fact that he printed on lined paper, all of it so reminiscent of grade school and sincere labor and the beginnings of putting feelings into words, and words onto paper. As an incarcerated adult, he was capable of anything Catherine could imagine; he might be the unknowing father of that daughter he had not known about. He hadn't mentioned the possibility, hadn't speculated upon it—and yet Misty could have kept such a secret, Catherine knew.

The fireplace was a working one, so Catherine placed the prisoner's letters, all except the one addressed to the daughter, in the grate. And then she sat once more on the couch and looked at the pile. She didn't have to decide now. She had time to see how she felt about it tomorrow. Or the next day. The one after that.

There had been an ice storm in Kansas, a snow that turned to rain, and then back to snow, and then, whimsically, finally, to sleet. Inadvertent perfect strata of disaster. The ground was treacherous, layered and slick, its surface deceptively benign seeming, snowy, with a thick scrim of ice beneath. Oliver slid as he headed for the newspaper at the curb, a swift flush of panic that he'd nearly fallen, then marveled at the tire tracks of the deliverer, who'd roved back and forth from side to side all down the block. Overhead, the trees were laden. They creaked ominously. Eventually, when the sun finally emerged, everything began to snap. All over town the branches crashed down—on cars, on houses, on power lines. Giant boughs. Devastating breaks. The streets were filled with broken limbs, electricity went out, windshields were shattered. What remained was a forest of strange topless trees, their severed appendages imploring the sky. Everyone stayed at home, built fires, used flashlights, listened to the radio.

Oliver looked forward to this odd day without obligations other than stoking a fire, opening and closing the back door for the dogs, relocating the refrigerated food from inside the dark refrigerator to outside in the bright hard light. On Saturday morning the Sweetheart trekked from her grandparents' house to his, four miles, in snowshoes. Her cheeks were red as cherries when she finally arrived.

"Unbelievable!" she declared. "It's like a war zone out there!"

As if she knew what a war zone was like. As if Oliver did, he scolded himself, he who'd been conveniently exempt, falling into a peaceful pause that made him too young for Korea, too old for Vietnam. It would not do to transform into a churlish grump, the complaining curmudgeon, one of the malcontents in their row of loungers at Green Acres. He kissed the Sweetheart's sweet cheeks, that flesh he felt like biting, it was so plump and ripe. Would he grow tired of her? Was she going to be his next, his last, love?

"She won't come home unexpected?"

He shook his head. The weather alone would have prevented his wife's return just yet. But Catherine was also settling an estate in Houston. She now owned a house, it seemed, one worth nearly a half million dollars. With it came a child who was at large, a delinquent who'd taken the opportunity of her mother's death to flee her boarding school. "I might like a kid who'd do that," Oliver had conceded. "I can sympathize with that." The privilege and private clubbiness of the East Coast. He recalled his own prickling resentment of that place, that it was mocking him, that it would never take him seriously.

Catherine had said, "So you should know why I have to try to find her."

"That part I'm not as confident about. That part I have some questions about."

He'd worked hard not to sigh over the girl, young Catherine. Could his wife not recall Miriam's complicated years? Or her own, for that matter? Teenage girls required the full attention of everyone in the house; they entered rooms as if strutting onto a stage, the eye-catching star with the biggest conflict in the production that was called All About Me.

The adults must have encouraged it, dressing them up, adoring their theatrics. First it was harmless, their favorite color pink, their preferred outfit the princess tutu and tiara, their venerated pet the kitten. They progressed through the rainbow, colors shifting from pink to purple to blue to green to, finally, black. From smiling affection and good humor and hugs and candy and fluffy kittens they moved to a sullen anger and ferocious affect that could sap the energy of an entire household. The piercings! The pet rats! The histrionics! Oliver shuddered. Teenage girls were graceless, moody, insecure, bad actors, annihilatingly melodramatic in the way of the suicide bomber: ready to claim collateral damage. What happened, he wondered, that allowed them to finally arrive at the lovely perfection of young womanhood? Something. A gentling. A dreamy distractedness, an unconscious maneuvering of their bodies, some stretch that came in their early twenties, the finishing touches. First love, perhaps, the initial inkling of a vast and untapped sex life. His daughter Miriam was an exception, her young womanhood somehow either truncated or pending; she'd gotten stuck in squalor and self-destruction. He hated to realize it, hated to know he could not cure it.

But the Sweetheart possessed that elusive young woman's charm. At times she became aware of his watching her, and she would stiffen, or oversexualize her movements. Yet at other times she inhabited the world like a very beautiful animal, without audience, a jaguar, a racehorse, muscles flexing beneath the flesh in every common gesture or exertion, head tossed in restless eagerness for what came next, a quality of excited readiness, availability, game.

Over and over he'd fallen for a young woman.

"I love you," he told the Sweetheart. Too often, perhaps.

"Me, too," she would say in reply.

The dogs were attracted to the snowshoes she'd removed, and had settled themselves on the floor mat where she'd left them, one on either side, identically flayed out with their back legs in what Catherine called the chicken drumsticks position, faces resting on their front paws, eyelined eyes staring intently at the people. If they could speak, they'd make insinuating, passive-aggressive remarks about his behavior; as people, Oliver wouldn't like them. They were busybodies, too clever, officious perky types who, anthropomorphized, would be beaming, freckled, bulky yet buff secretaries, gossiping and judging, fussy gay men or prissy spinsters.

But they made very fine dogs.

These days were a gift, an insular piece of stalled time. He and the Sweetheart had never spent more than a couple of hours together, never been capable of easy silence because they were accustomed to being rushed or being in public. The stories told after sex were not the same ones told after eating unheated English muffins. The banter in the kitchen of Wheatlands was not the same banter that evolved at the Scrabble board, where Oliver discovered that the Sweetheart was dyslexic and could not see the obvious words that practically made themselves on her slender rack of letters. The encouragement he offered was not the same as that he offered elsewhere.

Over the course of their strangely timeless interlude she grew more comfortable, or more weary of not being comfortable, or maybe she grew less in awe of his daunting gifts, those of experience and confidence, gender and power. She had, after all, the most powerful gifts of all: a long future and physical beauty; best of all, she also had no sense of how powerful those things were. Oliver had to be careful not to notify her of that.

In the afternoon they made love in Oliver's study, on the leather sofa in there. They lay afterward beneath a blanket, watching night fall outside, every now and then a distant crash as another tree dropped its exhausted freighted limbs. They drowsed in this cave of chill and dark, a forgotten peaceful space in the middle of a city-wide shutdown.

The phone rang much later. The house felt unfamiliar to Oliver, as if it wasn't his, as if he hadn't navigated it thousands of times before, dark or not. He realized as he stumbled in alarm from the study to the hall that he'd wakened thinking he was in his upstairs bedroom instead of downstairs on the sofa. He'd imagined Catherine in his arms rather than the Sweetheart. He only fully understood this when he followed the noise of the telephone rather than his spatial sense of where it ought to be. When he heard Catherine's voice there on it when he'd believed she was back in bed.

"Oliver, it's crazy, but I just got this bizarre call from the police in Wichita."

Now that he had oriented himself in the hallway, downstairs instead of up, Oliver had to reorient all over again: the police? Surely he wouldn't have been caught by them.

"Little Catherine," his wife was saying. "She's been found. She was driving a car somewhere off I-35, some place I never heard of called Freedonia, out in the sticks. Anyway, she's been found. She's fine."

The Sweetheart had made her way to him, silently. She stood with her head leaning against his shoulder, listening. Her face was bowed, as if to receive punishment, the cold light of the moon turning everything inside blue. Oliver had the urge to push the Sweetheart away, to shut a door between himself and her, to encounter this strange business on the telephone without distraction. He was having a hard time making sense of everything at once. An angry flare went up inside: this was age, his enemy, now disallowing him the ability to quickly adapt, to sync up one thing with another, to rise from a deep sleep into sudden chaos without suffering the slow machinery of mind and body refusing to fire at command. Napping synapses, sluggish muscles.

Catherine was still talking. Not all of what she was saying would adhere. He turned the phone slightly so that the Sweetheart could listen in. And it was she, when the call was over, who said back to him what he'd been told and not heard. Repeated to him his own part of the conversation, those things he'd agreed to do, those steps he would apparently be taking.

The girl was in El Dorado, twenty miles away, spending the night in a cell. "Your wife said they said Catherine was a flight risk," said the Sweetheart. "She said they said Catherine might have been suicidal, the way she was driving. She said she didn't tell them that Catherine probably just didn't know how to drive, she's only fifteen, and her mother died in a car crash not that long ago. She said she didn't want to complicate things by piling up a lot of extraneous details. But which one is Catherine?" the Sweetheart asked. "I thought your wife was Catherine."

"They're both Catherine."

"Well, no wonder there's so much confusion. You don't actually have to do anything until morning. Your wife said the forecast is for sunny and warm, and she said she thought the roads would be clear, so you could drive to El Dorado, to expedite. And she's going to get here as soon as she can. Tomorrow."

"Sunday?" he said.

"Today is Sunday. Tomorrow is Monday. And it's already clear," she pointed out. The resulting blue light contributed to the sensation of ice; the fire had completely burned out. The dogs stood by the back door, prepared to go outside, waving their stubby tails. Oliver held a flashlight and watched them tumble down the back steps like seals, seek purchase on the slick ground, quickly pee and then come skittering up once more. The moon shone relentlessly on everything, a cold gleaming landscape that looked as if it were all made of glass and could be shattered.

He asked Miriam to come with him because young Catherine was in possession of a car, and that car had to be driven away from the El Dorado dispatcher's yard. It relieved him to think that he could volunteer to take the clunker, allow Miriam and the stranger the luxury of his Saab. He had no interest in sitting in a confined space with an orphaned runaway teenage girl.

Not that driving with Miriam was very different.

Teenage Catherine would be acne-ridden, angry, and would smell awful. She might throw open the car door and roll out. Her ugly despair would seem contagious, and Oliver felt susceptible.

The Sweetheart had strapped herself into her snowshoes at dawn, ready to trek the distance between Oliver's home and Wheatlands. If the streets were going to melt, the restaurant would open. Brunch. And it would be packed, people sick with cabin fever, prepared to step back into the sunshine and spread their versions of their shared adversity. Already there'd been the slow spread of restored power; Oliver's microwave and coffee-maker clocks were blinking unset time at them in the kitchen, heat rising from the grates once again, various beeps resounding from all over the house as the technology came to life. From the curb, the Sweetheart had tossed his newspaper to Oliver, and then she disappeared down the block, steady and swift, a healthy young animal in motion.

Sure enough, by noon everything was a cheerfully dripping mess. Crews went from street to street piling fallen branches into a wood-chipping machine. Oliver took a Valium to calm himself, and then aimed the car for Miriam and Leslie's place. The roads were flowing with melt, patches of ice harmlessly slushing, people outside wandering and examining the strangely larger sky, all those pesky tree tops missing now.

"You're welcome," Miriam said, settling herself like a praying mantis in the leather seat. Her eyes were bloodshot, rimmed with last night's mascara.

The preemptive *You're welcome*; not an auspicious start. He willed himself not to bring up the man who'd been the last person to sit where she now sat, her naked friend, whose disposal, by the way, might have represented a favor Oliver had performed for her, his own unmentioned *You're welcome*, the exchange of transporting stinking strangers that would make them even. Instead he sighed.

"Got any ibuprofen in here?" she asked.

"No," he lied, unwilling to unlock the glove compartment for it.

She leaned her head back and used her palms to massage her bleary eyes. A few minutes later, she said, "No way you're adopting a child."

"Jury's out," he said. "Catherine's thinking of it as a moral quandary."

"But you don't think of it as a moral quandary?"

"Well, she wasn't bequeathed to me."

Miriam snorted, head wagging wearily as if she'd expected no better response from him. She could have said, "You never acted as if I was bequeathed to you, either." And she would have been sort of correct. Her mother was always trying to teach the lesson of kindness, not correctness, but Miriam would never be the proper audience for that. She was evidence, Oliver thought, of his and Leslie's supreme incompatibility. A child of such a union could never be whole or done.

The prairie outside town was more dramatically odd, more blindingly bright, after the storm, the devastation of ice and wind uninterrupted by houses and other human structures, the sun shining down without the shadows cast by those stronger, bulkier breaks in the landscape. It shone without warmth, merely brilliance, white now instead of last night's blue.

"Well, maybe Catherine will finally turn out to be a good mother," Miriam said. "Maybe she'll have a knack for it, this time. Maybe it'll be just what the doctor ordered."

"This time?" he said, then realized what she meant. He felt the familiar depleting tedious guilt. "Catherine was too young, back then. She was too young to know what to do with a teenager. Not just you, but any teenager."

"How hard could it be? I adored her."

He glanced over to see if she was joking. "You were always threatening to kill yourself."

"No, I wasn't."

"Yes. You were."

"Well, that's the way I must have felt," she said stubbornly. Oliver didn't think that she felt much different now.

"That's not easy to be a parent to, especially a stepmother." Nor for a father, not then, not now.

"No, you're wrong, that wasn't it. She was too smitten with you to pay attention to me. To anybody. Anybody but you."

"She was young," he repeated, although Miriam was right: he and Catherine had been preoccupied with each other. The intensity of the sweetheart. "Anyway, this girl, this current teenager, doesn't have a mother of her own at all. You had Leslie."

"Leslie," she said dismissively. "*You* got to divorce her. I didn't have that option."

"If you feel that way, you shouldn't be living with her, or working for her. I mean, feel free to hate her, but don't just take advantage. Don't take her love for granted," he said.

Miriam suddenly laughed. "Oh, please. As if you . . ." She shook her head. "Do not even *begin* to try to teach me how to not take love for granted." Oliver was on the verge of mentioning her friend the naked tattooed Adonis when Miriam went on, energized by self-righteousness, "You are such a fucking hypocrite! You with your mistress! As if you have any room to talk about 'taking love for granted'!"

Although he'd set the cruise control, Oliver now matched the acceleration in his heart with that of the gas pedal. Valium provided mild blunting, but still he noted his suddenly fluttering heartbeat in his larynx, the need to gasp as if to release pressure. "Excuse me?"

"'Excuse me,'" she mocked. "I should say 'mistresses,' plural. You are so fucking unbelievable. Do you really think it's such a secret? I've been watching you for a long time, Oliver. I know what you do. You find somebody, you marry her, and then after a while you get hooked up with somebody young enough to be your daughter. You are a walking, talking, big-ass complete cliché. You did it with Leslie. I mean, at first she *was* the younger woman, while you were married before to what's-her-face—HeeHaw? Fifi?—and then she was the one you left for a *different* younger woman, who was Catherine, and now you're doing it again. Do *not* try to deny it."

"YaYa," he said, when she seemed done. "First wife, YaYa." He wanted desperately to know how she knew about the Sweetheart, or *if* she knew, specifically, about *the* Sweetheart, particular, as opposed to *a* sweetheart, general. He wanted to know from which direction the assault was coming, which defense would have to be attended to.

"YaYa," she went on, "and the other discarded daughter. The first in the tradition. Or maybe not, maybe there were others? And also?" she said, not waiting for him to either refute or confirm predecessors to YaYa and Mary, "I knew about Catherine *way* before Leslie did, *way* before. When I was thir*teen*, I saw you and her one day. Skipping school at College Hill Park, I saw you in *our car* with her. You were making out like some kind of fuck-ing *teen*agers. And the really psycho thing about it was, I thought it was like you and *I* were doing something together against Leslie, that was my reaction, like she deserved it, me getting stoned and skipping school, and you with a girlfriend. I wanted to come be with you guys, you and me and the girlfriend against Leslie, against my mother. She was so innocent and upbeat and optimistic and . . . What's the word?"

"Guileless?" Oliver offered.

"Like that, times a hundred. So I never told her. I've never told her, to this day. And why should I? It's not like it'd help her. It isn't even *about* her, it's about you. This is *your* problem. I don't give a shit about telling Catherine. If she's too dumb to figure out who she's married to, well, that's just too bad. Why should I help? Where was she when *I* needed help? Being all obsessed with you, that's where. Let her get what she deserves."

The car shuddered beneath them. They were traveling at ninety-seven miles an hour on a road still patchy with black ice. Oliver lifted his foot, forced himself to breathe more slowly.

Miriam blew her nose on her sleeve. "Well, whatever," she said, more mildly. "I was thinking that you probably can't really help it. That it's some sort of addiction. And I know you hate that kind of jargonish diagnostic bullshit, and that you would rather die than go to some twelve-step meeting of sex addicts— you hate being categorized into any kind of group, I know that about you, Oliver, be*lieve* me—and sit there telling your story, but really, I guess it might be helpful to think of it as an illness rather than as a—" She left off again.

"Betrayal?" Oliver offered.

"Moral flaw," Miriam countered. "I mean, an illness can be cured. Whereas a moral flaw . . . So, anyway, just don't go around telling me that I take love for granted, okay? That is just *so* not going to be something you're allowed to do." She had pulled her long skinny legs up and was hugging them under her chin, the flexible self-contained gesture of a teenager. "You and me," she said blandly, staring out the window. "Not very different, huh?"

Oliver watched the road. The weekend seemed to have added a decade to him; Catherine's trip had set off some very strange days. When he glanced in the rearview mirror, his face seemed worried, panic of a specific type etched there, the panic of an old person losing control.

He'd never have guessed that he would be relieved to finally meet up with Cattie Mueller.

SPRING

CHAPTER 13

"WHY DID YOU run away?" Catherine asked the girl.

Cattie hadn't immediately answered. This pensiveness drove Oliver mad, but Catherine appreciated it. And even Oliver had to concede that Cattie was perhaps the only person he knew under the age of forty who didn't use "like" in every sentence she spoke. It was one of the first things he trained out of his elite squad of drones. That, and "you guys," which the upperclass patron did not like to be called.

"I don't think I *did* run away," she finally responded. Her silence had forced Catherine to consider the question herself, so that when she answered, Catherine understood. The boarding school hadn't been home. Wherever Cattie had been that wasn't her home, that wasn't with her mother, could not be a place from which she was running away. The sadness of the girl's situation was sadder still because Cattie didn't seem to find it sad. "She's so stoic!" Catherine cried to Oliver.

"It'll serve her well," he said dryly. He didn't respond to unpretty girls; he'd had a hard time with young Miriam, when she lived with them, so hell-bent was she on being ugly in both body and spirit. Since Cattie had moved in with them, he was taking himself away from the house earlier in the morning and returning later in the evening. In part this was because Catherine no longer had time to check in on his businesses for him. She also felt a purposefulness that had nothing to do with him, a new challenge for her charms, this girl she wished to befriend.

"It's nice to actually be needed," she tried to explain to Oliver.

"I need you," he replied.

When she faced him, she was shaking her head, aware that what she would say next would not be taken by him the way she meant it, seriously. "No, you don't."

He'd shrugged, lightly, but Catherine felt her words take up residence inside her.

"I actually really like that your dog's name is Bitch," she confided one morning to Cattie. "It's fun to yell it out the door." It was also fun to watch her husband flinch. Coarseness offended him, and somehow Catherine was enjoying that fact. It reminded her of the pleasure of tormenting her mother, once-upon-a-time, with the spectacle of Misty. Oliver had, however, helped distribute Bitch's puppies to his employees. The last two went to Miriam. The Desplaines' corgis, like the Desplaines themselves, were trying to adapt to this new addition to their formerly simple, coupled life, this strange dog named Bitch.

Catherine watched once as Cattie had encountered the fat corgi brothers splayed on their backs, white bellies soft and unprotected, confidently snoozing. Cattie had knelt and slapped those exposed bellies, alarming both dogs.

"Why'd you do that?" Catherine asked, oddly injured by the gesture, sensing that she herself was similarly undefended against an abrupt and hurtful assault.

"I don't know," the girl had said. "It just seemed like they were asking for it." A moment later she said, "Bitch would never leave herself open like that."

"True," Catherine said, considering. Like Cattie, Bitch seemed happiest to be left alone; like Cattie, she did not require pampering or privileges. She slept where she was told to sleep, ate what she was given to eat, displayed minimal enthusiasm or preference, yet also did not complain. She did not require a fenced yard; she had escaped the one in the back only to come around and sit on the front stoop. She didn't wish to run away, but she also did not wish to be penned. This subtle distinction appealed to Catherine. Cattie herself was like that, leaving the house on foot, without bothering to notify anyone, to wander around the neighborhood. She took Bitch, who did not require a leash. So far, she and the dog had chosen to return to the house. Both appeared to be taking note, waiting to see, making no sudden moves.

Dick Little and Catherine spoke every few days. Soon he would hire movers to store the personal belongings of Misty and Cattie Mueller, and rent their place furnished to an intern at MD Anderson. "I don't want to sell it," the girl had said, about her house. "But I don't need to go there right now."

She had not been running away, she'd been running home.

She had been headed there, but then she'd changed her mind. For one night she'd slept at Catherine's house in Wichita while Catherine was sleeping in her house in Houston. That night before the day they met in person, Catherine had lain in the dark under the skeleton mural, imagining the girl lying in the dark in her bedroom, in a bed once occupied by Misty, a girl who must certainly be imagining Catherine.

"And these were our lockers, senior year."

Cattie had trailed along after Catherine to visit two other sets of lockers, on the first floor, on the second, now on the third. To herself, she noted that on the one hand, the building reminded her of Lamar High, in Houston, and on the other, that here in Wichita nobody had to pass through a metal detector, under the eye of a security guard, and that the students apparently were permitted to use their lockers, whereas in Houston, there'd been a detector, a guard, and a locker ban. Row after row of chained lockers, student after student hobbling around under a fifty-pound backpack.

Cattie text-messaged Ito: *Back in the public sector, yo.*

Seek the geek, he responded. *The freak, the meek.*

The chic?

Never the chic!

Catherine was leading the tour the way she led all tours of her hometown: cheerful rendition followed by unfortunate sidebar. Everywhere, it seemed, had dual significance, heads *and* tails. "It's funny, isn't it?" she'd told Cattie one day in the car. "I've lived here my whole life . . . well, not *yet*, I guess." She laughed as she corrected herself. She had a habit of that, too, anticipating being corrected and doing it before someone else could. But Cattie wouldn't have. "Anyway, I've never lived anywhere but Wichita, so everywhere I go, every street I drive down or any building I go into, or whatever, there's about fifty different ways to think about it. Well, not fifty, but at least two. Like right there?" She had pointed randomly at a tall monument. "See that? That's a memorial for the football team that died in a plane crash, like in 1970 or something, but it's also where me and Misty got simultaneous food poisoning, we just screamed to a stop at the statue and puked out the car doors." The landmark passed. "We were working at Dog-n-Shake back then, eating free food every night. We called it Arf-and-Barf," she added, smiling.

Now, in the East High hall, she told Cattie about the puff science class of twenty-five years past—"Aeronautics! The teacher reminded us of the Pillsbury Doughboy! He actually wept when our weather balloon wrapped around a No Parking sign instead of becoming airborne!"—and then rolling out her lower lip as she provided the B side of that memory—"I felt terrible when I learned that his only child was hydrocephalic!" But quickly she rallied, reminded of the best friends' forays into choir, photography, drama, and something called Peer Leadership, at which Misty had failed by fighting with the facilitator on day one and bursting open a beanbag chair.

"Beanbag chairs!" Catherine laughed. "They were everywhere back then."

Hanging around with her, Cattie felt oftentimes as if the roles were reversed, that she was the grown-up and Catherine was the kid. Or that they were both neither, some new form of tweener. With odd titles; at the front desk downstairs, Catherine had rambled on trying to explain their relationship, settling on "I'm her guardian."

"I'm her charge," Cattie had said. The boy aide had looked up appreciatively as if for handcuffs; he seemed to think she was dangerous. Maybe she *was* dangerous, Cattie considered; there was nothing to prevent her from becoming so.

Over all, Catherine was loving their stroll around East; apparently she hadn't visited the place since graduating in 1979. "Your mom and I were on the softball team for about ten minutes," she said. "So we missed picture day." The team looked out from a black-and-white photograph in a dank hallway, feathered hairstyles, rows of bare knees bracketing a large trophy. "Miriam was on the track team," she said, moving a few photos down, and sure enough, there was the stepdaughter, rail-thin and scowling. "She was sleeping with the coach," Catherine said sadly. "Remember that street where the bar was that I showed you? Lucky's?"

Cattie nodded. The bar that had been Catherine and Misty's illicit hangout. Also? That same bar had once been a filling station, and Misty's uncle—what was his name? Bud?—had been a grease monkey there, much further back in history.

"Luther," Cattie said. She'd heard about her mother's uncle Luther.

"Right, Luther, he worked at that station that turned into Lucky's, and then Misty and I went to Lucky's, the place where the BTK might have visited, staking out his victim across the street. Her and her brother, the one who got shot in the head. Twice. And survived." On and on it went, her conversation style like the kids' song about the flea on the wing on the fly on the frog on the bump on the log in the hole in the middle of the sea. The neighborhood near the university, the university where the dorms were, the dorms where Catherine had lived, and before she lived in the dorms, she and Misty had made prank calls to the place. And also the playground on that street, where Catherine's parents had taken her, when she was very young, to participate in a peace march, and Catherine had stepped on a bee and her mother was furious that they were forced to miss the march.

Not so far from the airplane crash memorial, the Arf-and-Barf poisoning.

For Catherine, Wichita was a big bag of loose yarn, ensnared connections that knotted together the past and the present without clear cause and effect or pattern. Cattie couldn't make sense of it yet, but she was good at listening, patient at untangling. "Anyway, that bar and the playground are on the same street where Miriam's track coach lived. He was also the government teacher, but that's kind of beside the point, I guess. Miriam used to babysit for his two little kids. Isn't that kind of weird, her taking care of the kids, then sleeping with their dad? Poor Miriam, high school was more horrible for her than for me and Misty, I think."

"Yeah," Cattie agreed. She could certainly imagine that was true. Ever since their ride from the El Dorado sheriff's office in January, Miriam had decided she would make Cattie her project. "What was *your* jail like?" Miriam had asked, en route to Wichita that hard bright first day.

"Like a dog pen," Cattie told her. "It even had dogs." All night there'd been somebody just around the corner of the cell, the sound of turning pages to keep Cattie company. She tried to explain that a guard wasn't necessary. But like Miriam, the cops seemed to prefer dramatic possibility. "They thought I was going to kill myself," Cattie told her. "They took my shoelaces. They took Bitch's leash." Then Cattie had realized what Miriam wanted her to say next. "What was *your* jail like?" she complied.

Miriam's jail, of course, had been much much worse. Possession, intent to sell, a couple of parents who couldn't be reached, cellmates who wished to injure her.

This kind of exchange repeated itself on Sundays, when Cattie worked at the spa cleaning. Miriam followed her around pretending to be a big sister but actually just hoping to hear Cattie complain about Oliver. Miriam loved to hate her father, or maybe it was that she hated to love him, or both. At any rate, Miriam had recently adopted two of Bitch's puppies, so Cattie felt some obligation to be friendly. She allowed the sister act, although the woman was at least twice her age, and was apparently oblivious to the kinds of remarks that seemed insensitive. As in: "He might as well have been a sperm donor, for all the time he spent with me." Why, Cattie wondered, would you say this to a girl who had no father whatsoever? Whose mother had recently died? Nevertheless, she listened. She said, "Really?" when it seemed it was her turn to speak. Or "Exactly," because that was another word that occupied space and helped conversation roll along without uncomfortable silent gaps.

After their chat about jail, Cattie had opened the glove compartment of Oliver's car. Miriam was filling the tank, and Cattie, curious, had simply removed the Saab key from the ignition, unlocked the box lock, and quickly caught the clutter of pill bottles that spilled from the interior. Miriam was gleeful to discover everything that was wrong with her father's health. "Heart, prostate, cholesterol, anxiety, depression, erectile dysfunction!" she hooted. "He's just another old man!"

Not having known him very long at that point—all of the twenty minutes it had taken to have him spring her from the El Dorado sheriff's office—Cattie wasn't prepared to judge yet. But yes, he did appear to be a man heading toward elderly. His hair was white, his face was wrinkled, his teeth were yellow. However, he owned a nice car with heated leather seats and was willing to drive the stinking vehicle of Ito's so that the girls could take his. His mouth made a sour expression when he saw the dogs, but still he climbed behind the wheel.

Miriam and Cattie had each taken a Valium before restoring the pills to the box.

At Oliver and Catherine's house it was Miriam's old bedroom that Cattie now occupied. Guest quarters, Catherine's overflow closet. "*He* wouldn't let me decorate it," Miriam told her. "Catherine would have, but Oliver doesn't like real colors, only things that are variations on *tan*. Oatmeal. Ecru. Almond."

"He seems to be okay with black," Cattie had said.

"Yeah, the other not-a-real-color color." *Get over it*, said Misty in Cattie's head. *What are you, ten years old? Grow the fuck up.*

Last Sunday Miriam had offered to supply Cattie with hashish. "There's terrible stuff out there," she explained. "I wouldn't want you to end up in a coma from smoking formaldehyde, so let me know, promise?" Cattie agreed; again, it was easier to go along than to try to convince the woman she didn't particularly want drugs.

With whom, exactly, would she smoke hashish?

Soon enough, Cattie might matriculate here at this school where Miriam and Catherine and Misty had. The East High mascot was the Flying Aces, colors blue and white. The English teacher was the same woman who'd taught Catherine. "Misty and I were very rarely in the same classes," Catherine said now, blushing. Cattie knew why; her mother had followed the remedial track. Left behind in an early grade, her mother had been perceived as a girl who would thrive in the vo-tech halls, out in those outbuildings filled with budding auto mechanics, welders, carpenters, motel managers. In her future was a uniform and a name tag, some functional outfit that could be easily laundered to wash the unsavory yet essential fluids that would stain it. "She was really good at fixing cars," Catherine said, apparently trying to prop up Misty's high school image. "She could talk to guys really easily." Sometimes, however, Misty had been mistaken for one of them.

"I used to get that, too," said Cattie, knowing Catherine was interested in knowing. "Before boobs."

"People are insensitive."

"My mom would say the same thing," Cattie replied. *Dipshits*, her mother said in Cattie's head. *Assholes*.

At the heavy door of a room marked "Health," Catherine said, "This was where the pregnant girls took classes, them and the moms with their little kids! It was so hilarious having babies and toddlers at school. And Misty kept flunking PE, so she ended up in Pregnant PE one semester. All they did was walk around the football field for an hour. Her and a bunch of fat black girls." Catherine slapped both hands over her mouth, looking around the empty hall in case there were fat black girls anywhere nearby to take offense. "They *were* all black," she confided quietly.

"White girls get abortions," Cattie said.

"Really?" Catherine said, furrowing her brow. This wasn't an act, Cattie had discovered. The woman actually did not know some fairly basic stuff. "I guess that's what *I* did," she conceded. "Twice, in fact. But not in high school, just after. That guy I told you about who was a professor? Who worked with my mom at the U?"

Cattie nodded; probably she'd heard about him. Probably he was going to come up again, anyway, some other stray and dangling part of the snarl, another bump on the log.

"Well, him. Him and me at Planned Parenthood." Catherine sighed. "Downtown round the block from Kansa Karma. Anyway, those babies would be in their twenties. Good God. I might have ended up a faculty spouse."

"You'd probably be divorced," Cattie said. "By now."

Catherine laughed, and then went serious, and Cattie knew what was coming next, what motherhood made her think of.

"It's slightly difficult to imagine your mother as a mother," Catherine had told her when they met. "No offense." Cattie's response then was like her response now: a shrug that meant *none taken*. Catherine was only reiterating the same surprise Misty herself had been marveling over for as long as Cattie could recall. Never in anybody's wildest dreams had Misty Mueller seemed like a future mother. *Who'da thunk it?* she would say with the lopsided grin she called her village idiot face.

But if it was hard imagining Misty as a mother, it was at least as difficult for Cattie to imagine her mother with this woman as a friend. Catherine was pretty, for one thing, and moved in the way that pretty women moved, as if being observed, her simplest actions—rinsing dishes, starting the car, pulling fruit from bins at the grocery, touching her own face—laden with self-consciousness. See my pretty hair, her tossed head said. Look at my pretty nails, her posed fingers demanded as they touched any- and everything. She applied lipstick whenever she left the house, blotting, kissing, wiping away excess with her thumb, then applied it again fifteen minutes later when she turned off the car engine. She consulted a mirror with regularity—the one by the telephone, the one in the bathroom, the one by the front door, the one attached to the windshield. Why did she care what she looked like while talking on the phone, before retrieving the newspaper on the front porch, when visiting her mother at the nursing home? But because it mattered to her, it seemed to matter in general. Catherine often asked the opinion of both her husband and Cattie. "This one or this one?" she would say, standing with a different shoe on either foot, or with two separate panty-hose possibilities, a leg in mesh, a leg in something footless, the limp other halves hanging like tails.

The husband always had an opinion.

"Which is more comfortable?" Cattie would ask.

"Neither is actually comfortable," Catherine would say.

"Comfortable is sweatpants," said the husband. "Comfortable is giant T-shirts and plastic shoes. Comfortable is giving up."

"My mom wore sweatpants," Cattie said, just to get an apology out of him. He also enjoyed mirrors. *Gaylord*, her mother would have named Oliver. "Never trust a man who weighs less than you," she'd advise.

Her mother was a force around her, a series of impressions and thoughts that protected Cattie. She resorted to them daily. Would it go away, this voice that had become her constant helpful companion? Was it the fact of her mother's old stomping grounds, this city and school and former best friend, that had made Misty come so vividly to Cattie, to displace the anonymous narrator of her old life?

And did that voice explain why she and Catherine seemed so often to be thinking alike? For instance: the serial killer had recently revealed that an old cold-case murder was actually another of his victims. She hadn't been bound, this woman found beneath a bridge a decade ago, but she'd been his nonetheless. When Cattie and Catherine saw the victim's middle-aged son on television, weeping to have his mother's murder made at least one step closer to solved, they turned to each other and said, "He looks just like Dick Little!"

"The freckles," they went on, in tandem. And the earring, they added.

"Pretty soon you two won't have to talk at all," said Catherine's husband over the top of his magazine. "It'll be telepathic. Catherine and Catherine Junior." Cattie had texted Ito then: *This guy hates my guts.* Ito's sedan sat at the curb, a blight; the El Dorado police had kindly not impounded it, although its papers were not quite up-to-date. And Oliver had made a point of returning Ito's car keys to Cattie. Coming from Catherine, it would have been a gesture of trust; from Oliver, it seemed nothing more obvious than an invitation for her to get behind the wheel and drive away.

Not yet, she often thought.

Catherine hadn't known exactly what else to do with the girl, and so had begun their drives around the city, those places where Misty and she had spent their time, the junior high, Catherine's old home, the well-manicured park where their elementary school had once stood, and across from it, the grandmother's house.

"That's where the family was killed," Catherine had said. It was another bitter day; the wind had swept everything and everybody away, sky and sidewalk exactly the same cement color, some irritable gray geese plodding around. The shades at the dead people's house were drawn, their trees were bare. Misty's grandmother's home, three doors down, was nearly identical. "Innocuous enough, huh?" Catherine said.

"Which?" asked Cattie.

"Gosh, both, I suppose."

Stigmatized, Misty said in Cattie's head. "Yeah, pretty ordinary looking." In real estate, there was a dilemma selling houses in which something awful had happened. Some buyers—maybe most—were uneasy at the thought of living in a place tainted by tragedy. "Horror house," Misty would have said. Realtors were obligated by law to tell prospective buyers, but only if those buyers knew to ask. Most didn't, a fact that Misty had found surprising. "I would," she'd confided in Cattie. "I for damn sure know what can go on in a house."

"There was always somebody home at your mom's house," Catherine told her. "There would have been somebody there, that day the family was killed."

My relatives? scoffed Misty. *They wouldn't piss on you if you were on fire.* Cattie studied the two places. The only survivor of the massacre was the family's guard dog, but then he'd been put down the next day by the police. Miriam had told Cattie that. Miriam was an expert on the BTK situation. *Ironic,* said her mother flatly, in her mind.

"It's a whole new generation of owners," Catherine said, of both of the desolate-looking homes. "You wanna knock on the door? Get a tour?"

"Of which?" But before Catherine could say, Cattie declined wanting to visit either house.

Catherine had stared across the street at the geese strutting around, their abrasive honking audible over the car heater. "At that school that used to be there, your mom and I hated each other. Absolutely *hated.* Oh my God." It was another two-sided thing, Cattie thought. Like everything else in Wichita, its streets and buildings and people, even their friendship provoked in Catherine a knotted multiplicity.

A sudden bleeping alarm sounded at East High, and the doors of the hall's rooms banged open, releasing wave after wave of human noise and motion. Cattie and Catherine flattened themselves against the wall across from the hallowed senior lockers, watching as students surged by, nobody seeming to notice the two of them. In general, these students looked precisely like the ones from Houston. Cattie felt the familiar invisibility that she'd lost when she moved to St. Sincere. This school would not trouble her, nor she it.

And also? She could simply walk away. Having done it once,

she knew she could do it again. At night, as had always been her habit, she sometimes left the Desplaines' house and walked the neighborhood. Once, upon returning home, she'd found Oliver in his Saab, retrieving pills, she supposed. When he looked up and saw her, she froze. His expression had three stages: first surprise, next hostility, and, finally, smooth professionalism. "I, too, am an insomniac," he said. No mention of the potential harm that might befall a girl out alone in the night, no threat of punishment. He probably wouldn't mind if something did happen to Cattie. She certainly didn't have to worry that he'd concern Catherine with it.

"He could never have stood a son," Miriam had said of her father. "He can hardly stand *me*. But a younger, more handsome version of himself? Forget it. He has a mirror, if he needs to see himself."

In the crowded school hallway, Catherine sighed. "You could always just get a GED."

Why didn't anybody tell me at the beginning? Misty's voice responded. *If you could pass a test in a couple of hours, why in the name of God spend three years in this hellhole?*

"How is it that a little test could be the same as all that time in high school?"

"I was thinking the exact same thing," Catherine called out. "It's totally retarded, isn't it?"

When the halls finally cleared, the two of them found a different swirling tempest in the parking lot, where the wind tore Catherine's umbrella inside out and blew her dress up above her thighs. They ran to her car and sat in it watching the waves of sleety water break across its windshield, the wipers frozen to the glass in mid-motion. "Do you mind if we just sit?" Catherine asked. "I've never liked driving in this stuff."

"I don't mind." They both glanced upward as the hail began, pellets pinging off the roof and hood.

"Wow," Catherine said. "You never know what's gonna fall out of the sky here. Your mom and me, we used to get lunch out of the vending machines, like a Snickers and a Coke—my mom would have had a cow if she knew what I ate—and then come sit in Misty's car for an hour. Right in this same parking lot." Catherine waved at the water-drenched sea of vehicles around them. "Or sometimes we'd go downtown to our silly apartment." Catherine had already driven Cattie by the building. Which, coincidentally, was in the exact same building that one of Catherine's dentists' offices had been in, ages earlier. "You could still sort of smell that dentist-office odor, like drilled teeth, you know? He was called Dr. Tusk!" And one of Oliver's first businesses turned out to be on the ground floor of that precise same building, its ribbon-cutting probably going on at just about the time Catherine and Misty were renting the apartment on an upper floor, storing vodka and orange juice in its sad little refrigerator. A brown-brick high-rise by the river, a great location for a restaurant because it had a view. And that had reminded Catherine of canoeing in the river, she and Misty and two twins, Ron and Don, she told Cattie. The Twinkies. They had taken those boys to prom that year ("They had *bald* spots, they were so not the right age for prom! They wore *leisure* suits!") but then ditched them early and went to a cop bar, after hours. Naturally, strangely enough, or maybe not so strangely, one of those same cops ended up giving Oliver a ticket about ten years later. Catherine recognized him. Hole, sea, bump, log . . .

Cattie had begun braiding together the city as Catherine recalled it, one curious strand at a time, today aided by the icy blur the windshield view provided her. She knew that the bakery Oliver had opened last fall was previously the place where Catherine's father had bought his cars. Catherine had gone there with him every few years, dressed up, in order to trade for the latest model. Catherine's mother didn't believe in American-made cars, but her dad's dad was a Ford dealer, so for once he got his way. "He was brand-loyal," Catherine had told her, smiling wanly at Cattie.

Apropos of nothing obvious, Catherine now turned to Cattie and asked, "Do you think it's pathetic, to only have lived here?"

"No," Cattie said.

"You know that apartment downtown? Misty and I rented it under an alias. It was both our names. Catherine Mueller."

"My name," Cattie said.

"Yeah!" Catherine said happily. "I just realized that."

The sleet was slacking off, and the wipers, which had been straining all along under its attack, suddenly broke free and smacked away again.

"Funnily enough," Catherine said, "it was Misty who left Wichita, not me." And she was crying then, although Cattie didn't know why. Another of those two-sided things.

Funnily enough, she said to herself, knowing her mother would also have found the phrase amusing.

CHAPTER 14

PROFESSOR EMERITUS YASMIN KEENE passed away on a stormy March evening, "peacefully in her sleep," according to the obituary. Catherine couldn't fathom the woman going peacefully anywhere. She pictured the scary black walking stick, thrashing wildly about as its owner swirled below it into the after-life. Like somebody sucked into a cesspool. It was an image she would have happily shared with Cattie, had they been alone in the car, but refrained since they weren't. Yasmin's funeral service was being held at the same cemetery where Catherine's father had been buried. "Same place where I learned to drive," she chose to announce as they headed there.

"I had a driving lesson at a graveyard," Cattie offered. *Funnily enough*, they'd taken to saying to each other. She and Catherine sat in the back seat of Oliver's vehicle, while Oliver and Grace Harding occupied the front. Those two were like the parents, Catherine thought; every now and then her husband shape-shifted very briefly in her mind, to an old man, and when it hap-pened she felt a strange spasm in her chest. Shame, or something akin to it. Pity? She was about to postulate aloud that Misty might have gotten the cemetery driving idea from Catherine's family, and also that Misty herself had seemed to be someone born with the ability to drive. But then she realized that Misty had died in a car, and held her tongue. The irony was notable, but not necessary to point out.

"I could teach you to drive," Oliver offered. Catherine and Cattie exchanged glances; so far as they could remember, he hadn't been alone with the girl since the first night she'd spent at their home.

"Okay," she said.

Yasmin Keene's son the physician had called Catherine to tell her the news, then requested her mother's phone number so that he could notify her at the nursing home. Yasmin's daughter the professor of gender studies had written the obituary, citing Grace Harding as a survivor and "esteemed colleague of many years." Yasmin's son the curator of an art museum in Tulsa brought Yasmin's genius grandchildren to pay a visit to Dr. Harding at Green Acres. Yasmin's daughter the lesbian psychologist planned to endow a scholarship at the local U in her mother's name.

Catherine sighed, staring at the back of her own mother's head. When she died, what would Catherine have to offer as a legacy? Not only had Catherine not accumulated particular status or honors, her mother's only two potential grandchildren had been aborted, without her knowledge, decades ago. At the cemetery, Dr. Grace Harding's plot already existed, right next to Catherine's father, name and birth date engraved with an empty space beside it, waiting like a blank on a quiz to be filled in.

When Catherine told Cattie that they were going to a funeral, she'd made it clear the girl did not have to join them. "I'd like you to come," she confessed. "For one thing, I think it'd be nice for my mom to get to know you better." For another, she did not say, I would relish the company.

Cattie was amenable. The whole idea of family was a novelty

to her, a curiosity she had some unbiased interest in. Maybe she already understood that Catherine liked to have her around, that when Cattie was with her, she had an ally. Maybe the girl would grow as fond of Catherine as Catherine had grown of her. This wasn't the child she would have given birth to, she knew that; there'd have been rebellion and annoyance, from that child, by this point—anything but alliance. Yet Cattie was a teenager for whom Catherine had a lot of affection and understanding. Without consulting Oliver, they'd gone together and gotten tiny matching tattoos on their ankles, simple yellow and brown sunflowers, a tiny green stem with a single leaf.

"Kansas state symbol," Catherine said. "I always loved sunflowers."

Cattie nodded. "Yeah, not too feminine, for a flower."

"Hairy," Catherine agreed. "Woody."

Oliver thought tattoos were vulgar.

Now Catherine remembered something. She was about to mention it, the car trip her parents and she and Misty had taken to Colorado, during the summer of the bicentennial. The trip where the three Hardings had loaded down their traveling companion with more information than she'd known what to do with, one bit of which concerned sunflowers, the appealing way they always faced and followed the sun, a living demonstration ongoing alongside the two-lane highway as they traveled west.

Her mother the feminist, Catherine thought, might have appreciated having a not-girly girl. She might have enjoyed somebody like Cattie, or Misty, for that matter, had she been around early enough to influence them, love them. They might have been much more rewarding as daughters to Professor Grace Harding. She might have been able to shape them into citizens like those offspring of Yasmin Keene, serious people with unflinching facial expressions.

Yasmin's children had had their mother cremated; her ashes

would be placed, fittingly enough, in an outdoor vertical structure like a bookcase. Her children's father rested just above her on that marble shelf system, a man she'd never married nor lived with, but who'd remained the children's dutiful father nonetheless. Nylon Parker the Third, he was named; Catherine had forgotten about him, his timid presence now and then at some social occasion, a man who took up half the space of his partner, both literally and figuratively. Catherine wondered if the urn that held him was also smaller than Yasmin's.

Nylon Parker the Fourth began the series of comments that would comprise Yasmin's internment ceremony. Catherine had been handed the script her mother wished to contribute, a paragraph-length document that read more like a curriculum vita than a eulogy, and which contained not one shred of wit, affection, anecdote, or warmth. Yet she knew that her mother had loved Yasmin. What else could it be named? Even now, standing in a stiff wind wearing the same black dress she wore to every funeral she'd attended as an adult, Dr. Harding seemed better prepared to deliver a lecture than to offer mourning. When Catherine's father had died, she'd not cried publicly. She'd stood in the same outfit then as now, surrounded by many of the same personnel, stoic and composed. Later Catherine had found her with her head on the kitchen table, inconsolable, unable to stop sobbing. Yet when Catherine fell upon her in sympathy, prepared to join her in a cathartic tender moment, her mother had turned a distorted and inflamed face at her, furious at having her privacy breached. "Go away!" she'd screamed at Catherine. "Leave me alone!"

It seemed she would never be the daughter her mother might have wished for.

The four children offered their thoughts, as did a few of the surviving generation of professors and administrators who had made up the university's former society. There was chuckling affirmation of Yasmin's crusty personality, acknowledgment of her dedication and drive. Her children all commented on how fierce she'd been, and how much they'd resented and then been grateful for her tough love. Her colleagues had similar emotions; they respected her ferocity, they appreciated her contributions even as they sometimes found themselves on the wrong end of the stick. "Literally," Catherine whispered to herself. That horrible walking stick.

Then it was Catherine's turn to speak. She stepped forward, leaving her mother to lean on Oliver, and read what Dr. Harding had written, the list of accolades and honors and successes. They'd already been mentioned, more or less, so the group merely nodded. Then Catherine paused, looking up from the flapping paper in her hand. To Nylon Parker the Fourth, she addressed her final remarks: "Your mom terrified me," she confessed. "Really. And I'm pretty sure she didn't like me very much. I was not her kind of girl. Not her kind of person at all, actually. But she loved my mother. And I know my mother also loved her, and needed her, and will miss her. Your mother made a lot of contributions to the community, like everybody here is saying, but she also meant a whole lot to my mother. My mother can't say so, but it's true." Can't, and wouldn't, Catherine knew. *Tough*, she said in her head to her mother. *Tough titties.*

She chose not to step back next to her original spot beside her glowering mother but beside neutral Cattie; she had been naughty, and she now sought shelter. The girl pulled her hair from her face and squinted curiously. As another speaker stepped forward to add to the collection of comments, Cattie said in a low voice to Catherine, "Was there a funeral for *my* mother?"

Oliver had expected his ex-wife Leslie to attend the internment, since she'd taken classes from Dr. Keene when she'd matriculated at the U, passing through women's studies in her meandering quest for self-knowledge, but he didn't anticipate Miriam's being with her. And at first he hadn't recognized the man who accompanied them, a tall guy wearing a gray driver's cap. It was like Miriam to do something inappropriate like bring a date to a funeral. And then to cling to the man as if in heat, as if she simply could not wait to return to bed.

Then Oliver realized who the man was. The tattooed Adonis. Who, today, was dressed exactly like Oliver himself. Respectable citizen. Mourner. Miriam glanced at her father challengingly, tongue in the handsome guy's ear. So Oliver hadn't been doing her a favor when he disposed of the trash. In her black pea coat and tight black pants she resembled an aging male rock star, complete with taunting expression and dark-circled eyes, the hovering notion of concealed weaponry.

She certainly seemed capable of setting off a bomb in his life. She and her sidekick.

Beside the two of them, Leslie gazed serenely around herself, her usual bland smile on her lips. She'd greeted Dr. Harding by putting her cheek to either side of the woman's face, a strange gesture suggesting both Europe and felines. His ex-wife, the French kitty. Again and again, she'd insisted that Dr. Harding would enjoy a treatment at the spa, imploring Oliver to recommend it, to bring his mother-in-law to her. But he knew otherwise. Grace would never allow herself an indulgence like the one Leslie offered; she would decry anybody who chose to commit time or money to such a thing. Like Oliver, she'd been raised in the years following the Great Depression, back when *depression* meant a national economic crisis rather than a personal psychological one. Her generation, *his,* had been schooled in selfless rather than selfish acts. Leslie could not be expected to understand Grace Harding's stubbornness on the subject; she'd been born later, in an easier decade that had followed that tough one.

Moreover, undressing in a small room to allow another person

access to her body could never be anything but a medical procedure, at this point, for Grace. When her husband had died, Oliver understood, so had her sensual life. That had been almost ten
years ago, at a time when she was younger than he was now. In
the past, he might have congratulated himself on not having suc-
cumbed to the calcified ways of his old nemesis, this by-marriage
relative. But over the past weeks he'd come to respect her resolute
obstinacy. It seemed less like a limitation than a virtue, character-
wise, these days. He knew exactly how she would respond, and
why, and she was dependable as a result. He was learning to admire dependability, given how much seemed in flux around him.
His wife and her new pet the teenager; his unsettling daughter
with her arsenal of ticking information about him; his Sweetheart, who was returning fewer and fewer of his messages, with
whom he hadn't been alone in more than a week.

There were these two Italian bread-makers who were conduct-
ing classes in sourdough. Something about the way the Sweetheart had spoken about them . . .

When Oliver had last said he loved her, she'd murmured as-
sent rather than enunciating the words. It had been a mistake to
fantasize about leaving Catherine for the Sweetheart; in the
logic of love's magical thinking, sending his wife away with her
new venture—her sudden parenthood of Cattie Mueller—had
doomed the plausible reality. How remarkable it was that lovers
ever found one another; how astonishingly unlikely it was that
they would endure as a couple past the fitful business of first-
blush lust and sweaty secret assignations. He'd allowed himself
to envision a future with the Sweetheart, one in which Catherine joined the ranks of his ex-wives, that exclusive club. He had
fancied himself lucky that Cattie had arrived to offset his depar-
ture, the crisis of the orphaned girl effectively trumping that of
the philandering husband. Could he actually have thought that
he'd *blame* the girl for coming between him and Catherine?

Yes, he could. Now he looked toward the girl; she looked right back, as usual.

When Catherine departed from the written remarks Grace had provided, when she chose to conclude the dignified send-off with a gushy rush of sap, Oliver felt like seconding his mother-in-law in her grunting disapproval. "Hopeless," he leaned over to announce in her ear. "Absolutely hopeless. Dr. Keene would have understood, I'm sure."

He'd never have been brave or kind enough to do such a thing in his previous relationship with the woman. But he thought she appreciated his words now. Now that she had none of her own to offer in return. He vowed that when she died, when it was he at this cemetery standing before the stone that would bear her finished official data, surrounded by whatever-number of her remaining acquaintances, he would recite her worldly accomplishments, those and nothing more. People of their generation, people who'd been raised on the prairie or in the Dust Bowl, who'd performed their jobs in service of the greater good, did not require a public airing of, or praise for, their feelings. A lot could be said for not saying anything.

They all looked alike, soldiers. They all looked like Randall. So Cattie saw Randall everywhere, the military uniform entering the liquor store, exiting the grocery, a whole parade of them marching past East High. "PTSD," she would whisper to herself; his friend who'd celebrated himself to death. How else to explain? Who didn't have some version of that very same affliction? Down the empty road he'd walked, grown smaller, and then disappeared, like the vanishing point. A person could do that: walk away. At another grave, across the flat expanse of markers, a soldier stood among others on the bright green Astroturf. Randall, Cattie thought. No longer did it shock her to see him all over the place; it was him, and it wasn't him. Metaphysical. Syllogistic. This one at the cemetery had insinuated himself somehow into a family situation in Wichita, Kansas. Just as she had. And now they were both attending funerals. Tomorrow she would see him picking up a prescription, or jogging on a side street, or doing some other ordinary thing. For as long as there were soldiers wandering the world in his uniform, Cattie would see him.

He'd been at the press conference when the serial killer was finally caught, two weeks earlier. There at the sidelines, off-camera yet present while the officials were giving their endless bragging speeches and the cameras were clicking, the young man standing at attention, eyes focused straight ahead, at nothing. It took forever to get to the point—so much talking, so many thanks, such a lot of grandstanding and self-congratulation—and yet the soldier stood without blinking or yawning, without moving or mocking, there beneath a limp flag. In the audience, the victims' families: spouses and children, bereft, vindicated, enraged. Middle-aged, miserable, ordinary. But Cattie kept waiting for the soldier to reappear, that steady fellow

"It's always the guy next door," Catherine had said at the breakfast table the day after the announcement, studying the grinning face on the front page of the newspaper. "That gap between his teeth is disgusting." The killer had small eyes made smaller by his smile.

"He looks stupid," they said at the same time.

Across the cemetery the other group was disbanding, the soldier among the last to step away from the coffin and the Astroturf. That funeral's ritual was timed only a few minutes' pacing ahead of the one Cattie attended. She would hang back, too, because she didn't want to get any closer to the soldier. She didn't want him to transform into a specific other person who definitely was not Randall.

SUMMER

CHAPTER 15

H E TURNED SEVENTY in late July, and Oliver was deter-
mined not to care. His wife was due home from Colorado
by evening, and his Sweetheart did not know that today was
his birthday. Long ago he'd told her he was born in December,
and she'd nodded knowingly, smug about her intuition concerning his zodiac sign, unwilling to notify him of the literal
May-December relationship she thought they shared. She was a
Taurus. Her generation, or maybe just her current demographic,
believed in astrology.

Because his wife was out of town, he didn't have to hide his
other cell phone. The Sweetheart's messages made it shiver and
burr on the table. But it had been doing less and less of that, the
last few months. He was losing her. The feeling set off in him a
panic that afflicted him with the same intensity as his earlier
pleasure had—his heart running at a catastrophic rate, his nighttime riveted wakefulness during which he did not fantasize about
meeting but, rather, missing the Sweetheart.

The day was bright and warm; already the air was full of lawn
mower engines and children shouting, car radios through open
windows. To avoid the silent secret phone he left it on the table

when he took the dogs to the park and turned them loose to run. They collected affection out in the world, cheerful and confident, optimistic, pleased with themselves. They hadn't liked it when Catherine drove away with the other dog, the unfortunately named Bitch. Maybe it was Oliver's imagination, but he felt that their loyalty had turned subtly his way from his wife since the girl and her dog had moved into the house. Once, Catherine had been their favorite human, but not anymore. Once, they'd been the recipients of her indulgent affection, and that wasn't the case anymore, either.

"Boys against girls," the girl had said. She didn't say much, so you listened when she spoke. She was going to turn from an unattractive teenager into an unattractive woman, large-boned, unsmiling, unflustered, skeptical—a prison guard, a Mother Superior, a landlady. Oliver liked these qualities in men, but in women he preferred a bit of nervous laughter, a tentative element of inquiry, hesitation, and the capacity to blush or jump in alarm. The gestures of low self-esteem, that charming hardship, that sexy chink.

The Sweetheart, when she had been in the habit of tucking her head against his chest so that he couldn't see her carnal pleasure.

"She's so much like her mom it's weird," Catherine confessed concerning the girl. "I forgot how much I really liked Misty. The way she could keep her cool."

"She's cool, all right," Oliver agreed acidly.

"You can't be jealous," Catherine said. But not like a joke. Not as if she were teasing. She said it as if it were an ultimatum. He was disallowed. When he cast a glance in Cattie's direction, he found her already looking his way in anticipation, the unblinking gaze. Unlike most teenage girls, Cattie didn't seem to think of herself as the star of the show so much as an audience member. Or maybe reviewer. She seemed to be taking notes. When she turned sixteen, in August, she was going to wash dishes at Wheatlands. The Sweetheart would be her boss. Oliver had some nervousness about this plan. And also some faint hope that their affair would reignite. That this quasi-stepdaughter Cattie would provide a reason for him to see the Sweetheart more often. The Sweetheart, and those irritating Italian sourdough boys she'd hired.

But meanwhile it was a beautiful day, and nothing actually literally hurt, a sensation Oliver took a moment to appreciate. His heart was being broken, he understood, and his pride injured. Also he remembered that it was his birthday. And even as he thought it, he made himself reject the thought. No corporeal pain, he insisted to himself. All day this happened, a rotation: an absence of physical complaint, heartsickness, and dread that he then pushed away in favor of feeling fine. His wife phoned at four to apologize for the western Kansas weather: tornadoes. She and Cattie were stopping for the night in Great Bend and would see him tomorrow.

She paused, and Oliver said, "I'll go visit your mother," before she could request it of him. "I hate my birthday anyway," he added.

He no longer felt sour about seeing Grace Harding, yet knew it was more useful to pretend that he did. Let his capital grow, in his wife's estimation; he might need to tap into its reserve some rainy day. Whenever Catherine was busy with Cattie, Oliver performed the daily trek to Green Acres. He'd struck up a bantering relationship with the two remaining curmudgeons and often brought Wheatlands pastries for the staff. He purchased a small refrigerator for Grace's room so that she could have a cold apple whenever she felt like it. And he knew how to pick out apples, so he provided those, as well.

That evening he brought wine, not red, which would have been his preference, but white, because that's what his mother-in-law had always served. He did not mention that it was his birthday when they toasted coffee mugs. Everyone was arranging themselves in front of the television. The serial killer was being interviewed, in jail, on a national program. When he asked Grace if she wished to watch, she lifted her left, functioning shoulder: a shrug. She'd gotten hooked, as everyone had, by the local soap opera; this was its season finale.

Oliver was given the recently dead curmudgeon's Barcalounger. He made a point of draping an antimacassar over the headrest, that deeply stained place where another man's head had for so long rested.

At first, he could not quit studying the killer's looks—fierce, defensive, and aggrieved in the way of many midwesterners, eyes beady, expression challenged, men who appeared to have been born facing an oncoming high wind that was going to cause them no end of trouble, this one younger than Oliver by at least a decade but seeming somehow older, like the curmudgeons, wearing that hideous orange jumpsuit and the handcuffs.

He would be sentenced in a week. He could not be executed, as his killings had all taken place during a time when Kansas—briefly lax, temporarily liberal—had been opposed to the death penalty.

Nobody seemed opposed anymore.

The information was not new, the images were the same: the first family in its ordinary house made up of conventional members, Mom, Dad, Brother, Sister. But then the small chilling details. The man's voice narrating his work. When, for example, he'd begun to strangle the mother for the third time (inexperienced, a beginner at violent murder, an amateur—as Oliver had guessed all along), she said to him, "May God have mercy on your soul."

"Fantasies," the man said, "are what got me in trouble." By day he raised his family—a boy, a girl, a wife, that similar common dollhouse clan—and kept what he called "Factor X" at bay. He was obsessed randomly—out driving around, he'd suddenly be drawn to someone, a woman leaving her home or walking down the street. And then would come the stalking, the "haunting" of her neighborhood and life. From working in home security, he knew how to disable it. From studying criminology, he knew the habits of his ilk. His seventh victim he had killed and then gone to a pay phone to report the fact to the police, his voice on a tape.

He was a father of small children when he killed the mother of three small children. He wanted to be invisible, he wanted to be famous. Or infamous. "How many people do I have to kill before I get the recognition I deserve?" he'd queried of the news media.

"Our town was too small," the police chief lamented. "He would never get the celebrity he could have gotten in a bigger place."

"Yeah," said one of the curmudgeons. "He should of moved to California."

"New York," said the other. "Then he'd of been somebody."

"Jesus *loves* the little children," chanted the woman in the corner, her book as usual on her lap.

At a commercial break, Oliver turned to Grace. "This is like watching classic tragedy, isn't it? He's a type of tragic hero. Some crude and extreme version of Everyman, foiled by his own hubris. That damned Achilles' heel."

She looked at Oliver with startlingly uncomprehending eyes. They'd watched many programs together lately and been in complete agreement, which had surprised and delighted them both. He'd brought a DVD of *La Dolce Vita*, and they'd watched transfixed—transported, Oliver realized—entranced by the little white kitten, the blond beauty in the fountain, poor perplexed Marcel Mastroianni, a man out of his depths. "Mar*cello!*"

the radiantly wet angel called to him. "Hurry up! Come in here!" Oliver had been suddenly reminded of YaYa, an unexpected searing in his chest, his first wife's impulsive passion burning through his usual hardened opinion of her. In the beginning, when they were beginners, she'd have traipsed and danced and laughed and splashed into and through the early hours, too, and he would have found it charming, loving her as he did, helplessly. He wasn't accustomed to thinking of YaYa charitably. She was his long-standing and venerated enemy. Like Grace Harding. That afternoon of *La Dolce Vita*, her eyes had also shone.

But sometimes the old animosity between him and his mother-in-law popped up. He backpedaled. "I mean, the killer's desire to have it both ways, to be the upstanding citizen as well as the fiend. Dr. Jekyll, Mr. Hyde. You know? The rational mind versus the feverish heart?"

Her mouth hung open, as it did when she wasn't vigilant, when she was taken aback or thinking. A ragged gap of confusion. In this incredulity, in her utter incomprehension in the face of what seemed universally obvious to Oliver, he understood the distance between them: she did not believe in an uncontrollable temptation. What the BTK named "Factor X" was nonsense, in the mind of Grace Harding, an excuse that excused exactly nothing. How dare Oliver elevate the maniac to Everyman, to tragic hero? No, she declined to subscribe to a heart of darkness.

Why would he wish to convince her otherwise, he wondered? The interview resumed, and all Oliver could hear was the language of anybody in the throes of something urgent and insatiable, something that struck every now and then to sabotage, nag, and insist upon until it was fulfilled. And then to begin again, a cycle of . . .

The air-conditioning kicked on outside the nursing home's lounge window; the TV's volume was at its highest level. This wasn't the kind of entertainment Grace liked to admit enjoying, but she'd been agreeable enough when Oliver suggested they join the others. She would never acknowledge pride at having a visitor, a still-handsome man whose interest was solely in her, a man different from the others who occasionally appeared, the sheepish sons or grandsons in ball caps, men who shouted into the ears of their grannies, looking to leave as soon as possible, checking their watches, covering all the small talk and phony bonhomie bases. Her colleague Yasmin had been another exotic to pass through the doors of this establishment, and only because Professor Grace Harding was confined within. In no other circumstance had Oliver ever felt that his mother-in-law was grateful to him—grateful without qualifications. But he felt it now, and did not wish to ruin its glow.

On television, the killer's downfall was being chronicled, the final days and hours of his double life. And what had doomed this hapless villain? His own vanity. He'd asked the newspaper editors if a computer floppy disk could be traced to its user. He'd trusted them when they replied that it couldn't. Did all villains depend on the confidence that nobody else was as duplicitous as they? For instance, had Oliver himself ever really believed that his wives would be capable of having a secret love, a second life? That it would be he who was the betrayed? From the floppy disk the police had identified the computer and the user; from the church where the computer was housed, the authorities had found the man. A deacon, a codes enforcer, an upstanding citizen. To prove without a shadow of a doubt his guilt, they'd obtained DNA from his daughter. He'd left traces at the crime scenes— semen, naturally. The technology had developed over the decades since then. His daughter's DNA was a match. He was indisputably the man.

Brought down mostly by his hubris, but without any further doubt by his daughter. Oliver felt another shiver of troubling recognition. There was Miriam, out there armed to the teeth, ready to unleash what she knew and ruin his life. Having once been the sweetheart herself, Catherine would know the intensity of Oliver's passion for the current Sweetheart. She wouldn't forgive it. Or, rather, she wouldn't allow herself to be second to it.

Oliver looked at his mother-in-law, who wasn't watching the television but was watching him. She couldn't speak, but she could know. She, too, might have some information to share with Catherine. Of the man onscreen in the orange jumpsuit, Oliver said, "He's an egomaniac. A narcissist. A psychopath. A sociopath." He lined up as many catchphrases as he could pull from the air, anything at all to separate himself from his earlier statement. Not Everyman, no no no. A maniac. He could not afford to express kinship with this madman, not if he wished to hang on to his life.

Because the Sweetheart would not be there for him to begin again with. She hadn't been particularly thrilled when he notified her of Catherine's upcoming absence, the road trip to Colorado. The Sweetheart would leave him. This time, it wouldn't be he who chose. The time had come for him to be the one left behind.

"It's my birthday," Oliver said, changing the subject, lifting his coffee mug for a mock toast. Only then did he realize that he wasn't turning seventy but seventy-one. His math had been wrong. He was already older than he believed or wished.

In Colorado Catherine had found the place where Misty's car went off the road. There were rocks on the blacktop, an orange sign nearby warning of the possibility, falling rock as a persistent state, a chunk hanging suspended between cliff and pavement. They parked and stood on the shoulder. The mountains in the distance were beautiful, symmetrical. Had she seen them before? They looked familiar to Catherine. But maybe that was the familiarity of a clichéd standard: the pointed Rocky Mountain, with shoulders, capped with snow, as declared on advertisements for beer or automobiles, on truck sides and billboards and television. On cans and calendars and shirts.

"I had a dream about this place," Cattie said. "It looked just like this, and I was the pilot of an airplane."

At their feet and down the roadside incline a lush green patchwork of treetops waving in the evening wind, limber trees in summer, leaves making the noise of water, no sign of catastrophe. Bitch stood on the very edge, her black-and-white fur ruffling in the breeze.

"We came here the summer of the bicentennial," Catherine told the girl. "I was your age. Misty hadn't ever left the state of Kansas before."

"She was poor," Cattie said, crossing her arms. As if the comment had been a criticism. Catherine knew how that went, defending your mother one minute, complaining about her the next.

"We carved our names and the date everywhere. I bet I could find some of those." From the other direction, a pair of motorcycles whined by, their riders lifting their hands in unison. "And we drank river water," Catherine remembered. "We were trying to get giardia. We thought it sounded like a good diet. We were always inventing new diets."

The question here on the thin open place on the edge of the cliff was: had Misty killed herself? Had the woman decided she'd come to the end?

In the unnerving, extraordinary way the girl had of knowing what Catherine was thinking, Cattie now said, "She wouldn't have taken Max with her if she was planning to die."

Catherine hadn't realized she was still slightly unsure. Dick Little and State Farm had declared the death accidental; most of the ensuing evidence suggested that Misty wouldn't do such a thing as betray the only love she knew, abandon her girl. Yet now Catherine felt a physical relief at Cattie's assessment, a membrane of doubt borne off on the next gust of air. She'd shown Cattie the homemade asterisk on her shoulder, the one that Misty had carved there, describing the identical one that she had put on Misty's skin. Cattie had never been treated to that information, had never noticed a scar on her mother's shoulder. This, as always, had led Catherine to a whole associative trove of memories. The time they'd broken into a thrift store and stolen wigs. This man they'd followed in Misty's car. This dog they had rescued from an abuser. This apparent pact they'd made, so long ago, before either of them had believed in the necessity of a will or trust or future, before they were people who thought about growing old, about actually having something, or somebody, to bestow in case of emergency, in the event of accident, in the preposterous possibility of death.

Now the girl opened her cell phone and accessed her saved messages. She held the device to Catherine's ear. Despite the wind and the awkward angle at which Cattie rested the speaker in Catherine's hair, she could hear her old friend's voice, speaking to her from far away, a rambling message for her daughter about the dangers of being out in the night alone and needing to come home.

The summer was especially brutal in Arizona. Drought, heat, fires—fires begun by lightning strikes, fires set by arsonists, fires begun in witless innocence that resulted in extravagant mayhem. By the end of the summer, there would be a serial killer on the loose, some incendiary force just about to burst into flame. The Baseline Killer, he would be named, another in the lineage of infamy and notoriety. His first victims, not to mention his rapt audience, were still ignorant of his existence, of the conditions that were already conspiring to bring him to life and action. The city would be besieged and transfixed for years. It would happen again and again and again.

But for now the dog paced the confines of her backyard, its desert cacti on the other side, sand and rock and tennis balls, which she declined to chase, on her side. "Playing" was not something she understood. She panted, she waited, she slept with one eye open, all the scorching July day. This was the hottest yet in her time here in Phoenix. Left inside the house, she would do damage attempting to get out of it. In her old life, she'd had access to both, and spent her time pacing between, in and out, alert to the instant when the people returned, her own existence incomplete, on hold, without them.

Her new owner would be home soon, apologetic, loving. Anxious and guilty, too, fearful each day that she'd find the dog gone. For hours they would sit together in the cool house, the woman talking and talking, on the phone and to the dog, as well, the soothing and logical rhythm of routine. Affection, gratitude, ritual. Company. These were the components of reassurance.

For the woman who now took care of the dog, it had been the worst nine months of her life. First she'd had to break up with her boyfriend Lance, which had been rougher than she'd imagined, their having been together for some time, and the fact that everyone, including her parents, had grown accustomed to his presence in their lives. "You like him so much, you live with him!" Elise was tempted to demand. She wasn't young any longer, and her parents, who'd had her late in their lives, the surprise and accident after three planned children, wished to see her safely settled. They'd not felt great affection for Lance, but he was at least familiar. He was a locatable body to whom they could hand responsibility—not fiscal responsibility, but Elise already was in possession of that. They couldn't bear for her to be alone, and Lance was nothing if not capable of simply hanging around.

Lance himself had surprised her. His passionate anger at being dumped far surpassed any degree of passion he'd otherwise exhibited. Wow, did he *not* want to break up! So for a few weeks, back and forth Elise had gone, to his new room in a house of roommates, back to her town house with him. They argued over the phone, by e-mail, in person—and they made up the same ways.

He and the dog only tolerated one another. Neither was sorry to see the last of the other.

Of all the antidepressants Elise had tried, Prozac was the name that the dog responded to best. And the dog herself was a much better form of antidepressant than any drug Elise had taken. She would have probably preferred being in love, truly in love, but the dog made it possible to finally leave Lance and not look back.

And then after the breakup, her mother had grown gravely ill, and soon after, her father fell and broke both hips. This led to a nursing home, in which they both now sat, waiting to see who would die first.

Once, on New Year's Eve, Elise had gone home with a man she shouldn't have. In her absence, the night dissolved into disaster; the dog had escaped from her yard and been picked up by the authorities and impounded. For forty-eight hours, the duration of the holiday weekend, the shelter had tried to reach Elise, who'd made a heart-shaped plastic tag for the dog as soon as she'd returned to Phoenix with it. When those calls had failed—Elise at the party, Elise at the first bar, Elise at the next bar, Elise in this terrible man's apartment, all the while her phone ringing and ringing—the shelter had accessed the implant in the animal's neck. A new series of phone calls began. Long distance.

It was only luck, and her bright blond hair and her blue pleading tear-filled eyes, that had returned the dog to Elise. That other owner, that one in Houston, Texas, had not been the one who dashed at dawn to the Phoenix pound to sit for hours talking and conniving and begging and lying until the dog was finally released into her care. She'd bought it from the owner. She'd rescued it. She'd found it three years ago in her yard, she told the next person to whom she spoke. It was being beaten, she'd sneaked it out of a terrible situation. She'd inherited it from the previous owner, the previous owner had died, whatever manner of story seemed likely or useful or necessary. The point was: she could not lose this dog. It hadn't been clearer to her than the moment when it seemed she would. Ambivalence then turned to certainty.

And so the dog had been restored to her. Plush extravagant fur, expressive eyebrows, sinuous coyote body, meek sweeping tail. She would never risk losing her again. Her fence was secured; Elise installed a new microchip. In the fall, when she made her annual pilgrimage to Colorado, to her family's former land, she would take the dog with her. They would trespass together on private property, hike the hillside beneath Dracula's castle, and sit haunch to haunch at the edge of the fire in the dark. She attached herself as if in marriage to this creature, *health, illness, prosperity, despair*, to a life in which she would never betray it. *Do you promise . . . ?* She did.

Prozac, she had named the wild yet good girl. And by now she was learning to respond to her name. You weren't stuck with just the one. You had chances, there were choices. You could change your life.

ACKNOWLEDGMENTS

Thanks to my invaluable and tireless readers Bonnie Nadell, Anton Mueller, Kathleen Lee, Mimi Swartz, Connie Voisine, Sheila Black, and Robert Boswell.

And, for support, thanks to the United States Artists Simon Fellowship, the Atlantic Center for the Arts, Inprint, and the University of Houston.

And thank you ALC chum Laura Moats, singular shopkeeper Sarah Bagby, inimitable roommate Dana Kroos, and abiding angel Lillie Robertson.